The
Sky Thief

By
Wes Smith

I0589385

DREAM WIRE
PRESS

Physical editions printed by IngramSpark.

First Edition.

ISBN 978-0-692-58082-0 Digital; 978-0-692-58083-7 Trade
Paperback

To Brezlyn

In case you ever wish to go exploring

I

Before the fire, there was all the time in the world.

Near the bank of the Thames, clockmaker Hubert Thomas toiled away at his latest repair. Hunched at his work desk, his thick fingers tinkered at a watch below him with the deftness of the finest of surgeons. While many of his customers wondered why he spent such a vast engineering talent on an antiquated trade, few argued with his results. In truth, his father had been a clockmaker, his grandfather studied watches, and so on for many generations. As Hubert was not preoccupied with financial glory, he saw the work as his duty to continue an honorable family trade.

The London shop underwent many changes and moves over the years, starting as a booming corner space only to be slowly whittled down by technology to become barely more than a closet nestled in a dusty back alley. Still, Hubert persevered, managing gears and springs despite civilization's rush towards digital means. Those that shared his passion for the classic timepieces knew him as the finest of his time, and he enjoyed a small but loyal base of colleagues.

The aged master was not expecting company as closing time approached. Hubert worked unerringly on an ancient Rolex, his brown eyes exaggerated behind thick spectacles. Little distracted him most evenings, the only sounds coming from the rhythmic ticking on his walls and the slight clicks as he popped and set minuscule pieces of metal back into place. He relished the intricacies of such a classic model, losing himself in the brilliance of its construction, the certain magic held within its complex mechanisms.

So absorbed was he that he only noticed the two men at his counter when he picked up the restored Oyster to wind it. Hubert jumped at their appearance, clutching his tweed vest.

"Sorry! I didn't hear the door open. Was actually just

about to close up shop," Hubert wheezed, squinting from staring too long through a magnifying glass.

The men were dressed sharply in matching gray suits. The older of the two stood lean and tall, with stark white hair and a pointed goatee. His companion, a dashing young man with slicked brown hair, glanced around the shop with a judgmental sneer.

The white-haired gentleman smiled and adjusted the round glasses on his nose. "We arrived just in time then. Word has it you are the best person to talk to about acquiring antique timepieces," he said.

"Well, I hesitate to go that far," said Hubert. "I just do my best with what I love."

"I am Richard Deacon and this charming boy is my nephew James," continued the older gentleman with a nod. "We have been looking for quite some time for a clock that we believe might be in your delightful little store."

Hubert ran his hands over his broom-like whiskers, eyeing the one named James with skepticism. "You aren't one of those Steampunk fans, are you?"

Hubert had implemented a policy regarding younger customers after a teen had entered his shop with gears from a very rare and priceless Swiss clock bolted to cheap sunglasses as a sort of fashion statement. The aging shop owner did not keep up-to-date on the latest fashion trends, but he knew he did not care for "Steampunk" one bit.

"Nothing of the sort, sir," said James with a calming raise of his hand. "My father and I are collectors, as well. His birthday is coming up. We wanted to surprise him with a particular piece he has been after for quite some time."

Hubert beamed as he changed his tone. "Well, that I can do! What did you have in mind?"

"A German table piece. Late 1800's. Not exceptionally large, but has beautiful inlays along the sides featuring mountains. Gold numbers, if I remember correctly."

Hubert held back a cough. He removed his glasses and polished them with a nearby cloth. That his hands were shaking despite an otherwise calm demeanor was not lost on his guests.

"Sounds vaguely familiar. You'll have to give me a second to check my books," lied the shopkeeper.

Hubert knew precisely where he kept the clock. He also knew that such pieces required an artful dance of negotiation that was as much pretense and flourish as it was substance. From behind his counter, he procured a large, well-organized planner and placed it on his workbench with a large thunk. The book nearly dwarfed the stout clockmaker. With devout hands, he opened the cover in reverence.

The taller customer released an impatient grunt, but Hubert pretended he had not heard it. He leafed through the pages of notes, numbers, and spreadsheets worn brown by time and use. He flipped to a section of clock names and values, making sure to keep the registrar within full view of his customers. Though Hubert knew every entry by heart, the intimidating book of records weeded out the serious buyers from hobbyists, its pages filled with records that only the upper echelon of enthusiasts could afford. With a quick glance from the corner of his eye, Hubert could see the two strangers fidgeting, though they did not appear ready to leave. In his experience, such eager buyers often paid handsomely.

Searching through the list, Hubert's finger landed on an entry with an over-long number beside it. "It seems I do have something similar to what you are looking for."

"Wonderful!" Richard exclaimed with wide eyes. "We would be grateful to see it and confirm it is the clock we're after. There have been many impostors in our search, you see."

Satisfied that he had the upper-hand in bargaining, Hubert calmly closed his book and fiddled with a large keychain on his desk. "It's not often I get people looking to buy this kind of piece these days. You say you and your father collect?"

"Our family is full of hobbyists. My father has a knack for acquiring particularly unique and exquisite items of all kinds," said James. He raised his hand up to stifle a yawn.

"Then it's good to have a fellow admirer of fine craftsmanship in my store! It's a nice change of pace from repairs all day. Follow me, please."

Hubert shuffled out from behind his counter, keys jingling as he searched the ring for the correct one. James and Richard could not help but raise bemused eyebrows, as the shop was far too small to follow anyone anywhere. Their expressions widened when Hubert opened a thin door tucked secretly away between two grandfather clocks beside them. They turned sideways to enter, their imaginations flaring at what lie beyond.

Unlike the dim shop outside, the hidden room had all the care and management of Versailles. Along the polished burgundy walls and positioned on tables rested glass boxes, each containing table clocks, cuckoos, and watches of equally stunning age and value. Every display was lit by a warm light built into the case, letting the contents glint with gold and silver trimmings.

"My, my. Isn't this a surprise," said Richard, his mouth agape. "How immaculate. I'd wager this room is worth more than the rest of your store combined."

"It's a dignified collection," replied Hubert with a hint of pride. "My little vault reserved for customers that need a little more than simple decoration. Ah, ah careful not to touch!"

James paused as he bent down to admire one of the pocketwatches to his side. Only at Hubert's warning did he notice the small electronic lock pad and security sticker lodged onto the side of the glass.

He straightened with a reassuring chuckle, "Sorry, sir. Simply admiring."

"Quite all right. Wouldn't want us to be locked in here until the authorities arrive. Now, I believe what you were looking for is over here." Hubert pointed toward a distant stand.

Halfway back in the room, on a crafted oaken table embossed with swirls, a table clock beckoned to them. Hubert stroked his mustache as he pressed a long sequence of numbers onto the keypad. The glass popped as it unlatched from the table.

The clock had always been a special one to Hubert. He obtained it from a late colleague, who in turn had obtained it from a souk in Casablanca tucked among replicas and souvenirs. Though it commanded a fair price due to the fine outer craftsmanship of gold and Brazilian rosewood, the clock had long since stopped working on the inside. Hubert was tasked with its repair, but his friend passed shortly after and thus the shopkeeper found himself with a unique table piece.

The inner workings were like nothing he had seen before. Hubert spent months tracking down all of the parts needed to completely restore it to working condition. He found himself in love with the clock as he labored on it, guessing there were no more than a scant few similar pieces like it left in the world. He could never find a name or print identifying the craftsman, but it was truly the work of a master. The signifying element of the clock, beautifully rendered mountains inked with gold into the wood itself, reminded Hubert of the markings on a Stradivarius violin he had seen in a museum as a child. He debated for some time on whether to even sell it, but an economic downturn forced the ultimate decision to include it within the premium gallery.

"Well, gentlemen, is this along the lines of what you were looking for?" he asked with a tinge of sadness.

Adjusting his spectacles, Richard bent down to inspect the clock, spending a great deal of time observing the mountain drawings. Hubert noticed the refined mens' faces plastered with unnerving grins despite being wholly involved with the clock before them.

"Hand me the glass, James," grunted the elder of the two.

The young man, without the slightest hesitation at the command, procured from within his smoky blazer a bronzed magnifying glass with a series of knobs and buttons along the handle. Pale blue light danced along its length in swirled patterns. The instrument looked very out of place among the centuries-old time pieces.

"Now if you could, um, please be reminded…" stuttered Hubert as he sensed something awry with his buyers. His words made no impression on either of the two. He shifted on his legs, glancing at the nearest active alarm.

Richard studied the mountain range up close for a moment more before leaning back. Raising the magnifier, he pressed the top button and the glass lit up with the same glow as the handle, casting the onlookers with its sickly light. The shopkeeper could not get a clear look, but he briefly saw letters through the glass that were not visible on the clock itself.

"A-R-E-S," spelled Richard. James nodded silently but made no other suggestion as to what the letters meant.

Hubert stood flabbergasted, his eyes wide with wonder. "Incredible!" he shouted. "Is that UV? Blacklight? I would have never imagined an antique to have such a thing on it!"

Richard stood, turned the magnifying glass off, and handed it back to James where it disappeared once more into the folds of his suit.

Richard cleared his throat. "Normally, they don't. This is a special item we've been searching for."

"That is quite fantastic," said Hubert, pushing past the tall man's legs to run his hands over the mountaintops, "and a cause for celebration! I would love to hear more about what you know of it. After we talk price, of course."

"Mr… Hubert, correct? Do you have any children?" asked Richard passively.

The clockmaker furrowed his brows at the strange question. "N… no. Never was much of a charmer with the ladies, I'm afraid."

"Shame."

Hubert's lifeless body hit the ground before he even had the chance to see the gun drawn. James waited for the barrel to cool before replacing it to the inner holdings of his jacket. The two men stared down at the deceased shopkeeper, now with an extra orifice to his head.

"Artists like him are in short supply nowadays," said Richard as he patted his forehead with a fresh handkerchief.

"Shame he didn't have anyone to pass his knowledge

down to," replied James with a shake of the head.

"In today's world, you must be quick. New ideas travel at the press of a button. There's little room for antique, forgotten trades."

The two stood for a silent moment, watching as the hardwood floor became ever more crimson with blood. James glanced up at the precious clock, nodding towards it with a look towards Richard.

Richard strode towards the room's exit. "We're done. Go ahead and burn it."

When the local papers reported the arson, many in the neighborhood commented on how much of a craftsman poor Hubert had been but rumor had it a new electronics store would be going up in his place.

The greatest part about rural living were the back county roads. As Alexandra Stirling careened down one such winding highway, she was thankful that patrol cars largely stayed off the beaten path, kept at bay by small-town budgets. It would be a shame if, say, a newspaper intern who had passed out so hard she slept through her alarm got flagged for speeding.

Of course, the little joys in life were balanced, as they often were. In Alex's case, her poor Jeep Cherokee had long lost the ability to put so much as NPR through its speakers, leaving her alone to her thoughts as she blasted her way through the woods and into civilization.

While the rest of the world charged into the 21st Century, life in rural Missouri remained much the same as it had ever been. Smaller towns often bragged about how quickly their populations or businesses were expanding, yet that change was rarely felt as the sun continued to rise and set every day over the same green swaths of corn and meadows. The forests of the Ozarks granted peaceful solace, save for the beginning of deer season when underpopulated schools darkened for a week to enable families precious bonding time through predawn rituals and meals over firepits with friends.

In a town like New Delta, a bustling city by local standards, the coming of a new restaurant set gossip ablaze at a pace that could astonish even the largest of celebrity rag magazines. Though the people and technology of the area were by no means cut off from the rest of the world, Alex believed that the pace of life had mostly stayed unchanged since the time when Samuel Clemens wrote of a young boy drifting down the Mississippi River.

At least, that's what crossed her mind in the moments where she wasn't racing against the clock to make it to work on time, a circumstance she thought was universal to any area of the country and one she was all too familiar with.

New Delta's streets stirred with morning commuters as Alex barreled her purple Grand Cherokee towards the downtown area. Though traffic was rarely an issue for such a small town, the city limits sprawled for miles into rural farmland. Alex's journey along county roads and highways to reach the main thoroughfares involved a landscape that started with expansive fields merged subtly into subdivisions that sprung up in a matter of months. What started as a single cluster of homes grew into whitewashed monotony for the middle class. Eventually, the signs of fast food chains and convenience stores signaled a return to civilization. Lines of cars snaked around countless convenience stores, eager for drive-thru sodas and cigarettes. These shops of cheap pleasures were rarely far from one of the multitude of churches in the area. Living her entire life within this region, Alex had developed a very robust sense of irony.

She didn't hold those contradictions against anyone. Of course she disliked the hypocrisy. Seeing people speak out against their own interests had riled her up on more than a few occasions during her fiery high school years. However, as she grew older and increasingly eager to learn more about the world outside her normal boundaries, she realized that the issues facing the town were complex, the result of mindsets passed down for generations.

Her urge to wander was only partially for the learning experience. Alex was well aware that if she did not at least attempt to leave while she was young, she would become trapped and unable to escape in the future. Rural towns became a vicious cycle to those who did not move when given the chance. One excuse would lead to another, and before she knew it, she would have obligations preventing her from leaving. She may even come to accept her fate, afflicted with a twisted geographic version of Stockholm Syndrome.

The dichotomy of the city was no more apparent than Alex's turn onto Broadway. The first stretch was filled with small businesses, friendly buildings, and the local university. University Park displayed the first signs of Spring as joggers took laps around a shimmering lake highlighted with a stone fountain. Built onto a high ridge, a glass behemoth of a hospital kept watch over the morning traffic - a jumble of pedestrian bridges, specialty treatment centers, and parking lots. The complex was the only semblance of a truly modern city to be found for hours in any direction.

Traveling farther on, the street took a sharp dive that ended in the Mississippi River flowing lazily along its course, a steady constant visible from nearly every street. The downtown area avoided annual disaster thanks to a concrete floodwall along the river's banks. Murals depicted New

Delta's history as a trading town in the earliest days of Louis and Clark. The shops, however, languished with signs of age and decay. A few scattered businesses occupied leaning brick structures, but many storefronts had long been closed, displaying condemned signs over graffiti-covered windows. Some of the older residents tried to claim the downtown area had a rustic, river-town feel reminiscent of the trading post era; Alex considered it an eyesore, the last gasp for air over traditions that needed to move on.

Alex pulled into a parking lot behind one of the few buildings with modern renovation: the local newspaper and publishing house. The paper's distribution was not large, but the business was well-respected and covered a large swath of the region. Its building reflected local prestige with walls of white stucco and Spanish tile over wide arched windows looking towards the main thoroughfare. As Alex parked, she whispered a silent thanks for an uninhibited commute, arriving just moments before she had to clock in.

Punching her timecard, she rushed to join the staff huddled in a semicircle around their cubicles in the main lobby, a flurry of paper and scribbling pens. Alex threw her bag into her desk chair, grabbed the nearest notepad, and joined the back of the group. Though she was only an intern, she loved the atmosphere of those morning meetings, listening to her experienced coworkers running through the important topics of the day.

The Editor-In-Chief, Edmund Brown, was already well into the morning's events. He rattled off assignments and questions as though he were a barker at the local auction house.

"Jeremy, give me an update on the St. Louis murder by noon," he ordered. "Grant, keep up the good work on the storm damage. Another one is supposed to be on the way so be careful out there. Carrie, what do you have for me?"

"Got an email release saying utility increases are coming in May."

"Again? Ok, we'll work with it. What about you, Phil?"

"Jeremiah's is donating a lot of instruments for the veteran charity concert."

"Jessica's already handling the concert. We'll have her include that. Any other HI pieces?"

"St. Mary's is hosting a new therapy dog program."

"Eh, that slow today? Go ahead on it. We can bubblewrap the embezzlement. Alexandra, I'll have you make some calls about the Intrepid Theater deal."

His words sunk into Alex like stones. She kept her head down and scribbled into her notepad while trying to hide the agitation in her face.

When she was young, Alex had always been outdoors. She loved adventure, learning about new worlds, and digging through the ground. Her friends often joked that she was the only girl in junior high with a *National Geographic* subscription. She remembered spending nights endlessly pouring over stories of Angkor Wat, giant sequoias, and Egyptian treasures. She saw them as no different than the fairy tales her parents sang to her except these places were *real*, not some fantasy-land used for escapism. Exploration and journalism, writing truths about the world most of her peers ignored, seemed a natural fit as she grew older.

However, her hopes in becoming a journalist had been dashed repeatedly over her time stuck in the low-lying farmland of Missouri. Life happened. One day, she found herself alone and full of responsibilities beyond her age. Despite wonderful grades, she would not make it to Mizzou, the pinnacle of journalism schooling. She resigned herself to writing beat stories about kittens in nursing homes or the economic plight of yet another closed chain store in the mall.

When the meeting wrapped up, Alex dashed towards Edmund. He, at least, had Alex's admiration as a true newsman. Donning slicked black hair, a white shirt, and suspenders, the strong-jawed man was every bit the type of reporter Alex imagined existed in the days of Pulitzer and Hearst. All he needed was coffee and a cigar.

"Sir, can I have a moment?" she called.

He glanced at her then returned to the papers in his hands. "Hey Alex. How's our favorite intern doing?" he asked.

"I'm good, thanks. Hey, I was wondering if, when this theater deal is finished, you might take a look at some ideas I wanted to try before the semester's over?"

"What did you have in mind?" grunted Edmond.

"Well, there's word that Commercia is bypassing labor regulations for their merger. I've got several sources inside that…"

"You know we can't run that story, Alex. Our readers love Commercia."

"But, sir, this could be major," Alex pleaded as they walked through an array of cubicles. "They're local now, but with how fast they're growing, it's only a matter of time until someone takes notice of this. We should get on this first."

Edmund stopped and turned to her. "Alex, I get where you're coming from, but Commercia holds a lot of ad space with us. We can't run a story like that unless we all want to start looking for new jobs. Your heart's in the right place, but news is mostly a business like any other."

Alex's enthusiasm started dripping away. "Then something else? I'll be out of here in a couple of weeks and I still don't have anything. You know I can do it. I work my ass off here, but no one's going to hire me if my portfolio's filled with nursing home activities and real estate sales."

"There are several credible magazines for nursing homes."

"I'm serious, sir."

Mr. Brown rubbed his chin. "Alex, you're a good intern, and you're going to be a fine reporter one day, but you're trying to fly too close to the sun right now. I know your six months is almost up, but you know it's slow. It's just bad timing."

"I know, sir, but…"

"I'll find something more exciting - something publishable - when I can, Alex. That's all I can promise for now. Just take it one story at a time," he said.

They reached his office, which he promptly entered, slamming the door behind him. Alex gave a meek thanks and returned across the room to her bare desk. Banging her head down in a flurry of blond curls, she began crying softly into her arms.

She could not figure out why she felt this way on what was otherwise a perfectly normal morning. Since she had woken up, restlessness pulled at the back of her mind. It was as though her ideas had turned to mosquitoes buzzing just beneath her skin, daring her to scratch an itch she couldn't even see. All of the stakes in her life appeared so much higher all of a sudden, and she couldn't place why.

She knew the answer her boss would hand her before she even asked for the story, but the disappointment stung nonetheless. Alex hated being stuck in New Delta, but she never compared it to the Overlook Hotel until now.

One article at a time, she told herself, lifting her head off the table. She repeated the mantra several times in her head, wiping her eyes. She willed herself to start up her computer as she did nearly every day since she had started her internship. As long as she only focused on one story at a time, she could patiently let her future find doors to open for her. Trying to pound on them for attention would just drive her sanity away.

Picking up the phone, Alex absorbed herself in her work, stubbornly refusing to be held back.

The next day came far too quickly in an area stereotyped for its languid pacing. Like most mornings, Alex found herself in one of those sweeping meadows of the country looking towards the horizon when the smell of coffee grabbed her attention. She shifted around on the uprooted tree acting as her seat to greet a familiar face with dark, straight hair blowing gently in the brisk air.

"Hey, roomie. Figured you could use this before you end up covered in moss," said the newcomer, handing Alex a warm mug. "Couldn't sleep again?"

"Thanks, Becky. And no," replied Alex, brushing a tangle of yellow curls away from her face to blow away the steam.

The sun had just risen, its light sparkling through dew-soaked grass. Aside from the log and a few trees growing along rusted chain fences near its borders, the meadow was filled with nothing but low, brown hills patiently waiting to become alive and green once again as spring reared its head.

"I have to get out of here," Alex said. The voice was hers, but it sounded half a world away to her ears.

Becky glided towards the fallen tree and perched next to her friend with a dancer's grace. They wore matching denim jackets, but Alex welled with jealousy at how perfectly modeled it fit on Becky; she knew her own looked like a folded sack by comparison.

"Well, you only have a couple of weeks left of your newspaper internship. I'm sure you'll find something," Becky said. She wrapped an arm around Alex's shoulders.

"It's not that easy. I haven't done anything at the paper yet. They won't give me a story I can work with," Alex sighed with a shake of her head.

"So go and yell at them a bit! Make them give you something! They'll listen eventually, and you'll be so awesome, they'll wonder why it took so long to notice you."

"There's more to it than that."

"Oh? Like what?"

"I feel trapped, Becky. I can't just pick up and move. I have things that need taken care of here. What if I really don't even *want* to move on? What if this," Alex waved her hand towards the meadow, "is all that I'll ever have? Maybe I'm destined to just stay in this one little dot on the planet forever."

Becky tackled her friend with a hug. "What will we do here without your endless pessimism, Alex? Who will distract us from all the rainbows and sunshine?" she cooed.

Alex knew she was being ridiculous, but she couldn't bring herself to smile. "I just wish I had more of an idea what was going on with my life. We can't all be budding young models like a certain someone," she said.

Becky frowned. "You know that's just a means to an end. It's good money, and I'll meet a lot of great designers in

Chicago. Besides, it's not nearly as respectable as getting the word out about the problems of the world."

"Maybe…" Alex trailed off.

Becky grabbed Alex's shoulders and stared down on her. "It's not. You are going to be great at whatever you decide to do. You can't let these moods of yours win."

"But there's finances, no portfolio, no friends…"

"Alex!" Even stern, Becky's face glowed. "You are a dreamer. I am sure you will dream of something great to get you out of here. You just have to take it when it comes."

Despite the expanse around them, Alex's insides quaked with claustrophobia. Invisible walls bore down on her future. Everywhere she turned, she saw only more fields and an absence of humanity. Without Becky, she wondered how long she would have lasted, hopeless in the face of the self-inflicted prison that was a small town.

Alex stood up and stretched her arms high above her head, allowing the sunlight to burn off her fears as it did the morning haze. Her legs tingled as blood rushed back into them. She had no clue how long she had been sitting. An hour? Two? She didn't want to leave. The stump was her regular place of calm, a way to temporarily ignore her unhappiness, a place to daydream. Though the tranquil suburban neighborhood she called home waited only a few hundred yards away, the air felt cleaner in the field and may as well have been another country in the cool of night.

Walking with Becky back to their home, Alex distanced herself from her friend. She was grateful for Becky, of course. She had always been there to pull Alex out of ruts and set her on a straight path. However, they had always been inherently different. Becky looked every bit the supermodel: tall and lithe and popular. A city girl with a genuine Southern accent, her aura was otherworldly compared to the simple, honest living of the country they grew up in.

Alex, on the other hand, was not a big girl by any means, but she was stocky and moved in a brutish, direct manner that aided in her tomboy reputation. Even walking across the meadow, Alex stomped and plodded about in thick boots while Becky barely bounced at all, sliding easily across the ground without making a sound. Even the hair on Becky's head returned to perfectly conditioned bangs after being kissed by a faint breeze. Each strand had no doubt been carefully prepped before the coffee began brewing. Alex had not even seen a mirror yet.

A few loose threads of barbed wire and tangled brush marked the edge of the field. Beyond sprawled paved streets and manicured lawns without a tree in sight. Walking along the looping roads, they passed cookie-cutter house by cookie-cutter house, each with spotless vinyl siding, arched windows, and an abundance of square-footage for the families within. Signs of life for the morning stirred. The girls waved quick hellos to the few joggers and newspaper readers they chanced upon. A schoolbus barreled past them, teasing Alex with an easier time that could have been eons ago for how it felt.

At the far end of a cul-de-sac waited their own home, a two-story construction of rose brick and angled roof lines. The lawn was as neat as the neighboring grass, but smudges of grime marred the vinyl siding. The house was not abnormal on the surface, but it remained a subject of rumor and gossip for nearby families. That it was taken care of by two young women of college age made for a routine topic at community barbecues. Not that the girls minded; the two friends rarely attended such events.

Stepping inside the front door revealed an interior in much the same shape as the outside. Neatly arranged furniture went unused from lack of interest or care, as though waiting for owners that never arrived. Alex promptly stored her boots in the tiled foyer. Microscopic filaments glinted through rays of sunlight beaming through the windows, falling on pictures of the two in various stages of their childhood together. A few photos featured a man and woman laughing with the young girls, a layer of speckled dust covering the frames.

Becky turned to her roommate and placed a hand on Alex's shoulder. "You going to be ok?"

Alex rubbed her eyes and returned a weak smile. "Yeah, I think so. Just need the caffeine to kick in."

"Seriously, Alex. I know how you get when you miss them."

Alex bit her lip, eyes darting to the pictures beside her as if afraid to look at them directly. "I just wonder if maybe they would have had some answers, you know?"

"Maybe, but you are in control of your own life. I know it's hard, but you can't hold yourself back thinking about what they may or may not have thought."

"I know. I'm sure I'll be over it once I get to the office," Alex sighed.

"Alright. Well, I'll see you when you get home then. Are you going to see Jackson today? He's getting out, right?"

"Yeah. He's just waiting for a few final results to come back, and he should be good to go."

"It's so weird they kept him there for that long, but I guess that's why I'm not a doctor," Becky laughed, crystalline and charming. It knocked away the last bit of musty air that clung to Alex.

"Give yourself some credit. You heal people of their ailing closet selections," Alex said. Their giggling rung through the house for a moment before she reached over to embrace Becky in a hug. "Thanks, by the way."

The model's long arms wrapped Alex in return. "Anytime."

When they released each other, Alex lit up. "Oh, thanks for reminding me. Jackson wanted to borrow my poster for a project in his film history class," she said.

"Sounds about right for him. Anyway, I need to get to work. Call if you need me," said Becky. She hugged Alex once more before rushing out the front door. The sound of an engine starting followed. As her roommate's beat up Corolla sped out of the driveway, the morning's silence returned to Alex's den. Slinking down the right hallway to her bedroom, she regretted her insistence on waking up so early.

Pushing open the door to her room, Alex tiptoed around a heap of items on her floor. For a brief moment, she wondered if she should be upset about not tidying up the previous night, but the desire for order failed to grab her. Notes, pencils, a bright red bag, and her undoubtedly drained laptop were strewn across the unkempt mass of pink sheets on her bed. Magazines focused on literary and cultural impact, a rarity among Alex's people, were stacked hastily among no-longer-relevant softball trophies on a solitary bookshelf in the corner. The only straightened spots were along the walls: photos, rough penciled sketches, and article clippings. A framed poster for *Lawrence of Arabia* watched from above a messy computer desk, Peter O'Toole's piercing gaze acting as a silent protector over all he surveyed.

Digging through clothes piled about her feet, Alex found an acceptable pair of work sneakers, threw them onto the bed, and rushed into the attached bathroom to give herself a once-over with the mirror. Examining the bags under her eyes, she wished she kept more of a habit of wearing makeup, but it always turned out awkward on her despite Becky's tutelage. She settled with little more than a few quick splashes of water to get color back into her cheeks.

"What am I going to do with you?" she asked herself, praying that her reflection would answer back. Instead, she only saw an exhausted 22-year-old with a mop that made Einstein seem positively dapper.

Alex sighed, flicked off the bathroom light, and returned to her bed. She tried her best to fit the notes on her bed into her backpack. After no small amount of negotiating, she managed to close the zipper enough to hold in the contents. Turning, she stared at the giant film poster overlooking the chaos. She lifted the frame from its hook and laid it gingerly on the bed. Grabbing one of a multitude of cardboard art tubes leaning against the bookcase, she dismantled the back of the frame.

The poster was an original, printed on a thick material she had never seen for modern movies. Despite being over 50 years old, it showed little sign of yellowing or fading. A slight crease in the top left corner was the only sign of wear. It was one of the few material items Alex could honestly claim she loved. The image of Lawrence riding towards her, brandishing a scimitar as armies marched in the distance, never failed to ignite her imagination. As she painstakingly put the poster into the tube, she realized it was probably the first time she had taken it out of its frame in years.

A glance at the alarm clock next to her desk drained Alex of what little confidence she had of getting to her office on time. She resolved to at least not leave anything behind, a habit she found increasingly annoying in recent weeks. With one final look through the disheveled room, she carried her bags out of the house, turned the lock, and left without so much as a peek at her rearview mirror.

A few minutes of sunlight remained as Alex tore into the parking lot of the massive hospital. After attempting a story about a building purchase and staring at cat pictures on the internet for a few hours, she fled the office without looking back. Her relief in ending the work day almost resulted in several speeding tickets as she tore down the short stretch of Broadway towards the hospital. The gleaming windows looking out over University Park beckoned her inside.

Navigating the overly white hallways unnerved Alex. Her pace quickened to make it through the labyrinth as quickly as possible. Jackson's warmth would make her feel better, but the journey to him was Alex's worst part of the day. The antiseptic lights were too bright and artificial for the grim knowledge of hospital life. Growing up, she had not spent much time within the various buildings, but those few times were enough to etch a deep dislike for them. She did not mind doctors, but she wished she had a single, friendly doctor who made house calls like in old Western films.

Entering a hushed reception area several stories up, Alex turned right down a corridor and reached her destination. The door was shut, a small '429' embossed in black onto a sign above the door handle. She straightened her clothes as best as she could, took a deep breath, and knocked. A gruff "Come in" sounded from inside, signaling Alex to enter with a giddy smile on her face.

Sitting up in his motorized bed and surfing television was a man who returned an equally goofy smile at the sight of the tired writer. Alex's unease dripped away upon seeing him.

"Hey there, cowgirl. Come to tend the wounded?" asked the man with a warm, silky drawl.

"Why yes, Mr. Jackson," replied Alex in an exaggerated Southern accent. "Doctor's here for your treatment."

Dropping her bag, she met Jackson's embrace on the small bed. His lips tasted of cinnamon. Caught in his gray eyes, she was able to ignore the bandages and cuts decorating his features. She sat for a few moments, content to enjoy his warmth and run her hands through his scraggly brown hair.

Alex had been quite the tomboy growing up, constantly running around in a ratty baseball hat and jeans. She was known for helping her friends bale hay on their farms in the late summers. Where other girls her age were playing with fashion dolls or cooking sets, Alex was throwing baseballs or exploring rivers. She felt natural playing the rowdier games.

By the time she made it to junior high, the men she knew began to see her as something other than just a solid teammate. Alex even tried dating a couple of them but never felt a click beyond friendship. After she lost her parents, the extroverted tomboy began to fade away, replaced with a recluse too busy with work and school for love.

When she met Jackson, wandering lost through the university halls, Alex stopped worrying for the first time in years. He was tall, tan… a walking cliché of what a handsome man should be. He could take home any girl on campus, yet he nervously asked Alex out for coffee. Despite a confident city-boy exterior, he turned out to be a Film History nerd who was absolutely smitten with the country girl.

She was at ease around him, the first person aside from Becky to lay that claim since high school had ended. Jackson, in return, listened intently to what Alex had to say and gave an honest look at her endeavors. Their talks left her feeling confident in herself again.

However, Alex's lingering struggles made their relationship blossom slowly. Jackson never complained about Alex's hesitance to let people into her world. Eventually, she grew comfortable enough to lead him to her house. She remembered having a movie on but little else about her surroundings. She had been too focused on the smell of his cologne, the rough stubble that bristled in her hands. And the car accident after he left that hospitalized him for three days.

Sitting next to Jackson, alive and attentive, all her fears from that night had been replaced by an excitement in having him to herself again. No matter what happened in her professional life, she at least had Jackson as a rock to steady herself. With him, Alex never overthought things; she was content to lay down and channel surf from their medical lodging without having to worry about what the next day would bring.

"How was work?" Jackson asked from within their cozy haze.

"I just… I don't know. I think I'm going crazy."

"That's because you are crazy. You're a little viper just waiting to strike. It's in your eyes!"

Alex slapped his leg playfully. "I'm serious! I've been out of it all day for some reason."

"Aw, tell me about it. What's up?" Jackson wrapped his trim arms around her. Alex leaned into his chest, letting his steady breathing set pace for her own.

"I don't know. I've just been kind of listless the past few days. Like nothing I do really matters in the end."

"Is it work? Deadline or something coming up?"

She rubbed her fingers over her temples. "No. Just the opposite. I've been so bored there. I feel like I'm not going anywhere. This city's so slow, it's suffocating. And with all the bills and stipulations in the will it feels like I'm trapped. Like I don't have any control over my own life."

Jackson leaned forward to kiss Alex's cheek. Even through a hospital stay, he smelled of spice and sugar.

"You'll escape this place," he said. "Sooner than you think. You'll find a great paper in Chicago or New York or somewhere else big and grand and you'll never have to look back. Just don't let yourself get so down you can't remember how great you are."

"Maybe…" Alex trailed off. Her eyes burned from

lack of sleep and the sheer gratitude of hearing Jackson encourage her again. Even if she had trouble truly believing in those words.

The two aimlessly watched figure skating on television, mesmerized by the calming, flowing movements of the dancers. Only after several commercial breaks did Alex realize the sun had long set.

"You're sure the doctor said he'd be in soon?" questioned Alex, sitting up in the narrow bed. When she arrived, Jackson had already been dressed and ready. She couldn't imagine the hospital not wanting to get the room cleared out.

"Well, he said the results could take a bit. Gotta make sure my head's all right, hon."

"Your head's never been all right," she teased, thumping him softly on the forehead. "I just want to see you outside of this room, assuming you don't wreck every time you drive somewhere."

"Not my fault you live out in the boonies with fearless deer. Anyway, they should be almost done. We'll go back to watching old Audrey Hepburn movies soon enough."

The mention of the actress made Alex perk up. She leaned over the bed and grabbed the cardboard poster tube near her belongings.

"I almost forgot," Alex said. "You said you wanted my poster for your film history class right? Just bring it back in one piece or I'll personally put you right back in this room!"

Jackson gave a dramatic grimace as she bonked him on the arm with the tube. He gingerly slid the poster from the holster and unrolled it enough to see the main title scrawled across the top. "Thanks, Alex. I promise to be careful with it."

"You'd better be! And let me know when you actually watch it. I can't believe there's a classic I've seen that you haven't! It's amazing."

"I will, hon," he said, sliding the poster back into the tube. "I'd watch it with you tonight, but I've been sitting for too long already. I need to move around."

"I know. And, hey, speaking of…" Alex bit her lip, trying to figure out how to phrase her question. There had been only one thing nagging her in regards to their relationship. "Now that you've been to my place, maybe next time…" she let the question hang in the air.

Despite their relationship, Jackson rarely mentioned his home life, either his past in St. Louis or his current station. He noted once, briefly, that he was staying in one of the single-person dorms, but every attempt to bring it up again was met with disregard or a change in subject. Even when she was relatively close to his area, he insisted on meeting somewhere downtown, or the mall, or practically anywhere but his dorm.

Jackson's embrace stiffened, but his voice remained cool as ever. "Well, maybe soon, hon. You know how uptight they are about visitors. Besides, the place is just a mess right now. I promise not to keep you waiting, though."

Alex sagged and muttered a disappointed, "Okay."

Jackson, noting her tone, held her close to his chest. "Don't worry. Soon. I promise," he said.

Alex returned a sheepish grin, cracking under his earnestness. They kissed, and the matter was forgotten. As their lips parted, the beeping of Jackson's wristwatch startled the couple, and he fumbled to turn it off.

"Ok, you may be a little right. This is taking forever," Jackson said. "Hon, do you think you could go get me a coffee while we wait?"

Alex rolled off the bed. "Sure, dear," she said, going in for another quick kiss. She rifled through her purse for some change and left the room with Jackson waving behind her.

Jackson's room was nestled at the far end of a hallway in one of the newest sections of the hospital. The staff would normally be busy with movement, but the reception area disclosed a great deal of work being done to complete the building in the hallway opposite Jackson's. With the construction crews gone, the floor was occupied only by Jackson and a scant few others.

Walking back to the main atrium for the floor unnerved Alex with its silence. She made a point to ask for directions from the elderly nurse behind the desk, if only to hear something other than the hum of florescent lights or the squeaking of some distant, invisible gurney. The nurse, evidently as desperate for interaction as Alex, took her time reciting stories of the new building's creation before dispensing directions.

After several twists and turns from the reception area, Alex found a waiting room filled with cushioned chairs, a wall of vending machines, and a lone sofa with magazines piled on a glass table beside it. Like most of the building, the room was also unoccupied, and Alex wanted nothing more than to get her coffee as quickly as possible. She fumbled for the change in her pocket, the ever-present buzz from the machines overtaking her senses.

"Just get in and get out," she spoke into the air. "It's just a hospital. We'll be done in a minute."

As her quarters rolled into the coffee machine and

dark brew streamed into a paper cup, the white noise reached a crescendo. It burned through Alex's skull with an intensity that nearly drove her to scream. She reached up to cover her ears just as an explosion rocked the building.

At first, Alex thought an earthquake struck, that the doomsayers were right about the New Madrid fault finally waking up. The floor no longer held her feet, and she fell disoriented onto the cold tile below. Only the sensation of scalding water hitting her hand helped bring attention back to her surroundings. By the time she realized what had happened, the shaking stopped. The blaring of emergency buzzers sounded, strobes streaking the walls in blinding flashes.

Regaining her balance and nursing her throbbing hand, Alexandra made her way to the waiting room door. The doctors and patients that eluded her earlier were now scrambling down the halls in evacuation. Her assumptions of a mild quake were doused as thick, acrid smoke filled the halls as she entered the reception area. She coughed, eyes stinging, and found herself dropping once again to the ground as she had done so many times in drills during school. Scattered shadows continued to scream by, but they were impossible to reach in the haze.

Hissing rain poured down as the sprinklers clicked

on. Alex barely registered getting drenched. Earthquakes, tornadoes... she could handle natural disasters. Invited the change of pace they brought, even. However, she became increasingly aware that she had not been caught in a natural disaster. Panic seized her mind as she raced to find something familiar. She couldn't rationalize this new threat like she could an earthquake.

"Jackson!" she yelled, but there was no response from him or anyone else. She coughed again, and her next cry for help stuck in her throat, drowned amid the sprinklers and still-buzzing fire alarms. Somewhere in her memory, she remembered that a person should stay in one place when lost. Crumbling to the ground, she cried, holding her numb fist in the folds of her shirt. She begged for the universe to send Jackson to find her.

The emergency lights stopped. Three dark forms approached Alex between billows of white smoke. She thought to say something to them, to make herself known. As the figures took form and gained weight, she saw they were already heading straight for her.

Two rugged men strode on the sides. The man on the left was significantly older than his counterpart, an unkempt salt-and-pepper beard matching his hair. The younger was clean-shaven with dirty-blonde hair and a broad chest covered in tattoos. Sabers rested at the sides of bright clothes that hung like loose rags.

The third figure was one of the largest women Alex had ever seen. She towered above the frightened girl, exposed arms revealing an Amazonian figure of sinew and tightly knotted muscle. Alex sat captivated as the stranger knelt to greet her. A single, emerald eye pierced her with an illegible gaze; the woman's right eye hid behind a gilded eyepatch.

"You're the Stirling girl." The woman's husky voice left no trace of a question.

Alex pulled a wet string of hair away from her face and nodded, mouth agape. The stranger wore a dazzling, leathery armor colored in the richest azure Alex had ever seen. Golden markings woven into the fabric shifted and swirled on their own like glowing tentacles, mesmerizing her with their pattern.

The woman lifted Alex's chin with a coarse finger. "Your poster. The Arabian film. Where is it?"

Alex balked at the question, waiting for a punchline. When the tanned features of the woman failed to soften, Alex managed to squeak, "I… I gave it t-to my boyfriend."

The intruder cursed. She whipped herself up to the brutes behind her, causing Alex to jump in her skin.

"What should we do? He'll be gone by now," asked

the older man with a deep timbre.

The woman ran a hand through her crop of fiery hair and replied in a language Alex had not heard before. It sounded ancient and forgotten, the words flowing and dancing like fairies on a moonlit evening. They carried on for several seconds, the woman gesturing with such animation that Alex could only guess she was giving orders.

Alex willed herself to her own feet, trying to make sense of what they were saying. The only clear indicators were names being repeated; the younger man was apparently named Sorin. The older man was Fleet. The woman's name was harder for Alex to understand in their foreign language, but it sounded like 'Gwee-heh.'

The mist dissipated under the sprinklers. Around them, the atrium was clear of everyone except Alex and the invading trio. With the three chatting amongst themselves, a moment of escape flashed in Alex's head. Large as the three were, they carried only narrow blades for weapons. She may have been stocky, but Alex was quick, and the hospital was hall after hall of turns and dead ends. If she could lose them in the maze, she could find a hiding spot until the police showed up.

Amid the foreign conversation, Ghaoithe said, pointedly, "I advise you to stay put, Miss Stirling." The leader in blue had not even turned around, keeping the back of her blazing hair towards their captive.

Tears welled up in Alex's eyes as a string of possibilities ran through her mind, each progressively more terrible than the last. Her hand twitched painfully, which only served to make her sob more.

The group's discussion ended. Fleet, the eldest one, walked briskly towards the unfinished hallway where a few faint puffs of smoke continued to billow from within. The man in the open-chested shirt strode towards Alex and reached out a hand.

"You need to show us the room he was in," demanded Sorin. He boasted a thick accent, though far different and gruffer than the flowing dialect they had been chatting in. Was he Russian? Ukranian? At Alex's hesitation, he continued, "There's no time. We must hurry."

Scared but unable to see any other options, she grasped his hand, which was firm but not forceful. Slipping on the flooded tile as they marched, she led them down the hallway that had housed Jackson. The door to his room had been closed again, and the handle did not turn at Alex's command. Ghaoithe nudged Alex aside and bent down to the lock.

"Just a moment," said Ghaoithe. From within the

folds of the sash at her waist, she pulled out two slivers of metal.

"Please, don't hurt me. I don't know what this is about, but I was just visiting my boyfriend," cried Alex. She immediately regretted it. Bad guys never cared about the people crying for help in movies. It only drew unwanted attention to their hostage.

"We don't plan on hurting you. Just hold on," said Ghaoithe. She tinkered with the slender pins, now firmly entrenched in the door's keyhole until it clicked. The door popped open. She stepped in, flicked on the light, and began scouring the room.

Jackson had disappeared. Aside from sheets tossed about the bed and Alex's bag on the floor, no trace of the man existed. The cardboard tube holding the poster sought by Ghaoithe and her companions had fled with him.

The one-eyed woman made a swift pass through the room, checking under the bed and other tight spots. Her demeanor grew more dissatisfied as the search went on. Standing in contemplation in the middle of the room, she furrowed her thick eyebrows, grasping for an undisclosed clue. In a final gesture of hope, Ghaoithe swept up the tan folder of medical files at the foot of Jackson's bed and flipped it over. Blank pages fluttered to the ground. She burst into a series of long, gruesome expletives that startled Alex.

"Why do you want Jackson?" tested Alex once Ghaoithe calmed down.

"There's no time to explain," said Ghaoithe. "I'm sorry, but you'll have to stick with us for just a little longer."

"I was just in here 10 minutes ago! What did he do?" Alex's panic reached a fever pitch. Fear and confusion mixed to form bile in her throat. She needed to believe that Jackson escaped with the other patients, but something in her mind told her that he was gone for good.

He knew this was coming and left Alex behind.

"Just get your bag and come on," Ghaoithe ordered.

Alex's eyes glossed over at the leader. Ghaoithe and the two men were the only link she had to Jackson now. Was he some kind of drug dealer? A scam artist? She refused to believe that Jackson, her sweet Jackson, could be involved in anything so sinister yet here were these thugs hounding for his trail.

Not wanting to upset her captors any further, Alex grabbed her pack and held it tightly to her chest. If she managed to sneak in a call to 9-1-1 from the cell phone in her pack, then all the better.

The group ushered their way back down the hall to the unfinished partition as the sprinklers shut down and silence fell. Alex's unsure footing over the slick tile squeaked through the abandoned corridors as though she were exploring some long-forgotten urban habitat in a horror film. No trace of the doctors or patients from the earlier madness remained, leaving the entire floor to Ghaoithe.

The bearded man, Fleet, awaited them outside the plastic drapes marking the new construction. "Everything just as planned, ma'am," he said, uncrossing his arms.

"Absolutely sure?" replied Ghaoithe.

"No one hurt, and the only hole to the building is the one we put in it. The local law'll be here soon, though."

"Are we set to launch?"

"On yer word, ma'am."

As if on cue, the sirens of distant police cars screamed to life outside the building. Ghaoithe grabbed Alex's arm and led the team down the deserted hall. Most of the rooms had been completed but sat empty without furnishings or paint. Sawdust and a few scrap pieces of timber littered the ground, shaken loose by whatever blast shook the building. Without lighting along the path, Alex tripped over loose materials only to be held up by Ghaoithe's unwavering grip.

At the far end of the hall, light poured in from a doorway to greet them. They ran faster as they approached it.

Ghaoithe released Alex to run ahead. Searing pain burned Alex's eyes as she turned the corner to follow. She blinked, trying to remove her blindness.

The source of the dazzling light came from a massive opening blown from the wall. Rubble and exposed rebar blanketed the remains of the rooms that once resided there. A cool night breeze washed Alex's senses of the dampness within the hospital. As her eyes adjusted, the light faded, took form, and Alex lost her balance in disbelief.

Outside the hospital, floating several stories above the Earth, hovered a massive steel ship.

Looking back on the moment, Alex wished she could say that her drive as a reporter kicked in, that she had the ability to jump headfirst into danger for the sake of a good story. In reality, she stood petrified at the edge of the landing. All she could focus on was the drop from the battered hospital wall.

The physics-defying ship did not escape her mind; glowing blue markings covering the metal hull lit up every inch of the fall to the ground below like the lights on a baseball field. Only a narrow steel plank bridged the gap from the building to the sleek ship's deck.

Alex squinted against the light, trying to guess how many steps she could take before falling to her demise below. The ship silently dared her to cross. On the bow, written in intricate, sweeping letters, radiated the name *"Cloudkicker"* as if the ship were nothing more than an elegant bar one could stroll in to for an evening cocktail.

There is no way in Hell, Alex thought to herself. Far below, the police arrived, pushing back a growing crowd of onlookers. Worst of all, her coworkers stood next to their blocky news van. *I'm going to fall to my death on national television.*

Knowing she was on camera scared Alex as much as the drop at her feet. She at least wanted to be the girl successfully kidnapped by air pirates, not the unfortunate collateral damage in their raid. Headlines flashed in her head: **Attack by Unknown Airship Terrorists Claims Local Girl.** Alex was going to be a statistic.

Her visions of disaster were cut short when Fleet hoisted her onto his shoulder.

"Sorry, lass, but we can't wait around for ya to admire the scenery," he said.

Before Alex could protest, they were on the gangplank traversing the air. She clamped her eyes shut, more worried about becoming a pancake than acting as a knapsack for a stranger. Wind battered her face, sending panic through her body until her feet were placed on solid ground once more. The sirens and chatter from below disappeared as Fleet closed a door behind them.

Her eyes adjusted to a low, wooden hallway stretching to her left and right. Just beyond, voices echoed through the walkways. Beside her, the behemoth shape of Fleet waited. His eyes twinkled in amusement as he stared at her.

Alex glared up at him. "So what now? You torture me for info?" she asked. She figured that if her fate had been sealed, she wanted to get on with it.

"Now, I take ya downstairs and lock ya up in yer bedroom," Fleet said as he stroked his beard.

Alex could not tell if he was joking at first. As they made their way down a side staircase and into a long corridor, she knew he was not.

The hall was much brighter than the upper level with wood paneling emitting a soft glow without an apparent source. They passed several rooms, a galley, and storage areas filled with sealed crates before arriving at one of the final doors on the right.

"Can't you just make me walk the plank or something and get it over with?" asked Alex.

"No plank-walkin' today," chuckled Fleet. "We just

don't want ya wanderin' around. This liftoff might be a little rough."

Fleet opened the door, nudged Alex gently inside, and twisted the lock with a resounding *click*. Deep down, she knew the door wouldn't open, but she gave the handle a half-hearted tug anyway. When it didn't budge, she tried pulling harder and then resorted to kicking. The logical part of her mind had left in desperation until she wore herself out of energy.

Slumping to the floor, she pulled her knees up to her chin and began to cry. All of her fear, confusion, and frustration flowed through her, as much out of a need to do *anything* rather than listlessly accept her prison. She wanted the home and coworkers she had complained of. She wanted Jackson. Would she ever see any of them again?

The rhythmic bobbing of the *Cloudkicker* had almost rocked her to sleep when a sharp jolt forced her back to reality. The room lurched, and her stomach jumped into her throat. She knew that she was now airborne, sailing away from the only place she had ever called home.

Stiff and exhausted, she rose from the doorway to explore her prison. A bed covered with crisp vanilla sheets invited her to the corner. At its foot stood a vanity, Alex's hair frazzled beyond hope in its reflection. A private restroom had been tucked away near the room's entry. There were no windows, only the omnipresent light. All-in-all, it felt like some twisted hotel room more than a prison.

She plopped onto the bed, soft and fresh-smelling. Her bout of tears had dulled her immediate panic, but in its place came a sense of impending dread. Her crazed imagination flashed terrible images. She remembered reading that pirates sometimes trapped prisoners in barrels of brine or buried them up to their necks near anthills as a means of exacting information. She did not want to be food for ants.

Underlying her fear, however, was something else. As the full weight of her situation sank in, her heart beat with not just fear, but also excitement. She was on an airship. An actual, honest-to-god, straight-out-of-the-movies airship. Shouting with a tiny, desperate voice was her sense of journalistic duty. It grew louder, more powerful, as questions cascaded into her thoughts. Where had they come from? Why did they want the poster? How could something so massive stay hidden for long?

The answers had to wait. For the first few hours of flight, booms resounded at uneven intervals, followed shortly by turbulence that sent her rolling off the bed until she could no longer concentrate on her thoughts. Without windows, she had no frame of reference to where she was heading, how high up they flew, or if anyone attempted to pursue their ship. The vanity drawers contained no distraction. She regretted not keeping a book stuffed among her bag's inhabitants.

As a last resort, her phone came out unscathed in the breakout. An attempted call to Becky resulted in a screeching, piercing static that left Alex reeling in dismay. Her internet browser yielded nothing. She chalked it up to whatever mystical voodoo held the ship aloft and resorted to playing games instead. For once, she was grateful for being stuck in the news office all day, leaving the phone freshly charged as she sat at her workstation.

Destroying multi-colored blocks proved a welcome respite for her head. Time managed itself until the click of her door's lock brought her attention back to her captors. Bolting upright, Alex glared as the younger man, Sorin, stepped inside, his blonde hair and chest tattoos far too dashing for someone who just raided a hospital.

"All right, Stirling. Leave your things and come up," he said in his thick dialect. Alex tucked her phone in her pocket, nodded, and followed. Each step progressively tugged more on her soul. Finally, as she feared her heart would burst, the two arrived back at the stairwell that first greeted her.

"I really don't know anything. There's no point in grilling me over all this," she pleaded.

"That's not my decision."

"I'm just saying there would have been a lot fewer headaches for you guys if you left me back there. Now you're going to have all kinds of charges once the military catches up. If they don't blow us to shreds first."

She had no clue if the military was even going to get involved, but she did her best to sound as though she knew what she was talking about.

"Your military does not worry us," said Sorin.

The nonplussed response was not what Alex expected. She shrugged, trying to act cool and fearless, though her voice wavered. "Suit yourselves. But you're really wasting your time with all this. No point in keeping me locked in a room when you had all the info I could give you before I was even on this... thing."

"You were locked for safety," he replied. "Sometimes we fly close, and things get difficult."

Close to what, exactly, he left to her interpretation. As if she didn't have enough trouble understanding his rough, brutish English.

They climbed the stairs, passing by the main entrance and continuing up. Alex remained silent, pondering how a seasoned journalist would approach her situation. "An airship, huh? How did you guys stay hidden for…"

"Inside," Sorin cut her off. They reached the top of the stairs, which ended with a lone door. It stood slightly ajar, bathing their cramped stairwell with a warm glow. Shooting Sorin one last futile glance, Alex inhaled deeply and entered the captain's chambers.

Waiting inside at a large writing desk sat Ghaoithe. Cluttering the space around her were maps, books, tiki masks, carved statuettes, and other objects from seemingly every corner of the world. There was even an ornate spinning globe bolted down to the corner Ghaoithe's table. The decor caught Alex off her guard, forgetting for a moment that the gigantic woman was not a history professor but instead a commander who blew a hole through a hospital building.

Alex stepped in as the door slammed behind her. The horribles fates she had imagined in her bedroom came screaming back. Her hands trembled, and she worried her knees would buckle under the stress.

The rogue took her boot-clad feet off the desk and leaned towards Alex. Ghaoithe gestured and said, "Don't be afraid. Come on in. Take a seat."

Alex complied, and they sat staring silently at each other as they sized up their prospective words. Alex's original impression of a swarthy, dangerous terrorist began to fade the longer they sat. Without the smoke and blaring alarms, she noticed for the first time the sprinkling of freckles across Ghaoithe's nose. She could not have been older than thirty with only the faintest beginnings of wrinkles at the corners of her eyes. She was clean-cut, even pretty in a strange, exotic fashion that Alex had not been accustomed to in her white-washed hometown.

As they judged each other, Alex felt less like she was in a pirate captain's quarters and more like she had been called into the principal's office in school. Fidgeting in her seat, she decided to break the silence.

"Look, I really don't know anything. I'm just an intern who was visiting her boyfriend," Alex said.

"I know. Do you want a drink?"

Alex balked. She noted her thirst for the first time since she had gone in search of the coffee machine.

"Um, sure. If you're playing Good Cop, I'll take some water. Thanks," she said, her eyebrows scrunching in confusion.

Ghaoithe strode to a side table near the bed, her height shrinking the room considerably. She poured a drink from a clear pitcher cooled by fresh ice. It was the only drink without an alcoholic label on the stand.

"I'm not playing any cop," Ghaoithe said. "You are a guest on my ship, and we do not get many guests. As long as you are here, you will not be harmed by any of my crew." She handed the water to Alex and extended her other hand. "Since we never had formal introductions, I am Ghaoithe Loinsigh, Captain of the *Cloudkicker*."

"I'm, uh, Alex." Alex shook the captain's hand then then took a draught from the chilly mug. She tried to place the captain's accent but came up with nothing, it's raspy, lyrical movement not immediately recognizable. "Are you usually so cordial with your prisoners? Seems odd after you locked me up."

Sitting back down, the giant woman folded her hands beneath her chin and stared inquisitively at Alex with her one emerald eye.

"No, I guess not," she said with a chuckle. "I didn't want someone unused to our ship getting hurt during takeoff. It got a little rough once Whiteman spotted us, as I'm sure you felt."

Alex sputtered in mid-gulp. "Whiteman?! The Air Force base? That's what all that shaking was?" she asked. At Ghaoithe's shrug, she shouted, "Just what the hell kind of ship is this?"

"A very special one," Ghaoithe said. "Unfortunately,

we don't have a lot of time to talk about the *Cloudkicker*. I hate to get to business, but I need to ask you a few things."

She ducked and rummaged through her desk drawers. Alex sipped her water, boggled by the implications of the airship taking on a military base. She hoped whatever Ghaoithe searched for would bring answers, and she gawked at the captain with wide-eyed curiosity. Her disappointment was almost palpable when a poster for *Lawrence of Arabia* unfurled before her.

"That's it?" Alex sighed in frustration. "What is with this poster that's so important?"

Ghaoithe straightened the copy on the table. She leaned in towards her counterpart. "You had your copy for quite some time, yes?"

"A few years. I kept it above my computer desk."

"Can you recall it by memory?"

"Probably better than most, I guess. Why?" Alex asked, scratching her head.

"I need you to tell me what's different in this one."

"I didn't think Columbia Pictures really cared this much about errors in their posters."

"This is an actual poster. Your's was a very special duplicate. I really need you to look at this," Ghaoithe stated, straight-faced.

Alex sighed and stood up to look over the artwork. It was smaller than her copy but otherwise the same in every way. Lawrence's gaze bore through the canvas print, an army of men ready to join him in crossing the boundary towards reality. She had woken up to those same blue eyes every morning.

"There's nothing different," relented Alex.

"There is. Just think carefully. There has to be something," the captain said with the patience of a schoolteacher.

Alex strained her eyes, going over as much as she could remember. Every face, color, and brush stroke were exactly as she recalled them when she had taken her copy down in the morning. She was ready to admit defeat until a tiny portion of the print caught her eye, so small it blended seamlessly into the background to anyone not used to seeing it on a daily basis.

She pointed down towards the poster with a cry of excitement. "There! On the left, just at the edge of the sand dune. The signature is different."

Ghaoithe hunched over to get a better look. Alex tried not to look at the dizzying, swirling patterns on the chestpiece inches in front of her.

"You're absolutely sure?" Ghaoithe asked.

"Yes. I woke up to that poster nearly every morning for years. That is definitely a different name. Mine said 'Arias.'"

With the confirmation, Ghaoithe promptly rolled the poster back up, wrote a quick scribble on the white back with a quill pen from her desk, then shoved it back into the drawer.

"Thank you. That's exactly what I needed to know," she said. Sitting back down, she kicked back in her seat and smiled at Alex. "Now, where would you like us to drop you off? If there's anywhere in this country you've ever wanted to visit, I can get you close enough to set you down as a parting gift."

Alex blinked, unable to form words at first. She wanted the rush from finding the puzzle piece to continue.

"That's it, then?" she croaked after a few moments.

"That's it," replied Ghaoithe.

The anticlimactic end turned Alex's excitement into denial. She couldn't accept such a simplified tone, not after the day she had been shoved through.

"You kidnap me on your flying... Batmobile or whatever, scaring the living daylights out of me and all those poor people in the hospital, and tell me my boyfriend is gone. You aren't even going to explain why?" she said, digging her fingers into her palms.

"As cliché as it sounds, the less you know, the better. Your best option right now is to go on a nice vacation for a bit, be thankful you are safe, and continue on with a normal life," said Ghaoithe.

Alex smoldered in her seat. Ghaoithe did not appear to find anything wrong with the statement, despite the incredulous glare from Alex. Though in her mind, Alex knew that going home would be the logical thing to do, leaving without closure provoked a stubbornness bred from many years of country living. Her mind flickered with thoughts of her home, of Becky, of interviews with reporters over the unbelievable situation she had been dragged into. She imagined, sometime in the distant future, weaving a tale of her brief ordeal for her grandchildren after she was old and the world had become a much different place where flying ships were no longer a matter of fantasy.

She would go back to Missouri and finish her internship. People would discuss her kidnapping as A Thing That Happened Once before finding a new distraction in their lives. Life would return to a steady constant of paying rent and writing about the political affairs of local city councils.

It was not the future Alex wanted. Not truly. She was

on an *airship* in front a captain who wore *magical armor.* And she asked for Alex's help.

The pangs from missing wide-open cornfields had already passed.

"I'm not going," Alex said bluntly. The only sign of surprise from the captain was an arched eyebrow.

"Not going?"

"No. Not going. I am staying on this ship until you tell me what the hell is going on."

A smirk painted the corner of Ghaoithe's lips. "My crew brought you here. I'm sure they can escort you back to land as well."

"I'm not worried about Fleet or Sorin or any of your goons," Alex said. This time, the other woman did let a brief expression of surprise escape before regaining her composure.

"You picked up on their names that quickly? My, my, you are an observant one. I can see why you'd want to be a journalist," Ghaoithe said. "However, even if our destination wasn't incredibly dangerous - which it will be for a one-horse-town girl like yourself - what in the world would I do with you on my ship? I'm not offering a cruise here."

The captain made a point. Alex did not know the first thing about ships or flying, and she couldn't imagine a freeloader being welcomed with open arms.

"I will work. I'm not the kind of woman to ask for anything for free," Alex suggested. "I will learn what you need me to learn. I'm used to working long days and doing heavy lifting if I need to. It's just until I can see what this is all about. You can't throw this much at a person and not expect them to have questions."

Ghaoithe sighed and rubbed her eye. "What about your friends and home? You're willing to just leave? There's a good chance you'll never see them again."

Alex looked the captain down with the sternest of faces she could muster and said, "I have no friends. Well, I have one friend, and she's leaving too. My home is taken care of. Anything and everything I could possibly want in Missouri is already gone. You need to find Jackson, which means I'm tied to this ship until he's found. I need a story to tell, and this is it."

"You're awfully trusting to people you've barely spoken to."

"I thought I was going to die several different times today. I'm all out of caution at this point."

Ghaoithe threw her head back in a deep, husky laugh that vibrated into the walls. "Not many people with that mindset these days. You may not be a bad catch at all, Stirling.

Suppose I give you a shot. You sure you're up for this? Not at all afraid we'll end up stranding you on an island with a single bullet or anything?"

Alex's resolve steeled at the sense of progress. "I think if you really wanted to hurt me, you wouldn't have asked. Some writers risk their lives to get interviews with drug cartels. I'll risk mine to fly on a boat... ship... plane. May as well get used to risk early on."

"All right, then. I can't promise how long you'll last, and you'll need to stay out of the way when we get to business. But, I don't suppose it would hurt to have you along if you're certain. Welcome aboard the *Cloudkicker*, Alexandra Stirling," said Ghaoithe. She offered a coarse hand to Alex, which was promptly shaken.

They sat for a moment, letting the moment sink in. Alex had little idea what to expect, but the prospect of adventure started to excite her. She looked around the room, taking in the wild displays and dreaming of romantic journeys to foreign lands. Some childlike part of her wondered if she would begin a collection of her own.

"You seem a bit dazed. Any questions before we start you off?" asked Ghaoithe with a knowing smirk.

Alex's schoolwork kicked in at the opportunity. Reflexively, she reached for her phone and opened the notepad on it. She straightened into the best interview posture she could manage on the swaying ship. As she thought of questions, she blushed, finding her experience lacking far more than she realized.

"Well, to start off," Alex said, "um, how do you actually pronounce your name?"

The captain gave a patient smile not without amusement. "*Gwee-heh Lynn-chee*," she said.

Alex started jotting down notes but stopped after only a few letters, obviously stuck. Ghaoithe cackled and returned to the table lined with drinks, filling two crude shotglasses with an ominous brown liquid.

"It's Gaelic. Sounds nothing like it's spelled. I'll write it down for you, but first we have to start you off on this ship right."

The *Cloudkicker* interior was much larger than Alex had originally imagined, a monstrous amalgamation of wood, steel, and the glowing marks that, at her best guess, were either advanced technology or magic. The resulting aesthetic warped Alex's senses, leaving her feeling like she was simultaneously on both a spaceship and a pirate vessel from *Treasure Island*.

Ghaoithe started the tour with the bridge, what Alex could only describe as a ren raire mockup of the starship *Enterprise*. Morning light unfiltered by the clouds below poured in from the glass window that encircled the forward half of the room. Throughout the floor, crew members bustled about reading maps and checking instruments. Most of their work was familiar and tactile, but just as Alex would get used to the atmosphere, someone would touch the swirling runes at their desk, and the ship would tilt and sway at their command. Alex curiously investigated the sigils as they crossed the room.

"There aren't any computers or power cables under any of these," she observed.

"Nope! Just good, old-fashioned writing. You won't find a lot of modern technology here," Ghaoithe said. She became considerably chattier after a few shots of the sweet liquor in her room but otherwise seemed entirely capable. She moved confidently across the bridge, explaining nautical terms and introducing the crew.

Alex, no stranger to long nights of hard alcohol, had to stop after only a couple swigs of the drink. The buzz, combined with her lack of knowledge about anything Ghaoithe was saying, made understanding the ship all the more impossible. Still, she pounded away at her little keypad to preserve some kind of record, hoping she didn't slur too much in case a moment of clarity came later.

As the tour went on and her battery began to wear thin, Alex worried for her only connection to Missouri. She argued back and forth with herself about powering down the device, spinning it in her hands as she often did when thinking. It slipped between her fingers, smacking against the runes of a table beside her.

Reaching down to pick it up, she gasped upon noticing that the glowing runes had zapped life back into the phone. She shrieked with delight, showing the phone to Ghaoithe. The captain smiled at her with the same tepid interest a parent gives a child who insists on reciting the alphabet repeatedly upon learning it. Alex assumed that the people she had mixed herself in with did not use cellphones and kept to celebrating her small victory with herself.

Below the deck, three levels stretched on with a forth at the bottom of the hull for storage and briefly-mentioned mechanical areas of the ship. Each was fairly busy with people going about their business, playing cards, and otherwise taking it easy with their escape complete.

Alex stumbled into many of the inhabitants as her legs struggled to get used to the constant swaying motion. The vast majority of them simply laughed and helped steady her. Somewhere, the nickname 'Minnow' sprung up and spread like wildfire. Alex resisted at first, not keen on the title, but she had to admit their point; she was, by far, the smallest person on the ship.

"You know, I'm kind of surprised," mused Alex as she and Ghaoithe made their way back to her original jailed-turned-bedroom. Low mutters and a few echoes of laughter belted down the hall from her new neighbors.

"How so?"

"I figured there'd be more debauchery on a pirate ship. Everyone seems pretty calm on the whole."

"We're not pirates," replied Ghaoithe. A sneer crawled across her face at the last word.

Alex tilted her head. "You're not? Then what are you? I thought the whole kidnapping and attacking buildings thing was pretty much a pirate's job description."

"We are relic hunters, Ms. Stirling. We hunt down artifacts that have been forgotten by time or turned into myth. Every legend you have heard has its roots somewhere, and it's our job to find the source."

"So, you're like Indiana Jones?"

"Who?"

The response bewildered Alex more than most anything else. "He's a, uh, movie hero. An explorer. He goes into tombs to find golden idols and the Ark of the Covenant. Stuff like that."

"Never seen it, but yes, we're something like that. Although, I don't know why anyone would want the Ark. It's just an empty stone box."

"I… sure. Ok." Alex decided not to follow up, already too excited at the prospect of adventure to risk losing what little understanding she had. As they reached her room's doorway, one question did pop up. "So, if you guys are treasure hunters or whatever, why am I here? You still haven't explained what exactly you're looking for."

Ghaoithe motioned to close the door. "You'll find out tomorrow. There's a lot we need to go over if you're going to be part of this."

"Fine. Sure. Wait!" Ghaoithe stopped. "How do I turn off the lights? I can't even tell where they're coming from."

The captain chuckled and raised her hand next to the door. She slid open a palm-sized panel that had been perfectly hidden into the wall. The increasingly familiar runes were there, along with a long strip of the glowing energy. Ghaoithe slid her finger along the strip, and the lights began to dim. She gave Alex one last knowing glance and closed the door for the night. Absent was the clicking of the lock.

Though her room was small and mostly unfurnished, Alex happily claimed it as her own. The difference between having a locked door and an open one had a profound effect on her mood as she pounced onto the bed. Its mattress felt plushier, more comforting. She laid in it, staring at the ceiling not with fear of torture but giddiness for what the next day would bring. Only when she arose to the sound of gentle chatter in the hall outside did she realize that she had even fallen asleep at all.

Alex stretched before hopping over to the vanity mirror. Her hair was its usual mess with no hope of getting fixed until they landed. Her clothes, now the lone set she owned, were wrinkled beyond hope. At least the little makeup she wore rubbed deep into her face and gave her an appearance that somewhat matched her new companions. With a brief few moments spent making herself presentable, Alex opened the door and went on her way.

The decks of the *Cloudkicker* were vast but fairly linear. While not a luxury cruise ship, it was more than the pontoons and occasional ferries she had been used to growing up. Alex did not have to walk very far through the narrow hallways before finding the staircase that led to the other areas of the ship. A few of the sailors who recognized her greeted her, often with a Minnow joke, but most seemed to go about their business. She tried her best to keep track of faces, even names when given.

Her room and the galley were on the second level. She apparently slept through breakfast, as the room was mostly calm aside from a few scattered groups playing cards on the long tables. Upon catching a whiff of the meals, her hunger struck with a vengeance. She forgot that she had not actually eaten since her quick lunch the day before. The mess hall had been set up very similar to a buffet, and though he was done cooking for the evening when she met him the previous night, Alex's impression of the rotund Chef Richard had been delightful enough to trust his cooking. Most of the breakfast trays were cleared, but she still managed to scrounge up a hearty portion of scrambled eggs, a couple crispy bacon strips, and biscuits that tasted of fresh buttermilk.

In her starvation, she failed to notice Fleet sitting at one of the tables, rubbing his beard and staring at her with a wide grin. When she turned to take a seat, she caught his eye and blushed, embarrassed at how she must have looked clamoring over her wooden plate. Fleet waved her over to his table.

"*Dia dhuit, conas atá tú?*" he called as Alex approached him.

"Uh, morning?" she replied between bites of bacon. She sat down timidly, unsure of how to approach conversation with the giant man. "What language is that anyway? You guys were talking in it all day yesterday."

"Irish-Gaelic, lass. Not many speak it in the modern world, but Ghaoithe keeps the candle burnin' on this ship," Fleet said with a wink as he sipped on his coffee.

The shade over her mysterious captors began to rise ever so slowly. "She's Irish, then? Is everyone on the ship from there too?"

Fleet let out a boisterous laugh. His spirits were high for the morning, no doubt fueled by caffeine and a daring escape from the military. "No, Ms. Stirling, she's from a world between Ireland and Scotland. And we're not all from there," he said. "In fact, a good lot of us are from places you've never heard of, I wager. All over the world, really."

Alex nodded, appreciative of both the information and a hot meal. She gave the man across the table from her a quick once-over. In the light and out of the initial terror of the hospital, he stared back with bright eyes and sunburned cheeks above the curls of his beard. Alex almost thought of Santa Claus before she remembered how he lifted her effortlessly over his shoulder.

Cautiously, she extended a hand. "I'm Alex. You're Fleet, right?" she asked.

Fleet shook her offer with calloused but gentle hands. "That's my nickname, sure enough. After the river," he said.

While Fleet was forthcoming with answers, Alex tried

to test her boundaries. "Is it normal for you guys to take prisoners as crew members, then?"

Fleet grinned and reached down to take one of the several biscuits off her plate. "Last I heard, ya wanted to be here."

"I, well, yes. Sort of. But Ghaoithe didn't really seem to argue too much about taking on someone she didn't know."

"Ghaoithe has a good eye, Ms. Stirling," Fleet said between mouthfuls. "I think ya impressed her somehow. She likes thinkers and such."

"I didn't think she'd be so willing to let me on, though. All I can really do is write."

Fleet stared at her with playful inquisition. Under the gaze of his dark eyes, Alex's face felt warm, and she turned her attention to her plate. After a moment, the elder sailor chomped into his biscuit.

"We all came to the ship same as you. We had somewhere we wanted to leave, and Ghaoithe is happy to oblige so long as ya pull yer weight and don't try to overtake her ship. She's got a good sense for potential, and somethin' tells me ya have a lot more to offer than ya let on."

Alex's cheeks deepened a shade, but she tried to act natural. "Well, if that's the case, I can't complain."

She managed to talk herself into a corner. Now that she accepted that she was on the ship, her lack of experience marred her excitement. What could she contribute? She had no experience sailing or flying or whatever the *Cloudkicker* did. Her tour of the ship had been overwhelming, and she struggled with understanding most of the jargon thrown at her. Nowhere among the vast crew did there seem to be a generic "swab the decks" internship like she worked in the past, leaving her playing catch-up. Adventuring 101 was not a class she had access to.

Fleet sat patiently while Alex finished the rest of her meal. She hoped she had not made herself sick by feasting on so much so early, but the sway of the ship was barely noticeable. Her extended rest allowed her subconscious to adapt to the new motion.

Returning her plate to the front counter, the two made their way towards the bridge. The mood was significantly different than the night before. With their escape out of the way, the crew relaxed, filling the room with lighthearted chatter and laughter over several mugs of ale scattered among the inhabitants. Alex sneaked glances at the charts and graphs on their tables for a sense of their bearing, but they were an utterly foreign language to her. Sunlight poured through the gigantic curved window surrounding the room, revealing a bubbling sea of clouds, all cotton and fluffy amid the backdrop of blue.

Ghaoithe rose from her perch in the rear overlooking the ensemble. Still clad in her blue clothing, the captain let out a raucous laugh that very well may have been heard back in Missouri.

"Look who finally decided to work!" she shouted at the late arrivals.

"The only thing ya know how to work 'round here is the tap, ya oversized ginger," Fleet responded coolly. Alex grinned.

The response only made Ghaoithe laugh ever harder, if such a thing were possible. She clasped her burly partner on the back as they arrived near the captain's platform. "Get to work and find us our honeypot, you dumbass bear. And you," Ghaoithe pointed at a perplexed Alex, "You are the new Historian. Go talk to Sorin, and he'll get you set up. Meet me back up here once you've been given the basics."

"Historian? Is that even a thing on ships?" Alex wondered aloud. By Ghaoithe's noncommittal grunt and wave of the hand, she assumed that it was not. The prospect of getting to know Sorin excited her, at least, and Alex looked forward to having something to do.

Her bare-chested partner sat on the other side of the

bridge investigating what looked like the ship's manifest. Alex tried to make a note of just how much the ship held and of what, but Sorin closed its pages once he noticed the blonde's presence. He stood up and stretched, his body the perfect Olympian specimen.

"You're the research girl, yes?" he said. Alex took several moments to register the words through his Eastern European accent.

"Historian, I guess?" Alex shrugged, not really sure what exactly she was to the crew quite yet.

"History, research… it is the same. Follow me." Alex followed the bronzed hulk back down into the hull.

"So, what exactly do you and Fleet do for the ship?" Alex asked after several minutes of silence.

"Fleet is Quartermaster. He is Captain Loinsigh's second-in-command and helps fix big issues on the ship."

"And you?"

"I am First Mate. I coordinate all areas and crew of the *Cloudkicker*. Make things run smooth."

Alex hoped Sorin would expand what he meant, but he seemed satisfied with his answers and they walked along in uncomfortable silence.

"How long have you been on the ship?" she tempted.

"Some time. There are not many ships like us," Sorin

replied.

"That's an understatement," Alex nervously laughed, but it fell dead in the air. She tried to ask a few more questions, to detail where they were going or what they were after, but the only responses she could wring from him were grunts or to ask Fleet. By the time they reached the third level of hallways, Alex decided that Sorin was one of the least personable people she had ever met.

They eventually came to a cast-iron doorway a floor below her own room. When Sorin opened it, Alex could not see the difference between it and any of the other storage rooms in the lower holds. A few scattered boxes were secured on shelves along the wall, each of various size and shape. Only when she took a closer look did she notice that the locks did not have any keyholes. Where a clasp normally protected the contents at each crate's opening was a solid, smooth piece of steel inlaid with the runes common aboard the ship.

"What kind of boxes are these? How do you open them?" Alex asked. She ran her fingers over one of the inlays to see if it hid a latch but it was completely smooth aside from the markings. In charcoal on its top was the number '310.'

"These boxes are your job now," replied Sorin. He

handed Alex a thick, heavily bound book of parchment with a worn leather cover. Leafing through, she saw hand-drawn illustrations and notes on a swath of objects. Many of the early pages were crinkled and yellowed, but fresh, hastily added whiter paper brought up the rear. Most of the scrawling letterwork was in a mix of Gaelic and English.

Alex flipped through the pages in bewilderment until she came to a page with '310' headlining the top. As she took in the illustration, her eyes flickered back and forth between the page and the long, thin box next to her. Her mind swapped between making sense of what she was reading and the ludicrousness of the notion it implied until she slammed the book closed and pointed at the box.

"I need this opened," Alex stated bluntly.

Sorin shrugged and pulled a ring out of an inner pocket of his vest. Embedded in the center glinted an emerald filled with a faint light. As Sorin passed the ring in front of the metal plate, the runes burst with light. With a flash, the clasp disappeared, and the lid clicked open. A gleaming longsword, unmarked by any decoration on its reflective blade, rested among folds of vanilla-colored cloth. Alex's tutor passed the ring to her, its metal cool to the touch.

Alex turned to her surly companion. "Is this really Excalibur?" she demanded.

Sorin nodded without turning his attention away from his nails. Deciding to disregard her assigned mentor, she grasped the sword's hilt. It lifted from its container without the least bit of effort. Its length was nearly the size of Alex, but she managed to make a few ungraceful slashes, marveling at its steel slicing through the air.

"So, this is the kind of thing I will be researching?" she asked herself.

Sorin surprised her with an answer. "Yes. The book is your job here. Captain Loinsigh started it. Do not worry about the boxes already here; they have been cataloged. More will come."

"How do these things even exist? Most of what's in this book are just myths."

"Myths must start somewhere," said Sorin haughtily, as if Alex were a child to be scolded. "To fly on the *Cloudkicker*, you must forget what you think is hidden. There are many places and things in the world to be found, but only to those who want to find them. Your job is Relic Hunter, so you must start thinking this way."

His words rang with conviction and truth, but the logical part of Alex's brain rejected any flexibility to what she knew. How could she track down a myth? Surely, if artifacts based on legends were real, they would have been discovered ages ago by proper scientists. It didn't make sense. She could accept being kidnapped, even come to terms with a flying boat through some cartwheels in her logic, but Excalibur?

Still, she wanted to believe. She wanted it to be true more than the analytical part of her admitted. She spent much of her life idolizing explorers and their expeditions. The prospect of jet-setting around the world, finding things thought lost to time, thrilled her.

After taking a few more swipes through the air, getting used to Excalibur's balance, she gripped it tightly over her shoulder and returned to the book. Before Sorin could object – if he even would have anyway – she had both items in tow and made her way back through the hallways with strict determination.

She closed the door to her room with her foot, wanting a quiet respite from any rowdy crowds on the ship. She placed Excalibur softly on her bed. She nearly threw the journal down onto the vanity with an eagerness built up over years of daydreaming. It took up most of the countertop's space. Taking out her phone, Alex scoured through as much as she could to acquaint herself with the tome, often stopping to make notes or snap a photo of a particularly interesting page.

Items and artifacts filled most of the aging pages,

though a few locations were also dispersed throughout. Alex had never heard of the grand majority of them, an extraordinary collection of crystal skulls, dreadful amulets, and ancient cities. The Gaelic writing didn't aide in her comprehension of many of the listings. At times, she would run across a familiar inscription, transporting her back to her youth and tales of princesses or lost continents. Aside from Excalibur, she recognized pages for Atlantis, the hammer Mjolnir, and even an exceptionally detailed page for the *Cloudkicker,* its vertical wings rendered lovingly in ink.

As she studied, Alex noticed that several listings lacked any type of coordinates for discovery. Not everything in the book had been found, judging by the scarcity of information on many of the relics, but even those with a plethora of details hid any list of recognizable locales. There were a few names in bold letters and several mentions of the god 'Osiris,' but little else gave clues to the artifacts' whereabouts or methods of discovery.

Eyes becoming weary, she leaned back in her chair and rubbed life back into her face. Growing up, she fostered a knack for finding minute details missed by everyone else. She was even one of the few in school to enjoy filling out logic puzzles, going through each line of clues with a Sherlockian intensity. On the ship, however, with a book that defied logic, Alexandra threw her hands up in defeat.

A quick glance at her phone revealed that the morning had not passed as quickly as she thought. Despite feeling like she had been pouring over the pages for days, lunch was barely approaching. Fed up with her lack of progress, she tucked the book under her arm, grabbed Excalibur, and began the walk up towards the bridge again.

Fleet and the captain were engaged in a heated card match when Alex returned. Neither paid her any attention, instead yelling at each other over some obscure rule of their game. None of the others on the bridge took notice of the debate. Alex waited to see if the two would calm down at her arrival. When it became apparent they were not going to look her way, she slammed her newfound sword into the wood, where it held with a *thunk*. The two scoundrels stared at it for a moment as their minds processed the cloven table.

Ghaoithe's eye blinked then turned to the reporter. Alex straightened to her full height, which barely reached the top of the sitting captain. To Ghaoithe, Alex looked as though she was holding her breath for a dip in a cold pond.

Snickering, the captain returned her attention to the table, piling the strewn cards as best as she could. She carefully pulled the sword out of the table and rested it on the edge.

"I see you found my book," she said with a wry smile.

"Is this real?" Alex brandished the collection in front of the captain.

"You're holding it, aren't you?"

"Yes, but do these things exist? How in the world can that sword be Excalibur?"

Ghaoithe shuffled her deck, searching for the right words. "Legends start somewhere, even ones about magical swords. Civilization just tends to lose the fine details over time."

"What do you mean?"

"Well, that sword is most definitely Excalibur, but people forget that the Lady of the Lake was just a fisherman's daughter Arthur was shacking up with in his free time. When he told her didn't want to commit to anything, she threw him out and tossed the sword at him because it was the closest thing nearby. It wasn't even that special; just some rusty piece she had found at an abandoned caravan one day. Wouldn't even have been worth anything if Merlin hadn't dropped one of his potions on it a few years later. Old man was a bumbling idiot."

Alex stared, stunned and unsure whether to laugh or throw something herself. "So you're telling me this sword is the same one that was pulled from a stone and can blind its enemies?"

Ghaoithe rubbed her chin as she recalled her discovery. "The sword in the stone was a different version of the story we followed up with for a bit, but we had more luck with the Lady of the Lake angle. I haven't seen it blind anyone, but it can cut through just about anything and doesn't have any weight to it, as I'm sure you've noticed."

Fleet muttered to Ghaoithe, "If she's this excited over the sword, wait till she sees the hammer."

Alex ignored his comment. "How does that exist? How does any of that book exist? If these things are out there, they would have been found by now! These kinds of discoveries could change our entire culture!"

"*Your* culture, sure. But, *your* culture decided they were best left as myths a long time ago," Ghaoithe said, looking at Alex from the corner of her eye as she dealt a new hand of cards. "There are a lot of things unexplained on your side because modern society's lost touch with the world around them. Most people don't want to accept things they can't explain. If it can't be figured out scientifically, it must not exist, right? Meanwhile, they just handwave explanations on how Stonehenge was built or why just the sight of Yosemite can move people to tears."

"You're telling me to believe in magic?"

Ghaoithe shook her head. "Not magic, but you have to accept that there are very old forces at work in the world. If you have the conviction to believe in that, you'll discover all sorts of things that would never be seen otherwise."

Alex pulled up a chair and sat, rubbing her forehead. "It's that simple? Just… look for something and it'll be there? What about GPS and the Internet and all that?"

Fleet grunted and nudged the sword towards Alex to make room for his cards. "Dunno what ya mean by 'GPS,' but no machine's gonna be able to find most of these things. Artifacts are usually protected by very old sigils. Ya can't just walk in to someplace and take 'em off the shelf."

Ghaoithe nodded. "Trying to translate old directions is a lost art. The glowing runes you see around us can do all kinds of things in capable hands, and trying to read clues left by ancient generations is sometimes nearly impossible," she said.

"So you're saying that all this time, there's been a whole other part of the planet completely hidden away from everyone else? Just because we stopped looking?"

"Not just because you stopped looking, but because how to find us has been completely lost to modern society," Ghaoithe said. "Some explorers called our side the Lost Earth. I don't know when the split occurred, but somewhere along the lines, our civilizations grew apart until we separated into two; one that abandoned old language in favor of progress and technology, and one that rejected modernization in favor of using the natural powers around us. There's always been some overlap, which is why we share so many myths and legends, but how we approach them is completely different."

"A few like yerself make the jump," interjected Fleet, "but it's a small number. Even when people know how to find the other, it's not an easy switch. Most don't adjust."

Alex held the sword in her hands, staring at her reflection in its blade. The news of a hidden society was a lot to take in, yet she held the proof in her hands. When she drew her eyes away, she saw that Fleet dealt her two cards.

"Hold 'Em," Fleet grunted with a nod of his head. Alex obliged.

"What kind of power are the sigils then? Why hasn't it been used in our world?" Alex asked. Fleet shrugged and dealt the flop.

"Language of the earth itself, nearest we can tell. Most people can use it to power water and lights and whatnot. In the right hands, they can even hide things in plain sight or stop a bullet from doing any harm," he said, gesturing towards the captain's bright armor. "It has limits, though. We can keep a ship like this afloat, but we can't go into space or anything like that. Most cities in Lost Earth would be pretty old and rugged by yer standards."

"Don't you want to go into space, though? Why cut each other off?"

"Well, how many regular folks wanna spend their lives living without electricity? Or stay in communities cut off from most of the rest of the world and forced to hold their own? We're one of the few crews that can make trades with others, and we spend most of our time crawling through muddy holes in search of relics. It ain't glamorous, and some of yer kind would be bored outta their minds."

Ghaoithe eyed the cards in her hand, her face stonewalling any hint of what she held. "Sometimes people make the jump," she said, "usually genuine explorers like David Livingstone or people who have a heartfelt desire to escape back to the basics. Most don't give us any more than a daydream. It's the same for us. We like living close to nature. We're not interested in cars and glass towers and whatnot. Even those that are find themselves without any of the skills your society requires now, and they eventually come back."

"We ain't completely cut off from each other," Fleet said. "Just most people dunno about or choose not to admit when there's some crossover. The ones that do see 'em don't usually fit in. Folk don't like to think about things that go beyond what they know."

"I guess those people clamoring about UFOs weren't crazy after all," said Alex, absently watching Fleet deal the turn.

"No, the UFO people are definitely crazy," said Ghaoithe as the river hit the table. "Don't worry. We'll teach you how to tell the difference and read signs that others miss. It's easier to show you than try to explain, anyway. You just have to be ok with accepting that a lot of what you thought wasn't possible actually is to a point. Also, three-of-a-kind. You win. Since you didn't have any chips, I'll let you pick a prize."

Taken aback, Alex noticed for the first time that she held three Jacks in her favor without even paying any attention to the game. She wondered what the captain meant by a prize. Looking down, she stared at the warped reflection of herself in the sword's blade.

"I'll take Excalibur," Alex said.

Ghaoithe raised an eyebrow. "Do you even know how to hold it?"

"I'll learn."

Ghaoithe and Fleet exchanged quick glances. "All right. It's yours. We'll try and get a scabbard for it somewhere," Ghaoithe relented.

Alex beamed with elation. Already, she'd received more than she had expected from her first major victory aboard the ship.

She rode her wave of vigor for a few hours more, content to play cards and enjoy the company of her new employers. Though she still could not come to terms with everything they had told her, she chalked it up to Ghaoithe's insistence that seeing was believing. The last thing Alex needed was to start stressing over her new job and life before it even began, a habit formed long ago that only led to sleepless nights and dour moods.

If she was going to have a second start to living, she was going to do it right. It would start with a few rounds of cards, explanations be damned.

Before long, Alex was having a wonderful time. The transition from the hospital to her current state took her through a complete reversal. For their part, Fleet and Ghaoithe welcomed her with open arms. They asked her questions about her life, what it was like living in an electronic world, and what she hoped to accomplish with a genuine inquisitiveness that her past bosses never bothered with. In turn, she would ask them about their travels and distant lands. Through them, she started to see that even the world she was familiar with held much more than she possibly could have imagined. The *Cloudkicker* straddled a world between both worlds, she learned, existing beyond the boundaries of any ruling power all in the search for lost knowledge.

Ghaoithe was especially talkative and jolly, no doubt due to her mug never leaving her hand. The captain's propensity for alcohol was at the very least impressive.

"When yer stuck adrift, ale becomes yer best friend to pass the time," Fleet laughed when asked about Ghaoithe's libation, "and when yer as big as the captain, ya can take a whole lotta drink."

Alex lost her sense of time until a call of "Port ho!" reverberated through the bridge. Without hesitation, her card partners cleaned up the table in one swoop and made their way to their seats. Alex was still sitting, seeing for the first time that the sunlit sky outside the window transformed into a thick layer of fog, obscuring any visual of whatever port they were now destined for.

Alex asked, "What mythical land are we docking at?"

"Roanoke," said Ghaoithe.

Alex rubbed her ear, unsure she heard correctly. "Roanoke? Your hidden world is in the middle of Virginia?"

"Oh dear no, lass. We're off the coast of Brazil now.

This is the Lost Colony," snickered Fleet. The *Cloudkicker* sank below the layer of mists.

VI

For as long as she could remember, Alex had been surrounded by the Ozarks. Her family never traveled much, so her vacations consisted of the ancient forests worn by time. Their almost yearly pilgrimage across her home state to Branson offered winding roads through rugged territory of mist-capped hilltops. To her, the woods were deep and mysterious and old. The terrain formed over millions of years, carefully worn low by time and the elements, covered with mile-after-mile of thick forest grown in verdant soil. The hills of the Ozarks felt familiar, like home.

The mountains surrounding the *Cloudkicker* were

anything but familiar. Towering, narrow spires reached up from beneath the ocean like needles piercing through rough cloth. Green patches clung for dear life on their sheer sides. Looming in the distance, massive cliff faces turned into mountains that turned into clouds. This was not a world meant to be traversed by humans; this was wild, untamed, and exotic.

Alex had seen pictures of similar places from lands like China or Madagascar, but she could never have imagined how tremendous those worlds could be. She gasped as the ship traversed slowly through the alien landscape

Among the mountains ahead, Alex spotted signs of housing built into a cove. The buildings were hastily tiered into the surrounding steaming hills, roughshod exteriors snaking high above sea level and dotting the landscape with their tan and brown faces. Alex read about the favelas of Rio de Janeiro and Sao Paolo, and while the buildings of Roanoke expressed more care than those shantytowns, they still gave off an impression of a crowded, impulsive city.

The *Cloudkicker* slowed in its approach, allowing rain to begin pattering the windows and roof above their heads with a steady, measured rhythm. As the ship closed in on the main portion of the city, a sprawling affair on the low ground of the coast, a beam shot through the mist in their direction before moving on: a lighthouse. It was considerably out-of-place among such old-world aesthetics, a gigantic tower with poles branching out like thorns along its entire length. Along its side, two other airships rested in the air, neither close to the size of the *Cloudkicker*. Beyond them, the lighthouse looked empty from the outside.

Ghaoithe called for the ship to stop for a moment once they were within range of the building. After a few seconds, a blinking red light called to them from the end of one of the poles. The captain nodded, and the ship bounded cautiously forward. At the last moment of their approach, the ship turned to line up even with their dock. Two muffled thuds sounded from the ship's right side. The vessel lurched at the sound then became entirely steady, and Alex knew they had anchored.

"Stay close, and try not to fall off," Ghaoithe said with a wink. "Leave your stuff behind for now."

Alex was unclear on what Ghaoithe meant until they were outside. The long poles jutting from the lighthouse were actually flat on top, walkways leading to the main building. Alex struggled from the moment she stepped off the boat to stay balanced. Having become used to the swaying of flight, she found that getting her land legs back was very much a real thing. She did not stray from the walkway's safety rails but refused Fleet's offers of help. Even with her fear of falling, Alex's pride kept her from accepting help. She would go through the same rituals as her crewmates.

The inside of the lighthouse teemed with more life than the approach let on. Bright runic lamps ringed the walls of a flat entry area. Stairs spiraled down along the side, split by roomy floors filled with the hustle and bustle of the *Cloudkicker* crew and various traders trying to flag them down. Most of Ghaoithe's staff left the ship, leaving only Sorin and a few others behind for security and to unload crates from the holds. Alex walked past tables of sextons and compasses, cloth dealers, and even a few snack stalls piled high with sugary breads and smoked meats. All around, people were hauling away bags bursting with goods.

"Don't bother with any of these stands," warned Ghaoithe, as if Alex even carried money that would be useful in their world to begin with. "Most of the town is normal enough, but places like this are filled with nothing but swindlers and cheats."

Alex said nothing, contemplating what definition of normal Ghaoithe used.

By the time they arrived at the base of the tower, Alex's balance had steadied. Something in the solid, immovable earth beneath the ground floor helped to fight off her nausea, though she was still far from ready to test her appetite. She made her way to a long counter stacked with ledgers and papers. Ghoaithe was already in discussion with a squat tattooed man behind it.

"…and I told you I would hold it as collateral," the man said in a lazy tone.

"I'll be damned if I let you or anyone else keep my ship," grunted Ghoaithe. She slammed a heavy fist down, but the man remained unfazed.

"You know the rules, Ghoaithe. I've let this slide for a while, but you promised to bring repair supplies for the docks. I've got to keep you grounded until you can send some errand boys to get them."

"What's the problem?" asked Alex as she strode to Ghoaithe's side.

"Robbery, that's what! Dockmaster here likes to watch over his books like a hawk. No heart at all."

The dockmaster looked at Alex and stopped writing in his ledger. His eyes widened, and he slicked back his greasy hair with a free hand. "Well, aren't you a drink, missy? Don't tell me this good-for-nothing pirate roped you into working for her."

Alex blushed. "Why? Did she do something wrong?"

"Your captain promised us supplies to keep the

lighthouse up to par, but she hasn't brought any yet. We can't keep letting people dock who won't pull their weight," said the dockmaster. He ran his hands over his moustache and straightened so he stood slightly above the counter. "You know, we don't get many outsiders these days. If you wanted to have a look around town with an honest fella, I'm more'n able to assist."

Alex's face burned hot under his leering. Flirting had never been her strong suit, and she could feel her words tripping over themselves as she spied the man eying the folds of her shirt. She nervously straightened her collar and stood tall, coughing the man to attention.

"I'm sorry to hear that about the supplies," Alex crooned. "I'm sure the captain meant to get them, but she was caught up in an awful lot of trouble to bring me here. Are you certain you can't waive us this one time? I promise to make sure she remembers for our next trip."

A sigh of relief nearly escaped her breath when the dockmaster ran his hands over his mustache once more. "Well," he said, "I s'pose I can give you a first-timer's favor so long as you come say hi to ol' Finn once you're back in the area."

"Oh, I will. Thank you, Mister Finn," she said, willing herself to gently touch him on the arm. He blushed and muttered that it was no issue. He did not return to his books until the group was well out of the open-aired light-house entrance. The rain stopped, but warm, humid air clung to their clothes.

"What was that?" asked Ghaoithe.

"I don't know. Seemed like you were in a bind."

"You sounded ridiculous."

"It worked," said Alex. Fleet chuckled behind them. The captain's mouth curled up in a smirk, but she said nothing more on the matter. Alex felt she somehow won more points in Ghaoithe's favor.

The city of Roanoke was far less advanced than the outside of the lighthouse let on. Its streets were mostly paved with packed dirts or stone blocks, and every building looked like an amalgam of plaster walls and wooden supports. Many of the smaller buildings sagged with age and broken windows. The lack of any trace of electricity and the dreary weather made everything look like a painting of Shakespearean England. Only the occasional spark from inside a doorway or glowing panels on official-looking buildings gave Alex any indication that the city was quite a step beyond her own. There were no vehicles, and nearly everyone wore the same baggy, colorful clothes as the *Cloudkicker* crew. Only Ghaoithe stood out in her glowing armor. For the first time she could remember, Alex truly felt like an outsider.

"If this is Roanoke, what's it doing in Brazil?" Alex asked as her eyes darted about her surroundings.

The captain shrugged. "Dunno. Most people here don't care about their history much. It's just a place to hide away for a bit nowadays," she said.

"I thought you guys were all about history?"

"Our crew is, but the *Cloudkicker*'s one of the only ships searching for relics. On the whole, Lost Earth isn't much different than yours in that regard. Not everyone is an archeologist just because we use natural power instead of modern technology."

"So they just wrote 'Croatoa' on everything and got all mysterious and left for no reason?"

"No, lass," said Fleet. "They had a reason. Just no one knows what it was. And they told everyone where they was headin' when they wrote that. Just no one knew what it meant, and those that did probably ended up here and disappeared from yer end."

At Alex's perplexed expression, Ghaoithe said, "'CROATOA' isn't a word. It's a system of coordinates. Like Fleet said on the ship, not many know how to read them anymore. It's why relic hunting is so tricky, and that's just the first step to know. We'll have to teach you if you're going to be doing research."

It made perfect sense, when Alex mulled over the knowledge. That certain words could be used as a cipher for locations was one of the few logical notions in her new surroundings. It also answered a few questions about her book of relics.

"So, where is Osiris, then? That one seemed to be written down a lot in your notes," Alex asked.

The captain halted in the middle of the street. Her smirk was gone. "That's not a location. It's not something we can discuss here," she said icily. She continued on, leaving Alex feeling as though she had been reprimanded for asking.

"Don't worry about it," said Fleet, putting a broad hand on her shoulder. He leaned down to speak to her in a hushed tone. "Look, this city is alright for the most part, but it ain't a place ya want to be goin' around asking a ton of questions. Just give us some time to get situated, lass. Yer wonderin' is a fine thing, but ease up a bit for now."

The change in Ghaoithe's tone left Alex jarred despire Fleet's reassurance. It also planted the seed of curiosity that Alex knew would not go away until her question was answered. Whatever Osiris meant, it held some importance to the life of her captain.

Still, Alex dared not to test Fleet's warning. She roamed about in a new city, and the last thing she wanted to do was unwittingly invite danger. She could handle a little heat, but recklessly throwing herself to the wolves just to get one hasty answer did not figure into her gameplan. She at least had one goal laid out for her future, and it could wait.

The mist strengthened above their heads and signaled the return of steady rain as they followed Ghaoithe through the streets. No one spoke for the rest of their walk, giving Alex proper time to wish she had asked for a jacket before leaving the ship.

Despite being soaked, no one in the busy streets acted as if they were in a hurry. Friends greeted each other with hugs in puddles, shopkeepers continued hawking their wares to each passerby, and one man even dropped down for a nap at the edge of an ornate fountain. No one minded the drizzle in the slightest.

Ghaoithe's armor took on a glow once the drops fell. The golden inlays swirled with a faint yellow light. While everyone else trudged through the warm shower, the captain's armor remained bone dry. Alex no longer thought Fleet's comment amount the runes stopping bullets was an exaggeration. She got lost in staring as water bounced away from Ghaoithe's back when it came close to the material.

Walking through the streets, impervious to the rain, Ghaoithe took on the air of an untamed, tireless gladiator.

Wet and miserable in her normal clothes, Alex had no idea how far they walked through the city when the group stopped in front of a three-story building. A sign posted above the main doorway marked it as "Skyrunner Tavern" in an elegant font. A tiny man in winged shoes ran atop clouds that formed the two 'n's. Buzzing voices radiated from within, cut by sporadic hoots and whistling.

Alex went to her fair share of parties growing up. Drinking and cramming into friends' houses was nearly the official pastime of rural Missouri, trailing only behind going to church and baseball. In college, she spent plenty of nights in bathtubs and hand-me-down sofas. During a particularly hazy evening, she even laughed as one of her friends lost his eyebrows trying to light bonfire wood soaked in white gasoline. An unruly get-together was just another weekend to her late teen years.

Yet no party could match the inside of the Skyrunner Tavern.

The main bar and open area just inside the entrance greeted them with a combination of candles and torches lit by the ever-present runes of the world. The room was fairly normal by most inn standards, with several tables and a cozy fireplace at the far end. The contrast was in the clientele. Occupying every inch of the room were the most unsavory sort of brigands imaginable. Swords and knives cluttered tables otherwise piled high with poker chips and cards. Oily men struck out with dark-eyed women revealing ample cleavage. The stench of sweat and alcohol permeated through the air, causing Alex to choke for several moments after stepping in.

Ghaoithe and Fleet guided their new recruit to the bar and gave her a rare empty seat. The bartender, a scowling ruffian with ebony skin and arms the size of the young girl's torso looked at her with an arched eyebrow. He turned to Ghaoithe. "Gangplank?"

"Gangplank," the captain responded through pursed lips.

Ghaoithe and Fleet gave Alex heavy pats on the back before retreating to the end of the bar, leaving her all alone amid the crowd. No sooner had they disappeared when a gangly man with a hook nose and missing teeth approached Alex's seat.

"What in the world are you wearin', girl?" he asked, eyes lingering a little too long on her legs.

"Uh, clothes?" Alex muttered, trying to scoot away as much as she could in the cramped space.

"They ain't clothes from 'round here, then. What say we go get you out of 'em?" the pirate said with an untoward smile.

The bartender, noticing Alex's tense expression, approached the two and planted a firm smack on the back of the creep's head. Defeated, the man made a curse towards the barkeep and slinked back into the crowd.

"You'll be getting that a lot tonight," said the barman in a rich baritone. "Just give 'em a good slap and they'll ease off. Anyway, your partners ordered this for ya."

He slapped a mug onto the counter in front of Alex. Some kind of ale had been poured inside the glass, but the mug was so disgusting that it rid Alex of whatever thirst she had. Stains of wiped grease decorated the mug inside and out. A smudge of faint lipstick colored the rim, and the ale itself had bits of dirt and other globs of matter floating within it.

Alex hardly considered herself a tidy person, but when it came to food, she was easily nauseated by other people's leftovers or unwashed plates. She wondered, quite seriously in her mind, if this was the norm in Lost Earth taverns and whether she made a grave mistake in agreeing to joining it.

As she stared at the mug and croaked a quick thanks

to the bartender, the inn hushed to an eerie calm. Everyone near her seat looked at her in expectation. She knew she stood out with her clean skin and blue jeans. The thought of everyone laughing at the alien girl who couldn't handle a little beer frightened Alex more than the mug. Closing her eyes, she drained the glass in one swoop, trying not to taste it as it went down. For the first time in her life, she was thankful for growing up in a place where shotgunning cans was woven into the fabric of culture.

She finished, slamming the glass back onto the table, choking for air. The bar erupted with cheers, and she felt several friendly slaps on the back. From the far end of the bar, Ghaoithe was dark with laughter to the point that Fleet braced her to keep her upright. Alex looked around and noticed the bartender laughing, too, his original frightening glare now jovial. In his hands he held a wet rag. Behind him, stacked among kegs of lager and hard liquor, rested stacks of pristine, polished glass mugs.

"Welcome to Roanoke, newcomer. Rest of the night's on the house."

Alexandra's first feeling upon waking was the sharp throbbing in her head. She wanted to turn over, to forget the pain with the comfort of liquid sleep. She awakened, though, and that brief moment was all her hangover needed to prevent any possibility of returning to her pillow. She cursed the bright sunlight filtering through the window and cautiously sat up.

Alex couldn't remember getting into the room. She was in the inn, and decor was quite nice compared to the chaos of the main level. The bed was soft and piled high with sheets that had not been needed in the warm evening. She checked to make sure she still had all of her clothes on, and was thankful that she did.

Only brief flashes of vodka shots and laughter remained from her memory of the previous evening. At one point, she thought she remembered seeing Ghaoithe on top of the bar, her ginger hair almost scraping the ceiling, but even that was not a certainty in Alex's recollection. Somewhere in the back of her mind, Alex knew Fleet protected her from doing anything too terribly stupid for her first night in the lost city.

A long dresser hugged the wall opposite her bed. A washbasin filled with crisp, cool water greeted her on top. Her face tingled as she splashed herself a few times. At the other end of the dresser, someone laid out a pile of clothing for her overnight. They were in the same flowing, loose fashion of everyone else in the city: a white blouse with sleeves that curtailed into flowery red cuffs, full-length tan pants, a navy sash, and a pair of sturdy black boots.

Alex gave the clothing a wary look, judgmental of the odd fabric, before turning her attention to the restroom. Tears of glee nearly welled up in her eyes at learning that indoor plumbing was a part of her new outpost. The room's shower was little more than an aging pipe and over-sized bowl to stand in, but it was enough, and Alex wasted no time in stripping down to hop in. Her excitement tempered upon learning that hot water was apparently not part of the deal, her shrieks echoing down to the street.

Despite the chill, the shower allowed her mind to focus on things other than her need to lie down. It dulled the throbbing in her skull and helped sooth her stomach.

Rejuvenated and feeling the first pangs of hunger, she put on her new clothes and looked into the mirror above the dresser. Her new blouse had a deep, airy neckline she was not crazy about, and her pants hugged her form so closely she became astutely self-conscious of herself.

She had to admit, though, that they felt wonderful. The fabric was lighter than anything she had ever worn. It stretched with every minor movement, giving her a freedom in motion she never had in her worn denim jeans or bulky t-shirts. Whatever she thought of the fashion, her new clothes were certainly practical attire designed with heavy work in mind. With the final touch of tying the blue sash at her waist, she no longer looked like a stranger in the land; she had the guise of a true relic hunter.

After warily traversing the stairwell down to the main floor, Alex returned to the large entry hall. No sounds or hollers greeted this time; only a few scattered souls dotted the tables now covered with coffee and bread instead of cards. Behind the counter, standing as though he had not moved the entire night, was the bartender.

"Morning, Ms. Stirling," he welcomed her. She sat down at the bar, rubbing her head.

"Hey, uh…"

"Roy Hannagan, ma'am. Just call me Roy." The name was vaguely familiar.

"Alright, Roy. What do you have for someone who's still half-dead? And how did you know my name?"

"I know it because you told me last night. Just like I told you mine, though I figured you wouldn't remember," he chuckled. "We all said a lot of things last night. Best not to worry about that. Just hold on a moment."

Putting down his washcloth, he disappeared through a door behind the bar and returned several minutes later with a plate of two eggs and crisp slices of toast. He placed a steaming cup of black coffee next to them. Alex stared at the platter groggily, daring herself to test the limits of her stomach. A rumble declared the victor between her stomach and her head, and she gingerly nipped at the toast, savoring the milky-soft butter that took her back to early farm awakenings. The coffee was also welcomed heartily with a bold freshness that her instant, store-bought grinds failed to capture.

Roy picked up his cloth and moved on to another glass under the countertop. "So, you got roped in by the Sky Thief, eh? Been a long time since we had a visitor like you in here," he said.

"The Sky Thief? You mean Ghaoithe?" asked Alex between bites of toast.

"Yes, ma'am, I mean Ghaoithe. We call her the Sky Thief. It's her armor, you see," Roy said. He paused cleaning the mug and looked at Alex with a smile. Like most of her new companions, he scared Alex less in the daylight. "There are some people that like to act all flashy with runes in their clothes, but no one has anything like that blue getup of hers. When she drops down from that ship of hers, it's like the sky itself is falling, and anything she's after is going to drift away with it in the end. She is one of the best damn sneaks around when she wants to be."

Alex gulped down more coffee than she meant to. She sputtered, "Ghaoithe? Sneak? I wasn't aware giants had that ability."

"I know. It don't sound possible lookin' at her, but I've seen it for myself," said Roy, flashing his teeth. "Now, don't get me wrong. She's a strong enough fighter and can handle that rapier of hers just fine, but she doesn't like to if she can help it. Lucky, not many people are going to mess with a woman that's two meters tall. She'd rather dig around in some old cave than get her crew caught in a firefight somewhere. There ain't been a tomb out there she couldn't raid."

Alex remained skeptical of Ghaoithe's ability to fit into tight crawlspaces while adventuring, but even the young reporter noticed something incredible about the captain that didn't fit well into mere words. It was a presence, a gravity towards the Sky Thief that made it difficult for people to doubt her.

A question nagged the back of Alex's mind. "Am I safe with her?" she asked.

Roy pondered for a moment before shrugging. "Depends what you call safe. If you're asking if she'll harm you, then you'll be just fine. If Ghaoithe says you're under her protection, she means it. But the places she goes to are far from safe, and she's got a lot of enemies that think she's too soft. You'll have to decide how much of a trade-off that is."

Alex welcomed the news. Dangerous locations could be fun, but Stockholm Syndrome tugged at the back of her mind, nagging that she lost all reason by accepting an adventure with her kidnappers. Confirming she wasn't crazy with an outside source kept her doubts buried for a short while. She needed to justify the risk she had taken.

Her plate finished, she gave another thanks to Roy. When she patted empty pockets, he waved her off with a laugh, explaining that he and her captain had an arrangement. The image of Ghaoithe dancing on top of the counter flashed through Alex's mind.

"Oh, did she say where I was supposed to meet her this morning?" Alex asked before heading out the door.

"Make a left out the street and follow it until you get to the weird house a ways down. You'll know it when you see it."

Alex bid her farewells to Roy and left in search of what could be considered unique in a city that shouldn't even exist. Wispy clouds kissed the houses in the mountains nearby, but the sky held back its tears. The lighthouse, a distant gateway to the sky, glinted in early light. Smoking meats and the sound of vendors filled the streets around her with vibrant life. The day was still early, yet the crowds teemed with an electricity that countered the quiet sunrises in her familiar meadow back home. Roanoke was a real city with the façade of ancient times. Warmth filled Alex, a sense that she came to the right place, that her life, finally, was placed back on the right tracks.

The road continued without any sign of unusual buildings. Alex took her time strolling, her boots comfortable for a casual walk. She liked setting her own pace rather than hustling to keep up with the captain's enormous strides. She even thought about looking through the markets stalls, curious what currency the vendors would accept for their moist breads and ripened fruits. Whether it was Roy's coffee or the clear air, Alex's hangover nearly vanished and she became eager to explore on her own.

"...that red-headed bitch won't let anything harm her."

Alex halted. The prim and proper tone contrasted with the gruff language around her but it held the slightest hint of a drawl. The inflection was different, but she could not deny the familiarity to her ears. Drums reverberated through her chest, countless possibilities running through her mind.

Separating Alex from the speaker were several racks of clothing for sale along a thin alleyway. Curious, she stepped between the racks, pretending to judge the vendor's wares, her back to the speaker and obscured by a rainbow of fabric.

Another man's voice spoke, older and perfectly articulate, as though he were reciting Shakespeare with utmost reverence. "In any case, your recklessness has been most upsetting news."

"What's done is done, Deacon. I am working on damage control and moving on to more important business. The girl does not help those amateurs in the long run any more than a pet parrot."

If an argument was taking place, the two men took great pains not to convey it to anyone passing by. They spoke casually, like they were discussing morning stock prices. Alex edged backwards toward the rack between her and the mystery men. She had to look, to peek at the source of the man with the tinge of Southern speech.

"Any other time, she would be of no consequence, but you know this is being highly scrutinized. We've already had to waste massive resources covering up their theatrics," said the elder voice.

"And? I am not afraid of punishment here. Not with

the progress I've made."

"Perhaps, perhaps not. But you know how Osiris works. It will only take a few motivated individuals to disagree and scuttle the entire project. I am only asking you to use discretion, Ethan."

"I'll use discretion when we have time for discretion," the man named Ethan spat. "Osiris knows our priorities."

There was that word again: Osiris. She recalled Ghaoithe's expression at the mention of the name, the acidic tone in the captain's voice. Alex turned, her face down and covered by her still-damp curls. Pretending to be no different than any other shopper, she stealthily spread the shirts before her.

Through the waves of fabric, she glimpsed the two men. They both dressed in clothing that looked like an imitation of the city around them. The rich attire displayed the same bright colors as any of the sailors but with proper cuts and thick fabric made for royalty, not life in the air. The voice she did not recognize was an older man with purple spectacles, long white hair, and a matching goatee. He stood ramrod straight, with a long cane balanced before him.

The other man, the one named Ethan, was altogether too familiar. Alex muffled a cry with her hand. He looked like the Jackson she met with only days ago, but the similarities ended at his likeness. Gone were his timid slouch and bashful grin, replaced with a firm purpose and steeled eyes that dared the older man to continue testing him. This was not a gentle person she was staring at; this was a visage of fire and spite.

Alex froze, her head catching up with the moment. She wanted to call out to him, to ask him to explain what happened in the hospital and why Ghaoithe had been looking for him. She ached for the comfort he provided on so many occasions. However, her body would not – could not – move. Ghaoithe's warnings rang alarms in her mind.

Alex stepped back only to slip on a long coat that dragged on the ground of her hiding spot. She instinctively grabbed the clothing rack's bar to steady herself, rattling every item hanging from it. She lifted her eyes to see the two men staring at her through the upended clothing.

Whatever feelings Jackson confessed to Alex in quiet hours on the phone were not reflected in the hateful, loveless stare of contempt he shot her then.

"Ya plan on makin' yer way to us or ya spendin' the day shoppin', lass?"

Fleet's hand clasped Alex's shoulder. She jumped what felt like several feet into the air and whipped around. Fleet wore an oblivious grin.

Alex whispered to him, "The men behind me. They

were talking about Osiris. I needed to look in."

Fleet turned his head up and looked at the city around them. "Don't see no one but us and a few drunkards."

Alex searched the market, half expecting the two to leap out at her with guns drawn. However, Fleet was right. The two men disappeared among the thickening crowds and vendor stalls around them. Not a single flash of velvet to be seen.

"You have got to be kidding me! They were just here! A man with white hair and fancy clothes and… and I think it was Jackson, but the other man called him Ethan. You have got to believe me," Alex pleaded.

"Didn't say I didn't, but no sense in makin' a fuss now. Best get ya to the workshop," said Fleet. He nudged Alex towards the main avenue. She continued glancing over her shoulder for the remainder of the walk.

The crowds thinned. Alex sensed they approached the edge of the city, though the mountains and eclectic layout of the roads made it hard to know for sure. She paid most of her attention to the road beneath her feet anyway, dwelling on the Not Jackson that stared knives at her. She did not see Fleet stop and collided with his back.

They stood in front of what she could only describe

as a building in the loosest sense of the word. When she was in elementary school, one of Alex's friends had brought in a booklet detailing an upcoming Disneyland trip. Alex became fascinated with the polished rides and bright colors over everything. In one large detail, a picture of the Astro Orbiter beckoned children wishing to fly with its spinning rings and massive moving spheres.

The structure before her now looked very much like that wonderful ride. The top sparked with electricity between giant floating balls. Lines of energy swept along every wall of the rounded base. The sleek steel exterior contrasted with the other buildings, save for the lighthouse, a mechanical toadstool growing in an ancient forest.

"Roy wasn't kidding," said Alex, fixated on the spinning objects above.

"Just a workshop. Ya better learn to stop gawkin' at everything or yer legs'll grow into the ground," said Fleet.

Alex scoffed, "Sorry. It's a little hard to forget pretty much everything I've ever learned about physics and science."

As they approached the entrance, Fleet held out his arm to stop her. "Let's just keep yer meetin' today between us fer now. We can go over it when we're rightly well away from Roanoke," he said.

Alex began to object, but nodded curtly instead. The

earlier warning about the city listening in was no longer just a vague threat.

The inside of the building was one large room, dim and hazy. Alex blinked several times before her eyes adjusted. They entered a mad scientist's lair. A staircase beside the entrance spiraled up the sides of the wall and into the moving portions of the tall roof. Strewn everywhere were books, vials, bottles of glowing liquids, and crystals of every color. Most of the light came from an abundance of glowing designs with one solitary candle lit on a table opposite the entrance.

Ghaoithe hunched over the table with her movie poster, her voice carrying across the room. "You're absolutely sure about this?"

"Sure am, Ghaoithe. It's the only one that makes sense," spoke a gruff voice hidden behind the captain's frame.

"The first two letters could be read together. That would put us over Morocco."

"You know as well as I do there's nothing in Morocco. May as well just settle with the fact you're going into the Triangle and deal with it. You've done it before."

"Triangle?" asked Alex, coming up unnoticed behind the Sky Thief. Ghaoithe barely turned to nod at her before returning to the poster. Across the table from her sat a scrawny, bald man covered in tattoos. He tinkered with a miniature cube in his hands, screwing and unscrewing plates along its sides. It flared with light for a brief few moments before fading for good. The biker-esque man rolled it onto the table in defeat.

"Bah. Henry'll just have to get a new one. This one's out," he sneered. Turning his attention to Alex and Fleet, he raised a grease-stained hand. "Kirk, runic scientist at your service. You must the new girl that found the poster."

Alex hesitantly shook Kirk's hand, wary that someone that looked like a Judas Priest concert could really be a scientist. "Yeah. Alexandra. What's this about a triangle?"

"Bermuda. We have to go to Bermuda next," Ghaoithe said. She lacked the enthusiasm normally associated with the tropical destination.

"How do you figure that?" Alex prodded.

Kirk leaned back in his chair and placed a pair of thick boots on the table. "Your picture, darlin'. 'Arias' is a place in the Bermuda Triangle."

"I don't get what that has to do with a movie set in Arabia, though."

Kirk shrugged. "Dunno either. Probably has to do with whatever you've got to find there. But, it's all in the arrangement of the letters. Ghaoithe told you how to read these, right?"

Alex shook her head. "Not really," she said. "I know they stand for certain directions or something, but that's about it."

"Right. Well, these aren't typical directions like North or South or whatever," Kirk explained. He leaned back in over the poster, gesturing at the words as he spoke. The poster had 'Arias' written over the original signature. "Usually the letter arrangements stand for landmarks or visual clues. Depending on where they're placed, they could mean a ton of different places.

"The main thing here is the A and the R. If they had come later in the sequence, you'd end up somewhere in India. Instead, this specific sequence means it's somewhere near the Atlantic Ocean. From there, we have to use our own clues and judgment. Ghaoithe thinks the A and R should be read together, which would put you in Northern Africa. But, there's nothing there, and she knows it. I'm positive the first two letters are separated, which puts you in the Bermuda Triangle."

Alex still didn't get it. "How do I know what sequences mean what? There a list or something?"

"Used to be. A long time ago," Ghaoithe reminisced.

"It's a bit of a trade secret nowadays, and it's a long list. I have a few written in our book, but it's far from complete. A lot of the landmarks they refer to may have been lost over time, too, which means we not only have to find what we came for, but also find out where that landmark was. It's why relic hunting is a lonely art. You end up on a lot of goose chases around the world trying to find snippets of clues before you ever reach the endgame."

"Doesn't seem very helpful. Even narrowing it down to a country, those places are huge, and the directions don't sound very specific," said Alex.

"They're as specific as the writer wants them to be. Whoever wrote this one didn't want their hiding spot found easily. My guess is there's still more to this poster to figure out," said Kirk.

"Supposing we find all that out, just what is hidden in Bermuda, anyway?" asked Alex. The trio remained silent.

"Depends on who gets there first," Fleet said to break the tone.

Alex grew tired of the vague foreshadowing. She straightened up to her full height, which barely touched the chests of those around her, and stomped up to the table.

"Ok, look. I get it," she said. "This is important, but you're going to have to let me in on some details here. I'm not a kid; I'm here to learn. I don't think you let me stay on the *Cloudkicker* just to sit around and take up space, so if you want me to help, then let me help. If not, drop me off in Miami on your way to wherever the hell in Bermuda you're going and we can ignore this ever happening."

Ghaoithe straightened up at the outburst. Scratching her chin, she looked at Fleet. He nodded back.

"We can't give you all the details because we don't know them yet. However, we aren't the only relic hunters competing for treasures of the world. Just trust us that there are dangerous groups out there. We'll fill you in on the rest when the time is right," Ghaoithe explained.

Exasperated, Alex threw her hands in the air and paced off to look at a few of the shelves around the room and the vials they contained. The swirling, glowing liquids they held matched her thoughts.

Kirk stood up. "Well, that's that I guess. You'll have to figure out the rest on your own at this point."

"Guess so," replied Ghaoithe. "I could use a few spare rods if you've got any."

The scientist nodded and stepped near Alex, where a chest filled with colorful cylinders had been laid out. He picked up three rods glowing a soft pink and tossed them to Ghaoithe. "Should keep you going for a few more trips. All things considered, I'll waive your fee this time," he said.

Alex noticed a slew of parchment papers next to Kirk's feet and scampered next to him to get a closer look. Sticking out from the pile was a blueprint, its design strikingly familiar to Alex.

"You built the *Cloudkicker*?" she asked, picking up the paper before Kirk could object. It was not a typical blueprint, the outline and structure being crudely drawn. The markings of the hull, however, were intricately planned with notes scrawled over every portion.

"You just don't shut up, do you?" Kirk said, to which Fleet let out a short guffaw. "I didn't build the whole thing, no. I did make the damn thing fly. Working with energy is what I do, and there ain't none better than me at it. That ship was one of my best works, too. Shame it had to go to such a scoundrel."

"That's amazing! How does it work?" Alex desperately wished to take notes.

"Look, kid, I'm not going to spend time trying to explain to you how many patterns of runic energy there are or how to make them function in what ways," Kirk said, leading her to the front door with her companions. "All you need to know is don't touch those rods I gave your captain."

With the warning, the three were escorted outside to

be left among the crowds. Ghaoithe placed the crystals into a pouch tied to her sash.

"Well, that could have gone better," she said.

"Never said this'd be easy," said Fleet.

"So that's what a scientist is in your world. I figured they were all beards and spectacles and gizmos," mused Alex, not fazed by the news that dampened the spirits of the others.

"He's incredibly good at what he does. He looks like that because he's had too many people come after him for his 'services.' Someone with his skills wouldn't last a day out here if he was just another scrawny nerd," explained Ghaoithe. She trod towards the inn, leaving Fleet and Alex to catch up.

"Never seen someone so upset over a trip to the Caribbean," Alex said.

"We'll have to plan a little more than we was expecting. You've heard the mysteries of the Triangle, right?" said Fleet. He looked down to his companion.

"Yeah, but no one really believes them. Not nowadays. Besides, couldn't the *Cloudkicker* handle anything nasty? I thought that was the whole point of your special ship."

"To a point, lass. To a point. Just... read yer book and be ready."

Striding up to Ghaoithe, Alex felt the tension emanating from the captain. In their brief interactions, brooding had not been a regular part of the treasure hunter's personality.

Wishing to change the mood, Alex stated simply, "You know, I'm liking your home so far. It's really pretty."

"My home is very far away, and I haven't been there in some time. This is just a port of call. Thank you, though," said Ghaoithe without looking at Alex.

"Well, either way, it's fun enough. I'd love to learn a little more about it or go up into those mountains."

"We'll be able to do that soon enough. We have a couple of days before we can head out," said Ghaoithe. Her face softened and she slowed her pace. "If I remember right, you already have an offer for a private tour guide if you really wanted to explore."

"As if!" chided Alex. "You're the one with men at every corner. Roy says hello, by the way."

At the mention of the bartender, Ghaoithe let out a hoarse bark. "Roy? My man? I have no men. I saved his life once, and I trust him with mine. That's all there is to it."

"So you just dance on tabletops and flirt with the men buying you drinks for the fun of it?"

"No, I dance because I like to move around. I'm not

flirting; I'm telling stories with fellow travelers. None of them have or will interest me romantically. I do not spend my life pining for the affection of others," said Ghaoithe with a point of her thumb.

"Really? There's no one at all?" Alex couldn't hide her shock. Ghaoithe was a larger-than-life figure, but that was much of her appeal. Alex couldn't imagine such a confident woman having issues finding a relationship. "I wouldn't go that far. I'm sure you'll find the right person for you."

"No," Ghaoithe cut in. "Whatever part of the gene pool sparks the desire for intimacy must have skipped me. I have my crew, I have my ship, and I have this world we live in. I'm perfectly happy leaving it at that."

"So have you never… been with anyone?" Alex persisted. Her mind reeled at the thought of a celibate woman, especially someone as vibrant as Ghaoithe. In New Delta, most of her friends had been in perpetual relationships since they found out the concept existed, and having children before graduating high school was not unheard of. Alex's twenties were underway, and she already strayed behind the marriage curve.

"No one," said Ghaoithe without a hint of timidity. "I don't even think the damn thing works right, really. Wouldn't know what to do if it did. Guess I'm a pretty broken woman, huh?"

Her candid tone flustered Alex. She had not expected her superior to be so direct on personal matters. She ran a hand through her mess of hair. "No, not at all. I just… I've never met anyone that says they don't need love. Relationships were kind of the end game for people back home."

Ghaoithe arched a thick eyebrow in the country girl's direction. "I never said anything about not loving anyone. Just not in the way you mean it."

Alex stared at the captain as they walked down the lane. In the morning light, the sun glinting brilliantly off her blazing hair and blue armor, Ghaoithe's exotic beauty shone through her earlier frustration. She strode with confidence and grace, head above the crowd, a tigress surveying her domain. Countless men, and probably women, would give their lives to be with her.

However, Alex saw something else in the adventurer. She walked alone, within her own bubble just a few feet ahead of everyone else. It was hardly enough to be noticeable, and most would have chalked it up to the woman's long gait, but it was there. Just as the rain had failed to penetrate that inner sphere, so too did intimacy. Alex started to respect the captain, but she knew then that whatever world the rogue had come from would never be fully known. The runes on her armor protected more than just the captain's body.

The thought of never having a significant other also reminded Alex of just how much she missed her own. Knowing Jackson was in Roanoke and that he likely had answers to her questions caused Alex to second-guess her decision not to approach him in the street. She could not believe that he truly did not care for her. If anything, she needed proper closure, to find out why he held his true self at a distance.

"You were right not to talk to him. He's dangerous," uttered Ghaoithe.

Alex shot an accusing look at Fleet, who raised his hands in innocence. "How did you know about that?" she asked the captain.

"You're easy to read."

Alex's cheeks flushed. She realized how solemn her conflict over Jackson made her. She lashed out, upset mostly at herself for being so transparent.

"Maybe. Maybe not. You keep saying these things, but you haven't explained any of it. You still have to prove you aren't keeping me to sell in a market somewhere."

"Yer worth yer weight in trouble," Fleet chuckled

behind her.

Ghaoithe's smirk remained, but she did not laugh. "No, you're right, Alexandra," she said. "We have been vague, and I don't blame you for having doubts. It's easy for me to forget that you lost someone close…"

"More like forcefully ripped," Alex interjected.

"…but I have to ask that you continue to trust us for now," Ghaoithe continued without a pause. "I can't pretend to know what you're going through, but since you're still here, I'm guessing you took my warnings to heart."

The malefic stare from Jackson burned in the back of Alex's mind. She gave Ghaoithe a noncommittal shrug, but did not otherwise argue her captain's point. She breathed deeply, taking in the fresh, damp tropical air around her. She wanted to slow time and take a moment to unravel the possibilities open to her but settled for falling a couple of steps behind Fleet and the captain as they engaged in conversation about ship supplies.

A small kitten, all charcoal and soot, darted along the lane beside them. Alex watched as it climbed onto the windowsill of a butcher's shop and stared into the window with an eager tail twitching. The shop owner, just inside the glass, opened the window a crack and slid out a tiny cut of his current project. The kitten meowed, scampering off with the meager slice with all the joy a street cat could muster.

Smiling, though she did not realize it had crossed her lips, Alex bounded up towards her leaders. She shook her head, curls flopping like a shrub full of birds.

"Fine," she said. "You're right. I don't trust him, but don't think I trust you fully yet, either. You don't have to tell me everything, but you can at least start with how those crystals keep the ship in the air."

The quartermaster's baffled face was almost worth the argument. Ghaoithe, however, chuckled.

"Told you," she said to Fleet and motioned for them to follow, pulling one of the crystals out of her pouch.

When she was young, Alex loved dreams. She bounded into bed every night wondering what world she would be taken to and what strange creatures she would meet. When most kids reached the age where staying up late was a hard-fought privilege, she was still in bed early, staring at her ceiling until it parted into open skies.

That child had long since left, replaced by a woman who stared at the ceiling to keep it within her bounds. She did not dream, and she did not enjoy sleep. For some time in her early teenage years, she would practice the art of lucid dreaming, of becoming aware when she was dreaming so they could be manipulated. Rather than control them, however, she ended them swiftly and without mercy. Dreams were no longer kind.

When she thrust herself up in bed, sweating through her thin sheets, she panicked. Alex knew she dreamed, and that it had been terrible. It glided past the edges of her consciousness, lurking in memory as a shadow without proper form.

Alex needed a drink.

She slipped into her outfit, not even bothering to tie the straps of her boots. Her room swirled in the pale blue light of her phone. Notes covered its screen, an attempt to transcribe what she could remember of the day's events for future posterity. With the press of a button, the room went dark. Tucking the phone into her pocket to pass the time, Alex stepped out into the hallway.

The Skyrunner creaked with every footstep. She was not sure what she expected in the early hours of the morning, but the silence jarred her after hearing a constant drone of soft voices through her door. Snores rumbled from behind a closed rooms, and the candles lighting the building released a soft hiss, but no other sound echoed through the halls. The chaotic mess of her arrival no longer existed.

The main bar was no different. Not a soul remained,

sprawled across a table or otherwise. Had she not been awoken by an unknown terror in her imagination, Alex likely would have been wary of the empty dining hall. In her dream-addled state, she was happy just to find the ice chest nestled among the back counters; Roy gave her carte blanche access when the team returned that evening. Alex's mused over possibly finding some cold milk or even a soda hidden within its stores, if sodas even existed in her new home.

They did not. She settled with one of several unlabeled beer bottles that had been stashed inside the cooler. The caramel flavor of the stout brought a welcome chill to Alex's head, and she willed herself not to drink it too quickly. Sitting at one of the barstools, she chose instead to relish the quiet and the dark.

Sleep beckoned to her from a distance as her bottle drained. Alex was about to stand up and head for the stairs when the calming blue glow throughout the bar tinged with orange. Through the front windows of the building, a group of people edged towards the Skyrunner. Each figure carried an antique oil lamp as they strode through the center of the street.

At first, Alex gasped as her imagination sparked images of a mob come to burn the crew of the *Cloudkicker* for reasons unknown to her. She thought of shady dealings, or perhaps an argument over a relic. As the group came to a halt just beyond the entrance, however, she could see that the figures actually were the *Cloudkicker*'s keepers. They wore haunting, macabre robes that transformed their bodies into black pitch, but there could be no doubt over the figures of Fleet and Roy. Ghaoithe pushed towards the front of the pack, her unmistakable armor now backed with a regal ruby cape.

Alex dashed outside to greet the throng. "What in the world are you guys doing this late? And what are you wearing? You look ridiculous."

No one spoke. Ghaoithe lifted her lantern toward the mountains flanking the city and motioned with her hand. The ensemble began to walk again, leaving Alex stupefied on the street. She sighed, laced up her boots, and ran after them.

They walked in silence through the edges of Roanoke, the hissing of their lanterns cutting through the night. As they wandered, the lights guided the way through jungle interspersed with only the occasional shack until the city was behind them completely. Creatures cawed and shuffled unseen through the foliage around them, as curious of the humans as Alex was of the jungle.

The air in the mountains perked Alex up. She only noticed the clear skies and lack of rain after they marched for some time. Clear skies eluded them since their arrival, and she took in the renewed air with appreciation. Moonlight filtered through the tops of tropical forest, shining in patches along their route to give a magical, ethereal quality to the journey.

When they reached a clearing, the moon hanging near its peak, Alex rubbed her legs, suddenly aware of the hours spent walking through the jungle. A brush pile rose from the center of the field, a foreboding mark towering well above the grass. The surrounding forest no longer teemed with movement; the world consisted of the group and their open space.

One of the cloaked figures stepped away from the crowd and threw his lantern onto the brush. The wood roared to life, arcing towards the sky in a brilliant display. Alex raised her arms in defense from the blast. Figures swirled around her in a flurry as the group fanned out to enclose the bonfire. She stepped back, blinking, trying to reach cooler air. When she put her arms down, she found herself facing her captain, the two of them alone in the center of the circle.

Stirling twirled. The crowd stared at her, emotionless and omnipresent. She coughed, hoping to steel her nerves, but it only emphasized her fear.

"Ok guys. Nice with the voodoo cult thing on the

new girl. You can knock it off now," she said.

Ghaoithe, her regular smirk replaced with thin lines, stepped forward until she stood nearly on top of the young explorer. Alex backed up, nearly tripping.

"Why have you come to us?" the captain wailed into the night air.

"What do you mean? You're the ones who brought me out into the ass-end of the jungle!" Alex yelled back. Her eyes flitted around, searching for an escape, but she only found hooded figures at every turn.

The captain repeated, "Why have you come to us?" Her voice resonated off the trees with ghostly reverb. Shadows cut across the flickering light, casting Ghaoithe's figure with a demonic edge.

Backing up until she was almost at the ring of people, Alex lost her footing, crumpling onto the ground. Her knee throbbed, and tears welled up in her eyes from her pain and confusion.

"I don't know! I don't know what you want!" she shouted through trembling lips.

A deep murmur passed through the ring. They coalesced into a united chant, the words ancient and powerful. The heat from the fire sweltered to the point of being almost unbearable on the fallen girl's skin. Ghaoithe, cornering Alex against a wall of flesh, gazed down with her piercing eye.

"WHY HAVE YOU COME TO US?"

"I needed to escape! I had nothing left," Alex screamed. She was fully crying now and curled into a pitiful ball on the grass. "I wanted to see what the world offers. I want to find answers!"

The chanting stopped. A rescuing breeze lifted the scorched atmosphere and carried it above the forest for a brief respite. Ghaoithe's ruby cape rippled with it.

"So, you wish to discover the secrets of the world?" The Sky Thief's tone softened. As Alex wiped her eyes and the blur of the world came into focus, she looked up at Ghaoithe. The rogue's face remained unfazed, but the harshness in her stare had been replaced with a different glint: relief.

The fog in Alex's mind drifted away as she processed the question. She understood that Ghaoithe was presenting her with a choice she would not be able to back away from. Whatever decisions she made earlier would now be confronted with finality. She would be forever tied to her new world.

"Yes," said Alex. She stood, aching and sniffling, but eager. "I came to discover its secrets. I want to know what else is in this world outside of my front door."

"Step forward, Alexandra Stirling," beckoned Ghaoithe. The chanting softened, mixing with the breeze, whispering like spirits through the trees.

Alex hobbled up to the captain. A figure stepped away from the crowd and reached within his robes. Excalibur appeared from within the folds and was handed to Ghaoithe without a word. She nodded, and the member once again blended into the crowd.

"We are the companions of the *Cloudkicker*. You have expressed interest in joining our ranks. Is that still your wish?" Ghaoithe's voice rang clear amid the forest.

"Yes," Alex replied, no longer timid.

"Will you travel into unexplored regions? Search endlessly for knowledge even where there appears none can be found? To never give up on seeking answers?"

"Yes."

"And can you hold no bonds but to your ship and your crew? To be called upon with your life in brother- and sisterhood?"

Alex paused. Missouri hung over her with memories of watching the Mississippi drift lazily by and fields of solitude as summer storms rolled in. There would be no going back to simple country life and filing briefs over real estate sales.

A flicker of memory, and Alex gave another stoic "Yes."

The rogueish leader offered the hilt of Excalibur to Alex. "Why the sword?" Ghaoithe asked.

"It introduced me to this world. I'd like to learn how to use it."

"I see. A sword can do many things, Ms. Stirling. It can strike through your enemies, but it can also form bonds between allies. It can clear paths and act as a worthy tool. The gifts people choose from my ship tell a great deal about them. I wonder what Excalibur will say about you."

"Only one way to find out," Alex replied. She grasped the hilt, light and balanced in her grip. Another figure stepped forward, pulling out a bundle of leather scraps that, once untangled, turned into a new leather sheath with runes of its own stitched into the material. Alex struggled to fit it to her waist, the tip of Excalibur's blade digging into the soil. The figure in robes calmly took the leather and twisted it around to Alex's back, where the sword rested firm between her shoulder blades.

"You look positively courageous, Ms. Stirling," Ghaoithe said.

"Glad to hear it. But couldn't you have just, you

know, given it to me instead of walking us out to the middle of the jungle and scaring me to death?" asked Alex. She fidgeted, trying to find the most comfortable way to position the sword.

"Oh, let us have our fun," Ghaoithe muttered to Alex below the earshot of the others. She gave Alex a playful shove before circling around to face the surrounding crew. "Everyone welcome Alexandra Stirling to our ship! Now let's drink!"

Sometime between her first mug and daylight poking through a graying sky, Alex worried if joining the crew would be bad for her health. She initially stayed as sober as she could, trying not to drink too quickly, but the rogue's gallery never stopped trying to party. She couldn't even tell where the casks of alcohol came from, but they were constantly on the fringes of the clearing with music, dancing, and boisterous laughter attached.

A lull in the action allowed her to escape to a calmer side of the party away from the revelries and free drinks. Despite having such an exciting welcome to the ship's crew, Alex desperately craved a warm coffee to stave off the headache inevitably forming soon.

"Here, drink this," someone spoke in her ear. Alex

jumped, turning to see Ghaoithe beside her, steaming mug in tow.

"Dammit, Captain! I didn't hear you," gasped Alex. Ghaoithe shrugged and held the drink out again. It wasn't coffee, but it was thick and sweet, spreading warmth through the weary girl's limbs.

"Think you're awake enough to talk business?" asked Ghaoithe.

"Not really, but the drink helps." Alex strained not to gulp the honey-tinged liquid too quickly. It lacked caffeine's jolt, but the world slowly became clearer, her stance less wavering. The threat of pounding in her head started to dissipate.

"Close enough," grinned Ghaoithe. "Come with me, little Minnow."

They crossed into the tree line, now emerald-wild in the morning light. The enormous leaves and thick underbrush presented fewer hazards now that Alex could see, but it still painted an impression of traveling through a land that stopped aging when dinosaurs still walked the earth.

Once they were no longer visible to the party through the foliage, they found the others. Fleet and Roy waited on a gnarled root and stood when they spotted the two women. The group was well hidden within the jungle, but the sounds of the party rang within earshot.

"There's our lady of the hour! Been too long since we had a proper newcomer, I tell ya!" Fleet laughed. With a toothy grin, he squeezed Alex with a hug.

"Really? I figured this was pretty much everyday life for wayfarers," said Alex as she freed herself from Fleet's arms.

"This is a little different because of the circumstances. It may be a bit before we can let loose like this again," explained Ghaoithe. "Take a seat."

"That's ominous," Alex replied, but she sat on the plush grass anyway.

Captain Loinsigh paced for a moment before clearing her throat. "Do you trust us?"

"Mostly. I wouldn't have followed you this far if I thought you were terrible people," said Alex.

"We'll need more than a 'mostly.' Our little ceremony may have seemed like it was all flash and show, but we have an important mission ahead. We'll need everyone to be fully committed with us if we want to get it done."

The doubt hurt Alex more than she expected, but she could not blame the leaders for asking. They knew she had doubts. She strengthened her resolve, carefully choosing how to phrase her answer.

"I… do trust you. You also know I need answers, and I can't fully trust anyone who I know is hiding something important. What's going on?" Alex asked.

The tension lifted through the forest canopy. Ghaoithe smiled – not a smirk but a genuine, bright smile – and sat down on the ground across from Alex.

"Ok. That's fair," Ghaoithe said. "Now that you're sworn in as our Historian, it's time you get your details."

"Oh, hold up!" Alex tugged at her pocket, wresting away her phone. She pulled up her notes and nodded, much to the crew's puzzlement.

"You know we specialize in finding artifacts and relics," Ghaoithe explained. "What we do with them is a little more complicated than just sending them off to a museum somewhere. What do you know about Osiris?"

"He was the Egyptian god of death, and apparently a lot of hidden items around the world are related to him somehow. I thought the tag was one of your coded directions, but now I'm not sure anymore," said Alex.

Roy leaned forward, piercing Alex with a gaze more serious than the other two. "You ever heard of the Illuminati?" he asked.

Alex nodded. "Group of people secretly leading the worlds' governments, Freemasons, and all that jazz. Don't tell me they're real, too."

"Yes and no. Osiris is a group. Like us, they search the world for lost items, sometimes to sell, sometimes to keep. Unlike us, they're very rich and very business-oriented. They coerce entire governments with their hands in a lot of business and power, both in our world and yours," Ghaoithe explained.

"They're a rotten bunch o' ruthless thugs in suits, is what they are," Fleet interrupted. He spat on the ground.

"Maybe. They're dangerous. Very dangerous when they need to be, with a lot of people around the world looking out for their interests," said Ghaoithe. "As honorless and cutthroat as they are though, they've never caused us much trouble. We sometimes compete for the same finds, and we'll harass each other, but it's always been more a matter of competition and bragging rights than danger. Osiris knows the power they hold and sees us more as an annoyance than serious competition."

Her tone alarmed Alex. The fledgling journalist stopped typing and shot a quizzical look at her officers. "So, something's changed? What's Jackson's role in all this, and why are we staying so hush about mentioning them?"

"Pandora's Box," said Roy. The jungle hushed at his deep voice for several moments, the party little more than white noise beyond the leaves. Alex glanced at each of the others, confused, but their grave expressions offered no insight.

"Wait, like the Greek myth? We're going after the boxed source of all evil?" quizzed Alex. An image of her failed shop class projects came to mind. She would have laughed had she not been keenly aware of of Excalibur resting on her back.

"It's more of an urn really, but yes. That's the gist of it," answered Ghaoithe.

"Osiris is after it, too. Somethin's different with 'em this time, and yer old flame is at the center of it. We can't risk him getting any closer to it," Fleet said.

Ghaoithe rubbed her chin. "We don't know for sure what their plans are. We can't do anything rash. We aren't killers. Fleet's right, though; something is different about their approach this time.

"Your boyfriend's name isn't Jackson, first of all. As far as we know, it's Ethan Holt, assuming that's not a fake identity, too. It's the only name he has that's consistent throughout our run-ins with each other. He's a member of Osiris, and he's been tracking you for a good while, far as we can tell. He needed that poster and the coordinates on it."

Alex's gut clenched in defiance of anything other

than a case of mistaken identity. In hindsight, the news made sense. Perhaps she even expected it in a way. Jackson's refusal to show her his home, lack of family... even his accent resonated with the perfect Southern ideal more than realistic Missouri speech.

Her memories kept crawling back to the kindhearted man she knew. She spent intimate moments with him, learned his interests and passions, felt the tenderness in his arms. Could the answer really be so cut-and-dry? She had no reason to doubt Ghaoithe after the events of the past few days. Her lover obviously kept secrets from her, but nothing about his personality screamed out warnings that he was truly some conglomerate mastermind.

"They've been murdering people connected to this trail." Roy's pointed revelation gave the knife in her stomach a final twist. "A clockmaker, a few memorabilia collectors. We don't know everything they've found, but the coordinates on your poster seem to be at the center of it."

"Okay," was all Alex could croak out. Her emotions fought with her reasoning, and only through the application of her professional training did she manage to remain impartial.

This is it. This is the first test. Keep searching for answers, she thought. It helped to keep her grounded, even if only temporarily.

When Alex did not look up from her keypad at the news, her captain reached over and lifted a distraught chin. Her lone green eye rippled with compassion.

"You're not in this alone. It's a lot to take in, I know, but you dodged a bullet. Maybe even literally. We're going to find out what's going on here," she said.

Alex blinked several times, shaking her head to clear her thoughts. Ghaoithe's stare locked Alex with hypnotic magnetism so that she could hardly see anything else.

"I... we can talk about the mopey stuff later. Why is he... are *they* doing this? What's different?" Alex asked.

"We don't know," said Roy, clearing his throat. "They've been plenty shady before, but never so openly. They're dark, but they ain't that dark. Or dumb. Killin' people is messy and gets attention they don't wanna spend resources on to clean up."

"Was there a change in leadership or something? Anyone to hold accountable?"

"It ain't like that," Fleet said. "They don't have leadership. It ain't a fancy company where ya just send in a resume and whatnot. It's more like an idea, a religion to follow that's been around since the pharaohs. Sometimes they strike down their own for whatever reason and sometimes they all come together when they need to shift some power in the world."

"Whatever it is about Pandora's Box they came together for, they've been bloodhounds about it, and that's a problem," finished Ghaoithe.

"Well, the source of all the sorrows in the world seems pretty important, even compared to your collection," Alex reasoned.

"An empty source," corrected Fleet. "It's a nice thing to say ya have, but pretty useless now. Which means they know somethin' we don't, and they're willin' to kill for it."

Another silence. They were all thinking the same thing, but only Alex took the initiative to say it aloud: "Then we'll just have to find it before they do."

Ghaoithe cackled, "That's the plan! Glad to see you're on board, Miss Stirling!"

Alex blushed and fidgeted with her feet. "What's the first step here?"

Roy rubbed his bare head and leaned back. "I'll put ears on the ground once we get back to the inn. Osiris knows I'm in with your crew, but you never know what info some jockey will pass through. If anything, I can help move some goods in your favor."

"We've got maybe two days," said Fleet. "Three days

max before we need to be settin' off. Get things prepped and all."

"We'll just have to wing it," finalized Ghaoithe. "Sounds about right for us anyway."

Beyond their discussion, the atmosphere of the party changed. The gleeful hollers of drunken revelry sharply turned into screams. As the three rose to investigate, a hulking figure crashed through the brush. Ghaoithe drew her rapier before Alex even noticed her hand move, but it fell to the ground as the captain rushed to aide the figure instead.

"Sorin! What happened?" Ghaoithe yelled.

Sorin met her arms, his clothes tattered and charred. His body did not fare much better, collapsing onto a knee in a bloodied, bruised heap.

"Osiris," he gasped. "They're… burning Roanoke. The *Cloudkicker*'s blocked off."

Alex never wondered what a runaway train looked like until she witnessed Ghaoithe pummel her way through the streets of a burning Roanoke.

The captain's rage rubbed off slightly on the new recruit; Alex could at least move on her own rather than stand petrified and shrieking at the sight of a city burning to the ground. Fire normally blanked her senses, made her incapable of acting rationally, locked her mind away within a part of herself she never entered willingly.

Alex transformed into a scared girl trapped among equally scared citizens of Roanoke, driven by a desire to reach the only bastion of safety in the city at the lighthouse.

Only through the captain's relentless energy was Alex able to draw the strength to walk at all. Roy pushed her onward before rushing to fortify his tavern, if it still existed at all. Many of the party-goers rushed ahead, narrowly entering the city before the main entrances were cut off by the fire.

Fleet and Alex carried the ailing Sorin, an urgent need to bring him to safety the singular thought on Alex's mind. Ghaoithe forged a path for them, her body a battering ram against alleyway doors and shadows alike. Smoke towered into the mountains, hanging in pockets just long enough to choke the compatriots and leave them searching for the glowing runes of their captain's armor.

Most of the people of Roanoke rushed in the opposite direction, the *Cloudkicker* crew salmon in the stream. Their only respite came at a wide intersection where the smoke had cleared the streets enough to allow brief glimpses at their surroundings. Several blocks away, looming overhead, the *Cloudkicker* hung anchored to the lighthouse. Tiny figures clashed on the bridge, an assault held narrowly at bay and the only sign that the other crew members made it out of the jungle safely.

The wind shifted, and smoke veiled the lighthouse

once more. The window was enough, allowing Ghaoithe to get her bearings. She called to her companions to follow her down another wrecked alley.

The fires had already charred the path and moved on, leaving high, blackened walls on either side. With the escape from the fleeing crowds, Sorin groaned for a brief stop. His two crutches placed him against the coolest section of stone wall they could find.

"The one day it doesn't rain. 'Course this would happen now," Fleet said through gritted teeth.

"Osiris had this planned the moment we were spotted coming into port," said Ghaoithe. She stood over the injured First Mate, hand never leaving the hilt of her blade.

"Do they have a habit of burning down enemy cities?" Alex asked. Staying focused was her only way to stay distracted from the fires, and her attempt to sound brave was aimed mostly to herself.

"No, and that's the point. This isn't an 'enemy city' to them. They're getting desperate."

A blur shot out from the corner of Alex's right eye, a flashy streak from the window of a nearby structure. Another raced towards them from the other end of the alleyway. Ghaoithe jumped forward, yelling to the hampered trio to run. They wasted no time on her orders.

The two newcomers did not have any identifying marks, only wicked falchions in their hands. Whether they were Osiris or just profiteers of the situation, they launched themselves at the captain. Alex looked back to see Ghaoithe slam a fist into the leading assailant's torso before losing sight of them.

Flames roared alive and well outside the alley. It steadily burned closer to the heart of the city, creating blackened husks of the buildings it left behind. Alex blinked away the sting of falling ash, unable to figure out their location.

"This way. Don't stop, little Minnow. We'll make it if we keep going," Fleet reassured. Sorin grunted, though whether in agreement or pain was not clear.

They followed the streets in a vague line towards the lighthouse area. It popped up through pockets in the haze overhead but not long enough to see if the battle continued on the mooring.

They ran into crumbling walls that blocked their pathways, forcing them to backtrack several times along their route. Worse, the fire shifted with every change in the wind to rush towards the untouched kindling that filled out the city. The evacuating masses disappeared as the tower got closer, leaving the group alone in their hellish labyrinth.

Alex's eyes stung no matter how much she tried to wipe them. She could feel tears roll down her face only to evaporate on her cheeks. The straps holding Excalibur in place dug into her shoulders with every step.

They eventually found themselves entering an open square, but all of the opposite avenues crackled with flame. As they turned to backtrack, a snap ripped through the air, followed by the rumble of a falling building that destroyed the path behind them. With no streets available, Fleet grappled Sorin and lifted the burden onto his own shoulders.

"I can't hold him fer long. That building there! Knock the door down! We gotta run through," he shouted, barely audible above the roar of the city.

A mostly untouched home offered protection to their left, flame threatening to move in any second. Alex wasted no time in unsheathing Excalibur, but she balked once she arrived at the door. She struggled to move on the city streets to begin with; visions of becoming trapped inside a burning building kept her motionless.

Stuck for precious few moments, she could only react when the door shattered in front of her. Two more men stepped through the door and blinked, caught as unaware as the girl in front of them.

"'Ey, issat the blondie that the blue bitch was luggin'

around?" said one of the men. His confused expression seemed to be a regular fixture for his face.

"Aye, it is," said his partner. He carried a rusted sword as notched as his smile. "We get outta this alive, she'd make a fine ransom."

Alex processed what they were saying with enough time to step backwards and little else. She tripped and fell, narrowly avoiding a fist careening her way. Fleet placed Sorin on the ground as safely as he could and jumped into the fray with fists of his own.

The rookie sailor climbed to her feet, sword ready. Fleet was big and experienced, but he was also unarmed and could not get in close enough to the assailants to do any real damage. He took a jab at the closest fighter, who dodged about easily.

Alex came in from Fleet's left, making a wild, forceful swing at the first body she saw. The toothless criminal cried out as Excalibur landed in his leg with an awful squishing sound. He toppled onto the ground, rolling around in his own blood as it stained the dirt below.

The other man ducked past the Quartermaster, thrusting forward with his own sword at Alex's exposed figure. Fleet twisted, slamming an elbow into the man's back. The blade glanced off-target, slicing instead into Alex's right arm. The pain took a moment to register, but it hit with excruciating force. She screamed, holding her arm as a damp warmness spread through her fingers.

Fleet dispatched the remaining cutthroat with a blow to the temple. Yanking at the unconscious man's shirt, Fleet ripped off a long strip of cloth and hustled with it to Alex's side.

"You'll be fine, lass. It's not too deep," he said, inspecting the wound. "Stoppin' the bleedin' is gonna hurt the most though. Best bite on yer sword straps."

He did not lie. Pain shot colored specks through Alexandra's vision as he tightened the bandage over the wound. She worried she would chew through the leather or crack her teeth, but the moment passed, leaving her with a sore throb.

Fleet picked up her fallen sword and placed it swiftly into its cover on her back. The building they had planned to pass through was now ablaze, their moment of escape gone. He peered in the other directions, searching for a break in the surrounding walls, but none gave any insight to escape. Sorin lay nearly still on the ground.

"Help!" yelled Alex. "Someone!"

"Save yer energy! Last we want is another group of brigands hearin' us and waitin' fer the fire to die down a bit," scolded Fleet. "Least we're in the open and away from the fumes. We can hold out a bit."

Alex found no comfort in the idea. She called out another panicked cry. Fleet sighed, but did not comment. He chose to tend to his fading companion instead.

A moment of crackling wood and Alex let out a third cry. A faint voice shouted back, and she perked up. She attempted to stand, but the loss of blood sent her back to the ground dizzy. She called out to the stranger and waited.

From beyond the walls of flame ahead of them, a spark shot skyward. It arced high into the air, piercing through the thick smoke as though it were not there. The beacon lingered in the atmosphere a moment before fading.

"Stay close. We've gotta be precise for this," said Fleet. Alex looked to see Sorin already slung over a broad shoulder. "Seems ya got a knack for timing."

A familiar hum closed in overhead. Through the haze, runes fell from the sky, dim but rapidly glowing brighter. They gained weight and detail until they were clearly visible just beyond the rubble where the other voice called out. They hung there, ever watchful, before gliding towards the injured group.

From over the ruins appeared Ghaoithe, hanging onto the bottom a rope ladder that reached into the heavens overhead. Thick soot covered her body, but she looked otherwise unharmed. How she managed to survive her trek through Roanoke was anyone's guess, but Alex let out a grateful cry anyway.

Ghaoithe tugged on the ladder, and she drifted to a halt in the open square. She hopped down to allow Fleet to grab the rope and begin climbing with Sorin in tow. At the sight of Alex's bandaged arm, Ghaoithe let out a small chuckle.

"Looks like you've got your first battle scar," she said.

Alex simply nodded and fell towards Ghaoithe's arms. One gripped Alex tightly while the other reached out and pulled on the ladder a second time. They rose, pulled upward by invisible hands from the ship. Alex enjoyed the breeze that washed over her as they got higher and focused on Ghaoithe's protective embrace.

They moved beyond the smoke. Alex looked at the ground shrinking beneath them, at the city of Roanoke that no longer existed. Most of the ancient buildings were either on fire or smoldering, whole sections wiped out at a time. After centuries of hiding, the lost town ringed by beautiful mountains met its match in a precise arson attack.

"Are we safe? Did we make it?" mumbled Alex wearily.

"Yes, Minnow. We're safe for now."

Alex buried her face in her captain's chest and sobbed, the last bit of her stoicism eroded.

A soft hum emanated from the red crystal's stand. The stone bobbed up and down in tune with the ship it powered, three prongs below it siphoning whatever energy it held and pushing it through the runes that lined the ship.

"Runes can be used without one of these if you just want light or hot water," Ghaoithe had explained on their way back from Kirk's mad scientist shop, "but the crystals are what let us fly. Something about inert magnetism and runic conversion and yadda yadda. I just pop the damn things in when they run dry every few months and the rest takes care of itself."

"It's basically like a processor in a computer then," Alex said. The captain's blank stare relayed all it needed. "Never mind."

In the days since that discussion, the crystal room became a hideaway for the young woman. Fewer voices distracted her there than in her bedroom. The white noise from the crystal provided the necessary backdrop to process her thoughts. She poured over her notes, hellbent on avoiding too much downtime, but the leads in her relic book went nowhere. The scope of their mission grew heavier with each dead-end.

Twelve of their crew members had either perished or disappeared in the escape from Roanoke. They made stops over the ensuing hours, usually in remote villages so small that the only way to leave the *Cloudkicker* was via the rope ladder. News of the city's destruction had spread, but word of Roy or the others remained sparse.

The ship's supplies dwindled, as well. The fire interrupted their chance at resupplying in time for their mission. Ghaoithe traded for anything she could, but with dwindling petty cash and their artifacts already unloaded, they trudged on with only the basics. Morale plummeted, and eventually Ghaoithe dropped the search for survivors. Their priority returned to the Bermuda Triangle.

Sorin survived, providing perhaps the only good news since the attack. When Alex tried to check in on him, she was met with his usual gruff personality. She took his terseness as a positive sign and left him to mend.

Really, she left the majority of the crew alone. She felt that she hindered more than helped. Every turn led to structured chaos. Though Ghaoithe and Fleet made time for her, their conversations were clipped and out of courtesy. So,

Alex hid away in the power chamber with its bright ambiance and just enough room for a study table with two chairs.

She paced the chamber, scratching for ideas when the door slid open. Her captain strode in. Alex continued to pace while Ghaoithe filled the doorframe, watching with hands on her hips.

"I'm almost there, Ghaoithe. I know it."

"Alex…"

"If we just go back and consider the poster. I've searched for anything to do with swords, sand, the color blue…"

"Alex."

"You know, it would really help you guys if you would at least consider getting wifi."

"Alexandra Stirling!"

Alex's rambling stopped. She looked up at her superior as if just becoming aware of her presence, a short blonde possum caught in headlights.

"You need to sleep, Alex," said Ghaoithe. She crossed to the study table and sat.

"I'm fine," said Alex. "I just need to get this done. We don't have much time."

"You haven't seen a bed in two days. Won't do anyone much good when you pass out from exhaustion."

"You haven't had a drink in two days. We can both go without our vices a bit longer for the greater good."

The skycaptain loosed her boisterous laugh and pulled a silver flask from her sash. She wiggled it in front of Alex and motioned for the researcher to sit. Alex complied, sighing and feeling as though she should have known better.

"What's really going on here, Alex?" asked Ghaoithe. She downed a shot from the flask and passed it across the table.

Alex held her nose to the cap. Vodka. She shrugged and let the sharp taste of liquor bite at her throat. "What do you mean?"

"Something's bothering you. There's hard work, and then there's distracting yourself," Ghaoithe said. "Is it that guy's leg you're worried about?"

The memory of the crippled man flashed in Alex's head, crunching sound and all. Just the mention of it caused her arm to throb achingly. Yet aside from the scar that would show on her arm for the rest of her life, she gave the incident little thought.

"No," she said, "that's not it. I mean, it's not a pleasant memory, but it's not like we had a lot of options."

"Then what is it?"

"I don't want to talk about it."

Ghaoithe leaned forward, taking another gulp from the canister. "Look, we all have our demons. I get it," she said. "I hate needles. Can't go near 'em. I'll risk getting my limbs hacked off in a fight all day before I'd willingly get a shot.

"However, my crew knows that, too. We have to know what each other can and cannot handle before we get into situations where hesitation over something gets us killed. We got lucky in Roanoke, and what we do relies a lot on luck. However, we can't count on it every time and expect it not to bite us in the ass eventually."

Alex mulled the issue. Ghaoithe was right, of course. Logically, the openness made sense, but Alex no longer guided herself through logic. She knew the issue that kept her paralyzed as thugs rushed at her team in the flaming courtyard. All she had to do was name it.

"I can't," she said.

"Then I'll have to ground you once we figure out our destination," said Ghaoithe. "It's too risky having you in the field."

The captain stood, leaving the flask in Alex's hands. Reflected in the polished surface, a worn girl stared back, deep bags under eyes framed with blonde curls. She looked terrible, fatigued in more than just her body.

"Fire," whispered Alex. "It was the fire."

Ghaoithe stopped to place a hand on her partner's shoulder. Alex wanted to cry, to avoid explanation, but she continued to stare at her reflection.

"A few years ago, my family was about ready to move," she said. "We had built this nice house, had everything moved except the big furniture. We were just staying a couple more nights in the old place.

"I don't remember much. I woke up, and there was smoke everywhere. It was hot. I tried crawling out of my room, and I remember shouting for my parents as loud as I could. Then there were some men carrying me out, and I woke up in the hospital. I still can't do fires. Sometimes I wake up thinking I'm still trapped under all that smoke."

Ghaoithe sat back down and squeezed Alex's hand. Locked with Alex's, her eye did not waver. "You going to be ok?" she asked.

Alex shook her head, forcing her thoughts back to the present. "Yeah, I think so," she said. "I've come to terms with my parents being gone. It's just that I don't like talking about it much. Saying it out loud makes it true, you know? I can deal with it in my head and my heart until someone reminds me that it's not a dream."

Leaning back in her chair, Ghaoithe crossed her

fingers in thought. "So, that's what you meant when you said there was nothing left for you in your town."

Alex responded with a halfhearted smile. "Yes. They left me enough to keep going, but the house and the trust aren't that large. My friend Becky kept an eye on me over the years, but she's moving now."

Talking about what troubled her helped soothe Alex, but coping with the loss of her parents weighed down most of her actions since Roanoke. She understood, deep down, that her research merely provided a distraction from those choking flames.

The mission brought her back. Threats of being left out of future steps scared her just as much as her past. Being left to sit in her room while the expedition team explored unknown portions of Bermuda shocked her senses enough to slow her thoughts and approach the reality of the past few days.

Ghaoithe, for her part, nodded in contemplation. She leaned back and put her arms behind her head. "Well, I'm glad you decided to stay. I know it's not your home, and I'm not your parents, but I'd like to help you find what what you're looking for."

Alex blushed and fumbled with her hands. "Sorry if I was out of it for a bit," she said. "I guess life wouldn't be as interesting if it came with a roadmap, huh?"

As the words rolled off her tongue, a spark shot through her head. Roads. Bermuda Triangle. Her eyes widened as she knocked her chair over in the rush to flip through the book of relics. Ghaoithe, stunned by the burst, looked on in curiosity over her protégé.

Alex stopped on a page with fewer notes than many of the other entries. A rough map of an area covered in what looked like cobblestone had been hastily sketched in the center.

"What do you know about the Bimini Road? There's not much here," asked Alex.

Ghaoithe arched an eyebrow, interested in the turn of events. "Not much," she responded. "It was thought to be a road to Atlantis, but we ended up discovering the real city off the coast of Sierra Leone. There was never much reason to head to Bimini to check it out after that."

"I think this could be something. Everything refers to it as parts of an ancient building, but what if it's literally a road? Is that possible?"

"It could be, but we can't just go up and touch it. That's not how these things work. We'd need to approach it a certain way or have a key. It's just a bunch of limestone otherwise, even to us."

"We approach from the southwest. And we'll need two of those crystals, a red one and blue one," said Alex. Her body trembled from the excitement and fatigue, but her eyes burned with certainty in her explanation.

"Where in the world did you get that from?" asked Ghaoithe.

The rolled up *Lawrence of Arabia* poster rested propped up in its tube beside the table. Alexandra unfurled it across the table, pointing at it in various points as she spoke.

"Here," she explained. "This plane, flying from the bottom left to the top right, dropping a bomb in the desert. The two sides are carrying red and blue flags."

Ghaoithe laughed. "I knew I kept you aboard for a reason. Fine job, Alex!"

Alex beamed with pride at her captain's praise. With the mystery solved and her fears laid out, the full weight of her fatigue slammed into her. She began to collapse to the floor. Ghaoithe reacted quickly enough to catch the young girl in her arms.

"I think that means it's time to get you to bed," she said. Alex curled up in the captain's arms and did not dream.

IX

"Let's do this!"

Ghaoithe's drunken enthusiasm from the top of the bridge did not radiate through the rest of the crew. Her voice rang alone; everyone else sat on high alert as the *Cloudkicker* glided onward.

Ghaoithe didn't care for the Bermuda Triangle, Fleet had explained.

"Of all of the places in the world that can scuttle an airship, Bermuda's by far the most dangerous. Aside from the sudden weather calamities and magnetic variances the rest of the world's got, Lost Earth's realm of runes and crystals attract any number of random voodoos. No one in the crew knows what we're gonna encounter once we pass into the Triangle's grasp."

"How many times have you done this?" Alex asked. She shifted in her chair in anticipation. Excalibur rested across her lap.

"Twice," said Sorin. He absently rubbed his leg. The barrel-chested man returned to his post earlier that day. Though still a bit stiff with his movements, his irritable presence was welcome back on the tense deck. Alex swore he maintained a closer watch over her than before.

"First time we had a storm swoop in on us. Coulda swore we heard Thor's chariot itself runnin' beside us," Fleet continued. "Second was nothin' but clear skies fer whatever reason. Fickle place, this. Wouldn't be surprised if we were attacked by gryphons. Heard of stranger things happening here."

"Bring 'em on! We'll take 'em!" shouted Ghaoithe from her seat. Her cackle bounced across the room.

Alex stared at her captain, learning what the Sky Thief was like when afraid. Sure, the red-haired woman acted boisterous and stoic, brandishing her rum and rapier with flourish. Looking closer, her fingers fidgeted with her flask.

Her eye darted across the room, never stopping in any spot for more than a moment.

The woman known for purposeful movement transformed into a child wary of the closet at night.

"I've never seen her like this," said Alex. "It doesn't seem like her."

"Is not," replied Sorin. "This ship is her life. The Triangle is one of few places that can take it away."

The *Cloudkicker* shuddered, signaling its crossing through the mystical border. Ghaoithe's cackling grew to a peak, stopping only once she lost balance when the ship returned to its normal glide.

Throughout the room, the crew worked feverishly to get any information they could. The clock overlooking the bridge sped through numbers before settling all hands at twelve. A ratcheting sound came from the compass, which spun wildly about.

Then, silence.

Gray mist began to cloud a view that was clear but seconds ago. Within a few more moments, their visibility went non-existent.

Fleet rose and barked orders. "Do we still have our altimeter?"

"Yes, sir. It's holding fine so far."

"Keep our crystal output steady. The moment our altitude changes, brace fer impact!"

Alex gripped her sword to the point of pain, expecting the ship to be overtaken at any moment by some devious kraken from below the sea or a violent wind seeking to knock them down. She was not the only one; the deck entered a hushed state broken only by the odd hum or scratch of paper.

Ghaoithe hunched forward in her chair, waiting for calamity. When none came, she stood and paced across the platform. Still nothing. The groaning of the ship's hull added atmosphere to their plight but no danger.

"To Hell with this," the captain eventually muttered, throwing her hands in the air. She returned to her seat, hands rubbing her temples.

Minutes, then hours, passed by without incident. They hung in the middle of their clouded spectrum, daring not to travel any faster than absolutely necessary, if they moved at all. Alex could not tell.

Every fraction of movement became a blur. Whether it was the rotating compass or the motion of Fleet dealing a set of cards, a shadow followed like a television out of sync.

Alex thought she should panic, but the fear did not come. She accepted the ethereal shift. As the crew began, one-by-one, to fall into slumber, she knew that she, too, was already asleep. She turned, and lolling in her chair was her body, still clutching the sword in her lap.

A whistling swept through the chamber, a vicious wind she could not feel and the only sound to be heard.

"I'm here, Alex," called a hollow voice. Fog filled the bridge as well as the window. Alex searched for the origin of the words but lost sight in the milky haze.

"Where? Who?" she said flatly.

"Here."

Alex turned to the source, very clearly heard the second time, and began walking. She did not know if she was touching the floor of the ship or simply gliding. The glass wrapping the bridge materialized only for Alex to pass through as though it were water.

A chill sensation ran through Alex. Or rather, she knew it was cold outside the ship, and some deep part of her felt it, but she numbly continued her walk without acknowledging it. The deck was slightly clearer, and she followed the wooden beams to the prow.

The fog swirled as she approached, effervescent and alive. From within the boiling cloud stepped Ethan, standing firm at the tip of the ship. He smiled, a genuine smile without a trace of the malice or cunning of their last meeting.

Alex attempted to run up to him, to embrace him, but her body did not respond. She just stood there, gazing up at his handsome form.

"Is it really you?" she asked.

"It is. I figured it was time for us to talk," he said. He stepped down and placed a hand on her cheek. "It is good to see you again. You are so beautiful, Alex."

Infatuated, Alex smiled - or she hoped she smiled - and met with his twinkling eyes. They swam with the gentleness she recalled so well.

"What's going on, Jackson... Ethan? What do I even call you?"

"I... don't know. I have used so many names, I suppose my real one doesn't matter. I wouldn't even know if it was my true name anymore."

"So, all those things Ghaoithe said are true, then?" Alex stepped back, confused.

"To a point, but they don't know everything. Osiris does mean well, hon. We are doing what we can to try to save a terrible fate from happening to this planet. That's what we've always done."

Ethan's voice sounded genuine. He waited, giving Alex space to work out her thoughts. She was not sure what was going on, the mist crawling inside her head as much as surrounding the ship.

"I need to know what's going on... Ethan. What fate?" she asked. Her head throbbed, a very real sensation among the ghostly sensations before.

"We are here for you, Alex. I won't let anyone hurt you. I didn't before the hospital, and I won't now," Ethan comforted. He cautiously put an arm around her, testing her boundaries. She did not resist, falling into the embrace she thought was lost forever.

"I am happy here. Why are you guys fighting with Ghaoithe if it's so important?" she asked. Her mind wracked itself to make sense of things, but the more she tried, the more her thoughts seemed to slip away just beyond her grasp. How long had she and Ethan known each other? He loved music. Or was it sports?

"The Sky Thief is dangerous, love," whispered Ethan. He nuzzled Alex's neck. "You've seen how observant she is, how she always maintains control despite her outward appearance. Do not trust her."

Alex shook her head. She could see Ghaoithe's slumbering body on the bridge through the haze.

"She's saved my life. She welcomed me to her crew," Alex argued.

"That's what she tells you, but be careful. She hides a great deal. I am watching over you the best I can, but Osiris can only do so much. I love you, little Minnow."

Alex turned to face her lover. "How did you know my nickname on the *Cloudkicker*? Something's wrong here." she spoke to herself as much as to Ethan. The clouded memories started to crystallize once again.

Ethan held his eyes on her. The bright spark they held when he first came from the fog drained away to glazed lifelessness. They lost color. Finally, they sank into their sockets to reveal endless darkness. His face thinned to become skin hanging loosely from his cheeks. Hair fell in clumps, and his balding skeleton let loose a wail that pierced the heavens.

Alex tried to run, but her body held as firm as it had at his arrival. She could feel her heart beating again, life threatening to leap out of her chest, and she crossed her arms and cried.

She woke, violently and loudly. The wail persisted until she realized it was her own. Drenched in sweat, she stood up, trying to convince herself she was alive again. Outside the windows, bright blue sky hovered over the most gorgeous water Alex had ever seen.

She jumped as a hand held her shoulder. She jerked

around to see Sorin hovering over her.

"Is ok. You slept. We all slept," he said with an usual softness to the girl.

The rest of the crew woke up on their own terms, as well. Some screamed as Alex did, others woke softly and achingly, as if they were not used to real light. Ghaoithe grumbled and squinted at her flask before tossing it to the floor.

An immediate roll call was ordered. Two stayed in their terrible slumber, a mechanic and one of the galley staff, still locked with their personal battles against the Bermuda's magic. They were escorted to the medical bay, no one certain if they would see the sun again.

The remainder of the trip was subdued. The ship flew on course during the absence of conscious bodies as though pulled by an invisible hand, but the loss of two more weighed heavily on morale. Ghaoithe, hunched forward in her chair, glowered through the flight.

The only person who did not sit on edge was Sorin, who was no more sour than usual once they were on their way again. He even brought a deck of cards to the reporter.

"You need a distraction," he announced, pulling the neighboring table up to her chair. He dealt a hand before she could object.

"Thank you," Alex replied meekly. She took her cards and played a couple hands in silence with the First Mate. Sitting at an amiable card game, she saw that he was younger than she had thought, maybe his early 30's. His face still held a few scuffs, but he was attractive when he did not have a scowl painted across his mouth.

"Why are you always so quiet?" she ventured. Expecting a rebuttal, Alex was surprised when he answered truthfully.

"My people are not for small talk outside families and friends. We talk business and little else," he said.

"Where are you from, then?"

"Transylvania," he said. Sensing Alex's impending snicker, he added, "Romania. Very old country. No vampires."

"Oh," muttered Alex. She quietly watched him lay down three cards onto the table, not wanting to test his good will. "What's it like?"

Sorin grunted but did not speak. Alex feared she upset him, but he eventually spoke, "Very pretty. Is not large, but the land touches the sky all around. We have lots of traditions. Not too different from your home, I think."

Since her induction in the jungle, Missouri practically disappeared in Alex's memory. Sorin's description tugged at her spirit, reminding her of what she left behind.

"I think I'd like to see it someday," she replied.

"Is there a place you do not wish to go?" he said dryly. Alex was not sure if it was what passed for a joke from Sorin, but she smiled nonetheless.

"No, I suppose there isn't."

The two continued their game while the rest of the crew sat on pins as Bimini approached. Sorin remained somewhat gruff, but considerably more open than before the burning of Roanoke.

One thought bugged Alex, though, and she risked asking. "Sorin, what did you see in the mist? You don't seem upset."

For the first time since they had met, Sorin laughed, a warm and bellowing sound that burned with life. "Nothing I did not already know, little Minnow. Ourselves cannot scare ourselves when we know ourselves."

She made sense of his words, but remained curious to what obstacles the others had gone through. If a strong-willed man like Sorin could come out unhindered, then whatever Ghaoithe kept locked within herself must have been truly horrible.

The answers would wait. Within a few more hands of poker, the *Cloudkicker* spotted Bimini. A string of small islands approached, the mainland in Florida within sight from the ship's vantage point above. Alex gawked as the ship listed slightly to align with one of the smaller islands, teasing a view of the gorgeous seascape below. Crystal-clear water allowed glimpses of passing fish, rays, and incredible formations on the seafloor. As they approached the larger islands that made up Bimini, their destination sat unhidden, a track of stone blocks just below the water's surface.

"It's smaller than I expected," said Alex. From the air, the abnormal section of rock resembled a long cobblestone driveway more than a road. No one could deny that it stood out from its surroundings, though. It called for them beneath an aqua veil.

"Doesn't take much, so long as it works," said Ghaoithe. Alex jumped at the captain's voice in her ear. They had not spoken directly since the return from the haze. Whatever bothered Ghaoithe vanished as they caught sight of the islands, replaced with a lustful anticipation.

The ship turned, and the Bimini Road vanished beneath their sightline. With an easy slide, the *Cloudkicker* came to rest above their objective, hovering several hundred yards above the sea. With a nod of her head, Ghaoithe signaled Alex to follow her out.

"Feeling any better?" Alex tempted.

"Much," Ghaoithe replied. "Thank you. Nothing like a real job to get us going. Let's just hope your idea works."

They stepped out of the entry hall and onto the deck. Alex stretched in the warm Caribbean air, her body clammy after her dream in the mists. Already, a few seagulls tempted contact with the strange, silver bird in their territory.

At the side rail of the ship, Alex looked down to see they rested not directly over the road but slightly off port-side. Alex closed her eyes to stave off the vertigo she felt from such a high vantage point. When she opened them, two crystals were in Ghaoithe's open hand before her, one red and one blue just as Alex figured.

"Do the honors?" asked Ghaoithe.

"I just drop them? That how it works?" said Alex.

"We'll find out when we fly towards it."

Alex grabbed the crystals. They weren't much larger than the palm of her hand, but she lurched at their weight. She sensed that she was being watched from behind the windows to the bridge. Suddenly self-conscious, she readied herself to toss the rods overboard but hesitated at the last second, coming to terms with the significance of her appearance on that deck for the first time.

Since joining the ship, Alex assumed the way the crew treated her was typical for any new recruit, that Ghaoithe and

Fleet were extremely friendly to everyone under their command. Standing alone with the Sky Thief herself, the relic hunter actions towards Alex went beyond just the typical camaraderie aboard a vessel.

Alex seized her revelation. She looked up at Ghaoithe, who beamed at her, sun glinting off the golden eyepatch, almost as though she expected Alex's question.

"Before we do this, I need to know something. What did you see in the fog?" asked Alex.

"You first," said Ghaoithe as she crossed her arms.

"I saw Ethan," she said. "He said not to trust you, that you were dangerous. He was right about you in a couple of ways."

"Most people shouldn't trust me, I suppose," reasoned Ghaoithe. She leaned back against the rail and looked up to the cloudless sky. "I won't lie and say I got here by following the book."

"What did you do?"

"It doesn't matter anymore. What matters is how we act now, at this very moment. You'll have to decide what kind of woman I am. It's everyone elses' perceptions of us that shapes how we're remembered."

The captain's voice held no shame or remorse. She just continued to look up, hair blowing freely in the wind.

Alex placed her free hand on Ghaoithe's bronzed arm. It was soft, not at all as leathery or toughened as the captain's appearance conveyed.

"Please," repeated Alex, "what did you see?"

Ghaoithe 's hand closed over Alex's. She turned and gave Alex the same carefree smile that rarely left her face.

"My home," she said, and the conversation was over.

Nodding, Alex held the crystals in her hand for a moment more, then dropped them over the edge of the ship. The two explorers watched them fall for several seconds before landing with a distant splash. The ceremony done, they returned to the bridge.

The *Cloudkicker* pivoted and drew away from Bimini Road. Orders called for a lower altitude. As they turned one final time to align with the road from the southwest, the hull hovered only a dozen yards from the water's edge.

Alex sat and braced herself in her seat. "So what happens now? We just bum-rush the road?"

Fleet kept his eyes to their destination ahead and said, "We'll know when we get there. Different fer each case. With any luck, the sigils on our ship'll trigger the stones and the road."

At Ghaoithe's orders, the airship rocketed forward at a pace rivaling the best of roller coasters. Alex held tightly to

Excalibur's hilt to keep it from soaring off her lap. The underwater stones rushed to meet them. As they approached, little happened. No doorways opened or krakens emerged to guard their secret.

As they breached the leading edge of the road, colorful sparks flew from beneath their ship towards the crystals, now hot with energy. Searing light burst from below the hull. All visibility faded, drowned in a white flash.

"Y'all are gonna make me go blind," Alex grumbled, rubbing her eyes. When she opened them, the ship rested well below the surface of the ocean. Bimini Road stretched before them, longer than when they arrived and all contained within a tunnel of water rushing above. In the distance, the road stretched down into the earth and out of sight, a wall of liquid marking the end of their walkway.

Cheers erupted. Her companions swarmed Alex with pats on the back and congratulations from all sides. She couldn't believe it, transfixed by the newfound passageway she discovered.

"Don't be so surprised, lass. Ya got a knack fer this," Fleet laughed, granting a rough hug.

"Hopefully we live to see more of her ideas. Right now, though, we need to get to work," said Ghaoithe from her perch. She drew up to her full height and filled the room with ecstasy.

Sorin doled out equipment and assignments with methodical efficiency. Unlike the hospital raid or the docking in Roanoke, this was a proper expedition with ten crew members making their way into the passage. Alex never met many of them, a hardy bunch of brigands with dirt embedded in their skin.

Sorin insisted on joining the team, his bruises little more than an annoyance to his motivation. With Alex, Ghaoithe, and Fleet going as well, the ship was left in the hands of a quirky but fierce woman named Tory who immediately began barking orders from behind her tangle of dreadlocks.

Everyone carried a full bag of supplies. As it was Alex's first exploratory mission and Excalibur rested on her back, she was given a lighter load. A quick glance through her bag and she counted her phone, a decent coil of extra rope, several leaflets of paper, pencils, thin leather gloves, and a bag full of white plastic cylinders.

Pulling one of the cylinders out, Alex squinted at it a moment before recognition kicked in.

"Are these... tampons?!" she shrieked, heat rising into her cheeks.

"Best damn kindling ya can get, those things," Fleet

said with a wink.

"Kindling? Really?"

Fleet nodded. "Aye. The stuff inside 'em. We make a point of loadin' up anytime we have the chance. You'll see."

"Well, glad to know these still exist here," Alex muttered as she fumbled to return the tube back to her pouch.

As they left the ship, the adventurers stopped to marvel at the wonder they discovered. The tunnel was bright and dry, as though the ocean had always flowed around it, and the air without a hint of staleness. Life of all colors and styles swam above and beside them as they walked.

"This is incredible," Alex gasped. She tested the wall. Her fingers tingled as they went into the warm oceanic wall. "What happens if some divers come this way?"

"They can't see it. It would be like we never landed. Unless they can turn up some magnetic resonance crystals and an airship of their own, anyway," explained Ghaoithe. She was the only one not wearing a bag strapped to her back. Alex doubted ego was any part of that decision.

The ten of them started the trek towards the falloff at the end of the road. Wary eyes darted upward every few steps out of fear the world would crash in on them at any moment.

"It's like the shark tunnel at the zoo," said Alex.

"Perhaps, but this is not glass," cautioned Sorin. He failed to deter Alex's wonderment.

Ghaoithe vanished among the blue walls ahead. Only the shimmering of the sigils ingrained on her armor offered glimpses of her whereabouts. At times, she stood completely still as she scouted the terrain, easily blending in to as part of the sea and coral.

Chatter filled the tunnel. Spirits were high with a new discovery lying in wait. The men wove stories of their past expeditions to their partners or dreamed of what they would do upon return (most of which involved copious amounts of ale). Alex blushed when comments about some of the women among the *Cloudkicker* crew were brought up in vulgar conversation.

"Everyone seems to be in a pretty good mood," said Alex to Sorin.

"Yes. It has been some time since we've gone to task," he replied. "Should be a good run."

"Do you really think Pandora's Box is down here?"

To that question, Sorin only shrugged.

They came to the end of their liquid tunnel. Ghaoithe paused, examining the road ahead as it took a sharp dive underneath the sand and rock. A black maw before them offered no insight to its secrets.

With a wave of her hand, Ghaoithe led the charge down into the depths. At first, the darkness blinded the crew. Their movement slowed to a crawl. As they descended, the intricate patterns on Ghaoithe's armor flowed with light and, before long, the sand walls surrounding the team were flickering with yellow and black shadows.

A fine layer of sand covered their path and slowed their progress down the gentle slope. The air, dank and musty, swirled with particles that lay undisturbed for eons.

They followed their leader as the path leveled out. Unburdened by a pack, she continued to buzz ahead and back, a rhythmic dance of vigilance. The crew's fervor died down, not replaced by solemnity but a rather focused concern for the mystery ahead.

Alex daydreamed of what await them at the end of their path. She walked with an actual mission to find a lost artifact. Each step forward, she shook with such excitement that she worried she would yell out in jubilation and cause the entire tunnel to collapse.

The change in the walls was ignored at first. By the glow of Ghaoithe's armor, the crew spotted runes etched into the sandstone's surface. Dark and lifeless, they stretched back far towards the entrance. Pressing on, the runes gained a glow of their own. The light was anemic - nothing compared to the charged signs Alex experienced elsewhere - but it offered ample support to their human lantern. Whatever they were trying to reach was close.

Their answer met them in the form of a massive door. Towering well over their heads and into a blackened void above, its steel plating depicted a grand oceanic scene. Dolphins and sharks swam by warriors armed with javelins. Tidal waves crushed unprotected homes. An octopus stared at them from its perch, front and center.

The crew fanned out around the door's entry chamber, taking the discovery as a sign they could rest from their backpacks. Alex continued to stare up.

"This is amazing!" she exclaimed. She ran to meet her captain. "I thought you said you discovered Atlantis."

Ghaoithe inspected the door with ravenous curiosity. Her brows furrowed at what she saw.

"We did," she said to Alex. "That's what worries me."

"Worried? This is huge! It's an entirely unexplored area!" cried the reporter. She set her bag down, grabbed her phone, and began snapping pictures. Ghaoithe ran her fingers over some of the embossed figures, pressing lightly every few inches.

"That's the problem," Ghaoithe said. "We have

nothing on this place. No notes, history, anything. We don't have a clue what's inside or what kind of protection it has. We're blind."

"Then we'll have to make history this time instead of just uncovering it," Alex said. The determination in her voice invited a pause in the Sky Thief's search for a clue.

The party huddled together in the center of the chamber while Ghaoithe searched for a way to open the path. When it became apparent that time was in no short supply, Fleet leaned over to the rookie explorer.

"Hand me one of yer plastics, lass," he grinned.

Alex scrounged through her pack until she found the white cylinders nestled at the bottom. She pulled one out and handed it to her mentor.

Fleet rummaged through his own bag until he found an assortment of fine twigs and a pair of stones. After arranging the wood into a small pile, he ripped the applicator from the tampon to take out the stuffing inside. He placed the fluff underneath the pile. With a few sharp clicks of the stones, a fire licked the inside of the brush.

Small as it was, the fire cheered the crew. They sat, telling stories or singing shanties forgotten by most of the world. Cards were dealt, and Alex warmed up to the companions she rarely talked to.

They were as interested in her as she was of them. Aaron Huff, a lanky fellow who once wrestled a crocodile, sat enthralled when she tried to explain television. That led to a detailed description of what video games were to a heavyset man named Jonas Karlsson. She laughed as the middle-aged explorer sat mulling over the description of *Donkey Kong.*

"I tell ya this: ain't no monkey gonna toss barrels at me and live," he flaunted.

"Well, there's a lot of them. And you have to memorize just when to climb the ladders. You only get three tries."

"I only need one. Yes ma'am," he replied. He sat back, clearly upset and imagining a hypothetical barrel situation in his head.

"I don't see what's so fun about sittin' around and staring at a fake gorilla all day," said another explorer, a younger chap with a pointed chin and hair covering his eyes. "Is that all you guys do?"

"No, not really. I mean, games are popular and people watch a lot of television – those stories broadcast on a screen. There are sports and stuff too."

"Do y'all do things with other people? Like go drinkin' or travelin' or anything?" asked Aaron.

Alex thought for a moment. Her town wasn't the best

example of bustling cultural activity. "Sometimes. I used to go hiking with a couple friends. We'd go to the bars downtown every now and then"

"A couple? That it?" Aaron scoffed.

"We try to get together more when we can! Between work and school and stuff it's hard to find time to do anything more exciting for a lot of people."

"Sounds like all ya ever do is work and then sit at home with yerselves."

Alex searched for a way to explain her home, about bailing hay with friends' families or sitting at a baseball game. In the end, all she could stammer out was, "I… I guess so. Most of us don't do a lot with strangers."

"What about yer history?" asked Jonas. "Our history. Don't ya ever go out to find more about it?"

"There are some people that do that, yes, but it doesn't pay well. Most people find it boring or not interesting enough to make a life of it, I think. We had a movie called *Jurassic Park* that got people into dinosaurs for a bit, but that's about it."

The group stared at her, incredulous at the thought of such an insular world. They could not imagine a place so scared of their own neighbors and upbringing; that modern society had no desire to change such a mindset saddened them.

"Come now, lads," interjected Fleet. He placed an arm on Alex's shoulders. "We all need time to ourselves now and then."

"Only if we ain't got a proper lady around!" shouted one of the others. The rest of the group erupted in playful jeers.

Fleet held Alex close. "They're just curious. I bet they'd be jumping over barrels too if they could."

However, Alex wasn't upset at the group. She bit her lip, pondering their words.

"They're right, though," she said. "Most of the people I knew only cared about what was in front of them or what could make them money. Anything outside their own traditions scared them. That's why I left, really."

"To each their own. They won't be able to stop time forever. Besides, we're glad ya chose to come with us," said Fleet.

"Me, too. Hopefully I can do something worthwhile here."

By the time the cacophony died down, the fire existed as little more than embers. Rest called to the adventurers, and only Ghaoithe remained vigilant.

The chamber doors did not yield. She tried everything

she could at the base of the structure with no luck. Crystals and sigils were useless. None of the flowing artwork near the ground disguised a hidden panel. So, she resorted to the next level of exploration: she went up.

Heights never scared the Sky Thief more than the possibility of letting a tomb go unopened. Her size, however, made the climb tricky. Her boots outsized most of the footholds on the face of the door. One dolphin slipped away from her, and she hung by a desperate hand as the ground beckoned three stories below.

Guess that's what I get for not using the damn rope, she thought to herself. Her sleeping family triggered a brief but powerful wave of envy. *Maybe if I break a leg, they can climb this stupid thing.*

Shoving aside her jealousy, she swung to grasp one of the spear-wielding men. It clicked at her touch. The rush of discovery flooded her head like a powerful lager. *Found you.*

Her hands fumbled along the edges of the figure. When she reached the javelin, it wiggled just enough for a trained hand to notice. It did not flip like a switch, but upon pulling it, the spear left the man's hand and slid along a track in the door. Ghaoithe tugged the spear until the pointed tip reached the octopus in the center of the door.

The heavy sound of locks reverberated through the

door, shaking the frame. Ghaoithe raced towards the bottom as quickly as her footholds would let her. She dropped the final few feet with a hard thud onto the ground just in time for the door to begin raising itself.

Its monstrous grinding woke the resting team. Salt-thick air rushed in and blew out what remained of the fire. So pungent was the smell of the ocean, Alex held her breath thinking she would be caught under a tsunami. Only when the door was fully open and its contents revealed did she release an awed gasp.

Before them, a city of marble columns stretched into the horizon. Water swirled overhead, just as it had at the *Cloudkicker*'s arrival. Green orbs cast pale illumination scattered throughout the cryptic structures. Nothing moved.

Ghaoithe stood, spitting out a mouthful of sand. "I found it, guys."

X

Whatever society built the underwater city vanished long ago. The only signs of life came from the expedition team passing from lantern to lantern. Doorways opened to darkness. The tiled streets sparkled with undisturbed sand. All overcast with a filter of blue as sunlight trickled through the water overhead.

"You'd think we would have found skeletons or something," observed Alex. She spoke without looking up, her nose buried at the parchment in her hands. With all the precision she could muster, she traced their steps as a rough map of the city.

"I couldn't tell you the name of the city, let alone what happened to it," said Ghaoithe. She hovered nearer to the group since their entry. When she wished to scope the sections ahead, she ordered the team to a halt until she returned.

"Could this be a sister city to Atlantis?" asked Alex. "I can't imagine they were the only city to be swallowed by rising tides over history."

"No. Atlantis was a normal city that had a bad ending. This city was always underwater," said Ghaoithe. She waved her hands over the horizon. "There's no method to the buildings. They didn't build towards higher ground anywhere. It looks like the city was built mostly by what was easiest at the time, not out of fear of rising tides."

Alex jotted down the captain's observations. The city did have a hectic design to it, with ramps, long bridges, and structures on platforms built with seemingly no order in mind. They found no parks or communal areas of any kind. It stretched with unadorned sameness for miles under the ocean, a blanket of pointed marble tops.

Alex stopped to investigate another home. A large statue stood next to it, vaguely in the shape of a human but featureless otherwise. A few similar statues watched over the crew as they explored the ruins and stark white domiciles. The crew shuffled past a low structure with a gaping circular entrance. Ghaoithe held up a hand and peeked inside. Finding only another pile of ancient dishware, she moved on.

"Seems like every society needs plates and bowls to give future archaeologists something to do," she mused. Alex chuckled and peered into the shadows as well.

"It's strange," Alex said. "Even those other societies tried to make pretty bowls and plates. Aside from the door we came in and a few of those weird statues, there's no artwork or detailing anywhere."

"Well, wrap 'er up! We found the world's most boring civilization. Can't get no bigger find than that," laughed Mar Olmstead, a brutal lunk who wanted to outwit himself with every sentence.

Alex shook her head and continued without acknowledging him. "What are we looking for anyway?"

Sorin glanced over her shoulder at the map. He said, "A vault. Secure place. Like a bank."

"A bank? I figured something like Pandora's Box would be somewhere important like an altar or something."

"Powerful items are not for the public. The Vatican hides its secrets. The U.S. Constitution is under heavy guard. Here will be the same. Everywhere it's the same. This is not some artwork for regular people to stare at," said Sorin.

"It'll probably be a nondescript building," added Ghaoithe.

Alex looked around. "They're all pretty nondescript."

They passed over a bridge. Their path ended with a ramp spiraling downwards around a tower. The narrow windows offered the same dim view as the other buildings, but a shiver ran up Alex's back nonetheless.

The sensation continued once they reached solid ground. Movement shimmered at the edge of her vision, but with each turn of her head, nothing appeared. She blinked, believing her subconscious to be playing tricks, but her fear stayed just behind her.

"Does your world have any weird creatures I should know about?" she asked timidly.

"What, like dragons and stuff? Not many. Animals are pretty much the same everywhere," said Ghaoithe.

"What about ghosts or werewolf types of things?"

"A few, but they're not what you really expect. They don't bother anyone unless you go looking for trouble in their territories. Why?"

"Because it feels like we're being followed by something."

"That's because we are," Ghaoithe said simply. Alex

noticed for the first time that the other crew members gripped their hilts and bags with twitching fingers. The captain slowed her pace.

Nothing crawled out of the shadows or abducted team members from thin air. Their pursuers kept their distance as Ghaoithe's team trekked on. They searched building after building, never more than a few seconds at a time, while dread followed suit. Images of giant spiders and lurking vampires stuck in Alex's head, but they were met only with silence from each doorway.

The group stopped at the front of a squat, round building. A shriek in the distance wailed at them like nails on a chalkboard. It hastened, and as the sound grew more frequent, the ground shook with plodding thumps.

The color drained from Ghaoithe's cheeks as she muttered a quick, "Oh shit," followed by a very loud, "GOLEM!"

The wall of the round building exploded into a hail of marble chunks. Scattering at Ghaoithe's warning, the team dove away just as a stone club crashed to the ground where they were standing. At the other end, one of the giant stone figures hunched over the prone crew. Its faceless body turned towards them and deliberately swept the ground for a second strike.

The *Cloudkicker* force leapt into action, drawing their weapons and leaving their supplies behind. They surrounded the gigantic statue, confusing it just long enough for Ghaoithe to leap onto its back.

Alex wrestled with Excalibur, stuck in its sheath in her panic. Another swing from the statue's bludgeon soared over her head as she took another dive. Her arm burst with pain, the wound not quite healed.

"The actuator!" called Ghaoithe. Her arms wrapped around the automaton's neck as she attempted a distraction of her own.

"The what?!" called Alex.

"The actuator!" A blow from Fleet to the golem's knee disrupted its balance, knocking it down. "Its controller! Big crystal nearby! Can't miss it!"

Two more of the tremendous statues thundered from the distance. The men not occupied by the downed golem split to take on the newcomers in a frenzy of steel.

Alex scrambled to her feet. She reached into her side bag and threw the coil of rope at her friends just as the golem began to rise.

"Tie its legs!" she called before disappearing into the ruined doorway.

Surmounting the pile of rubble left behind proved a

difficult task, and Alex tripped in the attempt. She tumbled and ended face-down over a steep pit. A stairwell, decorated with the footsteps of the golem, hugged the outer wall.

Edging away from the ledge, Alex stood and started the careful journey down. Within a few steps, she lost the ambient light from outside. The light of her phone was now her only guide, and it ended only a couple short feet from her.

Now she knew this city had dangers. Now she had reason to be afraid of the dark. She heard the battle upstairs and used her friends' battle shouts as motivation. Her head spun, and she wished for nothing more than to sleep off the nightmare.

The bottom of the staircase landed in a circular room several stories below the front door. A speck of blue left the only mark of an escape above. Sliding Excalibur from its sheath, Alex held the phone screen ahead and marched forward.

Only one doorway led away from the landing. Beyond, a grand hall with rows of marble columns stretched on. A dot of red light shone from the far end, a vast stretch of darkness between it and Alex's phone.

She tiptoed in. Nothing stirred as she began to cross. She worried that, if there were no dangerous creatures, the room may still be filled with traps. Death from poisoned arrows or worse occupied Alex's mind. She looked at the ground with paranoid regularity the farther she journeyed into the hall.

The crystal sat in a siphon much like the one keeping the *Cloudkicker* afloat. It sat alone, just a few yards from Alex's grasp, when she heard the familiar scraping sound. Both relieved and frustrated about avoiding poisoned arrows, she had just enough time to leap away before a spray of marble rained down.

Her phone slipped out of her hand. The golem's club snuffed what little light Alex had on her. She panicked, unable to see anything beyond the pale light from the crystal. The creaking from the stone warrior forced her to her feet. She jumped back even farther from her objective as another swing rushed by. It passed close enough for the wind to brush her clothes.

Alex eyed the crystal, losing ground with every swing and her arm growing heavy under the throbbing pain of her scar. She knew she did not have the stamina or the strength to take down the giant. It moved through the shadows, allowing only brief appearances as its bulk passed in front of the siphon. With only her ears to judge the golem's location, it was only a matter of time until its club squished her like a gnat.

With every path she attempted, the figure blocked her route. It predicted every step she took, by some empowered sight or hearing of its own. Desperate, she froze in thought. She expected another swing, but nothing happened.

An idea popped into her head. With her options running out, she struck Excalibur against the nearest marble pillar. It let out a clang that filled the room. The column shattered under the golem's club seconds later, drawn by the strike.

The golem's shadow stood at its full height, silhouetted against the crystal. The machine was too large to skirt around without getting caught in its assault. Alex only had one chance.

Reaching into her bag, she grabbed a handful of the tampons and charged at the guardian. As it began to swing, she tossed the plugs into the air. They landed with tiny clicks around the statue, confusing it enough to pause its action.

Alex seized the opportunity and raced between the golem's legs, bee-lining for the crystal. At the last moment, she slid herself headfirst at the wall. The golem's club flew in an arc inches over her body and crashed directly into the actuator.

A shower of rubble covered Alex. Rolling over, she

reached a hand up and felt the pockmarked surface of the stone club frozen directly over her. She laughed.

When the *Cloudkicker* team found her, she sat alone in the pitch black chamber with her back against one of the golem's legs and Excalibur across her lap. She squinted against the proximity of Ghaoithe's glowing chestpiece.

"You guys owe me big time," said Alex with a wide grin.

Ghaoithe placed her hands on her hips and looked around. Nearly the entire chamber sat in ruin, the still automaton front and center.

"Looks that way," Ghaoithe said with a whistle.

Fleet helped the blonde to her feet. "How in the nine Hells…?"

"Guess tampons can put out fires as well," Alex said. She counted the group and sighed in relief when she noticed everyone alive. "Whatever happened to 'There are no mythical creatures?'"

"There aren't. Golems are different. They aren't alive. They're more like… what do you call them? Automatic machines?" said Ghaoithe.

"Robots? Your world has giant fighting robots and you didn't think that was worth mentioning?" accused Alex.

"Yes, I suppose that should have been mentioned.

Here, look."

Ghaoithe pointed towards the bottom of the statue. Trapped in mid-swing, the heel of one of its feet lifted up. Etched into its sole were runes not unlike the writing in their airship's control room. Alex didn't expect to understand the language, but she was surprised when Fleet spoke up.

"What do ya reckon it is, ma'am?" he asked, lost on its origin as well.

Her hand brushing through her orange crown, Ghaoithe sighed. "Your guess is as good as mine. It's nothing I've ever seen. This place gets more nuts at every turn."

"Least it looks like we may be on the right track," called Jonas. He stood in a corner opposite the entrance. With proper light, he discovered a doorway that had been missed in the mayhem. A low corridor bent left and down, deeper into their abyss.

"Not like we have many other ideas right now," Ghaoithe shrugged.

The expedition took a short rest. Alex retold the fight to her comrades. Once they had time for their adrenaline to fade, they hit the hallway.

Ghaoithe kept close to the group in the narrow quarters. Alex stepped beside her as they wound their way down the path.

"You did well, Ms. Stirling. I thought we lost you for a bit there," said the captain.

"Only thing I lost was my phone. I guess I'll have to try and remember everything I wrote down," sighed Alexandra.

Ghaoithe patted the hair of her newest hire. "Just makes you that much closer to really being part of our world, hon."

"I love being with you guys, but I also want to be accurate when I write about it. The phone had all my notes."

"Let's focus on finding Pandora's Box before working on an award-winning exposé."

A soft dot of light in the distance signaled an end to the hallway. Ghaoithe slowed once more and searched about the walls for anything unusual.

"What do you think is so important about it?" Alex gulped.

"I truly wish I knew. Osiris has always been predictable, if nothing else. For this, though, they've left behind any reason. No telling what they've found out about it," said Ghaoithe.

Their path brightened and gave way. They stood on the edge of a rock face, surrounded by a moving sphere of water. A single marble bridge stretched before them. At the other end, a columned building hung suspended in the air at the center of the bubble.

Alex, absentminded from the sight, took a short step towards the bridge. Her captain pulled her back with such force the wind left her lungs. Ghaoithe reached into Sorin's pack and pulled out a handful of colored round stones. She rolled two of them towards the bridge where they fell through the illusion and into the torrent below.

Shaking at her narrow escape, Alex grasped her captain's helping hand. "I'm sorry," she blurted. "Thank you."

Ghaoithe brushed the dust off Alex's shirt and nodded. She returned her attention to the chasm. Two more stones left her hand, this time rolling to either side of the bridge. They continued rolling well into thin air.

"Stay in a line. We're taking our time on this," Ghaoithe announced to the team.

They gathered and ventured onto the invisible pathway. Alex gripped Fleet's backpack, fearing the first step only to find solid footing. Up front, their leader stopped every few moments to pick up the marbles and roll them ahead to ensure the path was straight.

After painstaking minutes, they reached the suspended chunk of earth bearing the temple. Alex fell to her knees and let out the air she held for the walk across. The temple loomed before them, larger than any of the other buildings they had seen, a Parthenon from a lost culture.

"Hate to tell ya, lass, but that may just be the start'," said Fleet.

Alex groaned, "As long as we're on solid ground, throw whatever you want at me. Darts, fire, bees… anything is better than falling."

The temple entrance had no door, only an open entryway inviting any who sought it. Unlike the rest of the city, its walls were well-lit by the glowing ivy-colored orbs. As they passed inside, they found a hall that consisted of just one massive room supported by the plain supports seen elsewhere. It was empty but for the far end. An altar, turquoise and brilliant, rested along the wall.

Sitting on top, sporting a rich violet suit, a tall man with the white goatee greeted them.

"Good afternoon, Ms. Loinsigh! Always a pleasure," he said with a grin.

From behind the pillars and entryway, swarms of guards appeared. Some wore the same seafaring dress Alex had come to know from Lost Earth, but most wore modern body armor and pistols aimed directly at the shocked crew.

"Deacon," Ghaoithe said through gritted teeth. She clenched and unclenched a fist, her eye smoldering with hate.

Deacon jumped off of the altar, and paced down the steps towards the middle of the room with a carefree gait. He twirled the staff in his hand as he walked. He stopped almost nose-to-nose with Ghaoithe, matching her height with his own skeletal frame.

"A step behind as always, I'm afraid," said Deacon. "One of these days we may let you have one out of pity. Boost your crew's morale and all that. The world is so boring without some competition, however miniscule."

Ghaoithe moved to rush her adversary, but Alex's hand on her arm held her back. At the sudden movement, one of the officers in Deacon's guard discharged his gun. The bullet whistled by Alex's ear, bounced off the captain's glowing runes and forced everyone to duck as it ricocheted through the temple.

Deacon rose without haste. He adjusted his circular glasses and looked around the chamber.

"Gentlemen, may I ask which of you fired that?" he asked.

No one spoke. Deacon stared at his army patiently until one man raised a quivering palm. With little more than a shake of his wrist, Deacon drew a revolver of his own and shot the offending bodyguard. The white tile stained with crimson, the first splash of color on the marble canvas in eons.

Returning the revolver to his inner pocket, Deacon coughed. "Please excuse their lack of protocol. Many of them have only heard of you by reputation," he said, returning his attention to his hostages.

"I should run you through," spat Ghaoithe.

"You could try, but I remind you that while you have runic armor, your companions do not. I promise the next shot will be under my authority."

Guns shifted to aim at the remainder of the team. Ghaoithe held her tongue back, contempt burning in her eye. It darted about, counting the number of guards, searching for possible exits and coming up empty.

Deacon walked along the line of trapped guests. At seeing Alex, he stopped and raised an eyebrow. "Ah, you must be the girl Ethan has been so infatuated with. It is a pleasure to meet you, my dear."

He reached out to Alex's hand and brought it to his lips with a gentle kiss. She grimaced and wrested her arm away. Deacon shook his head in disappointment.

"You're Ms. Stirling, correct? Let me guess: the captain here has convinced you were are the great evil, a corporation bent on power and finance who will stop at nothing to achieve its goals?" he asked. He knelt down to

Alex's eye level.

Alex straightened. "Yes. You haven't done a great job to prove otherwise."

"I admit we have been getting lax as of late, but I admire your naivete," Deacon laughed. "She probably didn't mention the hospitals we build or our vaccine research. That is what we do with our relics. We make the world a better place. All while your beloved Sky Thief inebriates herself with a bunch of thugs babbling on about keeping history as public knowledge."

Alex fought for a response, some chide remark, but her wit left her. Deacon's cunning eyes bore into her soul until he finally patted her softly on the shoulder and stood up.

"You know, this is truly an amazing place. Have you figured out where we are?" he asked.

"Please, enlighten us," said Ghaoithe dripping with sarcasm.

He ignored her tone and continued, "Eden, or at least as close as we can figure. A world before human evils." A hand motioned at the hall before them. "A world completely devoid of sorrow. Imagine how content its citizens must have been!"

"About as content as I will be when I stick your head

on a pike."

Deacon's grin held. A slender, gloved finger brushed Ghaoithe's cheek. His eyes flickered to the front of her armor. "Now, now. Mind your manners, captain. You and I both know the value of... proper study."

"Did you get what you came for? Was it worth torching Roanoke for?" asked Ghaoithe.

"Yes, we got what we came for. It is quite the world-changing discovery and a bit of a surprise, I must admit," said Deacon. He removed a cloth from within his jacket and polished his glasses with it. "As for Roanoke, I agree that it was such a tragedy. You must understand that desperation requires certain actions to escape it. And the world is quite desperate."

"Go sit in your high-rise and let the rest of us decide whether we need your help or not," Ghaoithe growled. Alex held her arm in check.

"I want nothing more than to return to my high-rise, Ms. Loinsigh, but work comes first. If you'll excuse me..." Deacon said. He gave a curt bow to the expedition and signaled to his force. They amassed, forcing Ghaoithe and the rest out of the temple.

Outside, on the temple grounds, Deacon turned to Alex. "You know, you are wasting your talents with this band of scruff. Perhaps you should not be so afraid to talk to your former lover next time."

"You make it sound like you aren't going to kill us anyway," cried Alex.

The older man laughed. "Kill you? Oh heavens no. Ghaoithe has been quite the sport over the years, and things have been set in motion outside her grasp as it is. We've already won."

Deacon held up his cane and pressed a switch on the handle. A few seconds passed, followed by a monstrous splash from overhead.

Alex thought the *Cloudkicker* was a considerable ship. Looking at the Osiris vessel, she realized she had been traveling on little more than a cruiser the entire time. The airship coming down to greet them, a mass of black steel blocks and sharp sigils, dwarfed even modern military carriers. It descended through the bubble and came to a rest beside the acropolis. Water cascaded down its sides as a bridge lowered to take on its owner.

The troops filed on to the deck, their sights never leaving the *Cloudkicker* force. With a final bow, Deacon stepped aboard. The sigils on the hull burst with light, and the ship ascended once more into the swirling water above.

Once Osiris was well out of sight, Ghaoithe yelled

out, frustration filling their bubble. The crew watched helpless as she walked to the temple and started punching one of its walls. Alex stared at the ground, flinching with each successive thud.

When the captain returned, her knuckles were raw and bleeding. "We're getting it back," she said.

"They beat us, Lynn. Ain't the first time, ain't gonna be the last. We'll get 'em on the next piece," Fleet said. He placed a hand on his friend's shoulder, but she brushed it off.

"I mean it. This isn't like the other times," Ghaoithe hissed. She fumed all the worse than the arson with no catastrophe to distract her energy.

"Yer makin' this difficult. We can't get it back and ya know it."

"We will get them," Ghaoithe screamed. Even Fleet sank back from her rage. "I don't know what the hell they need that urn for, but it's something big. You know. I know it. Whatever they are planning with that thing is more important than anything we've ever fought over. I will not let them get away with it."

No one dared respond at first. Alex had no issues with attempting to get Pandora's Box back, but the subtleties of the rivalry flew over her head.

Eventually, she tread the dangerous waters to ask

Ghaoithe, "How do you think we should do it?"

Ghaoithe flashed a daring eye, as if she expected an argument. Once she processed the question, her features softened. She rubbed her forehead. "I don't know. We'll think of something."

"Well, we better be quick. The longer we wait, the more time we're giving them to finish things off."

"You're right," she said with a sigh. "Let's go, everyone. Careful crossing the bridge."

Their return trip was silent and featureless. The husks of powerless golems littered the tops of the entry tower, now cold and dead. As they passed through the ruins of the city, Alex took in the unadorned architecture with a new perspective.

"Do you think he's right about this being Eden?" she asked Ghaoithe.

"It makes sense. That would explain why none of us knew anything about it," said Ghaoithe. She wrapped her sore knuckles in a piece of cloth handed to her by Fleet.

"Seems like it would have been a pretty boring place," Alex said. Deacon used 'content,' but the city looked joyless to her. Its basic structures sat without any signs of possibly harboring life, a sterile environment built solely for practical purpose and little else.

A world without art or individuality? Alex shuddered at the thought.

Word spread through the *Cloudkicker* about Osiris' ambush almost from the moment they boarded. Their ship launched, rising above the ocean tunnel and into the clouds.

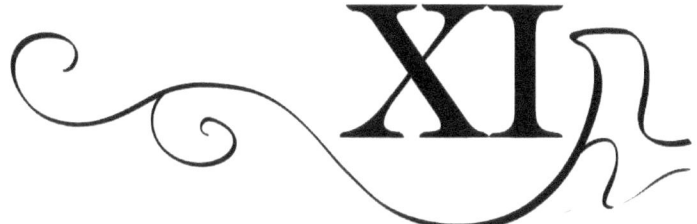

Alex concentrated on following Ghaoithe's motions. The captain told her to look at the opponent's eyes to predict where the next strike would land, but Ghaoithe's eye kept flashing towards the ground.

Daring a swing with Excalibur, Alex's footing slipped on the polished deck. She fell face-first, her nose bouncing on impact. She yelled and flipped her sword onto the deck. She tested her nostrils with ginger fingers. Not broken, as far as she could tell.

"I can't do this, Ghaoithe," she said. "You keep

looking at the deck, and you've got to find a better place for this."

Ghaoithe helped Alex to her feet. "Sorry. I would have Fleet help but he has work to do."

"Why do you keep looking down?"

Ghaoithe tugged at her golden eyepatch. "Depth perception is off. Counting how many feet I am from someone is the only way I know my distance. I don't even think about it anymore."

"Well, it's a bad habit if you're trying to train someone else," Alex grumbled. She reached down to retrieve Excalibur. Her arm stung from the training, and she was ready for a warm meal.

Ghaoithe set Alex into a fighting stance and called out strikes, making amendments to her form when needed. "Thrust. Moulinet. Remember, you have a broadsword with the weight of a foil. Use that to your advantage."

The country girl begged to learn how to properly use her famous blade, but she struggled as her teacher called out numbers and motions. The fluid, agile movement contradicted Alex's build meant for strong-arming through situations. Besides, even with lessons to distract them, both their thoughts wandered elsewhere.

At long last, Ghaoithe's tenacity gave way and the two

returned to the ship's hold. Sailors ran about, active as ever through the bright hallways. Alex said hello to a few of the more recognizable faces, happy to be a full-fledged part of the ship.

By the time she finished showering, her body longed for the bed. She passed out, not even bothering with her clothes or bedsheets. All she knew was the soft embrace of her pillow.

When she woke, Alex was wrapped snuggly in her comforter. Fleet sat at the vanity, staring out to a sea of billowing cotton beyond her room. He jumped at the waking girl's shriek.

"Fleet! What the hell, man?!" she screamed.

He coughed and scratched his beard. "Don't get yer knickers twisted," he said, keeping his eyes averted.

"I'm not wearing any knickers! Get out, and turn off the window on your way!"

The quartermaster flipped a panel next to the vanity, and the view of the sky transitioned back into a panel of wood. He strode out, grumbling something about insular societies and public showers. Alex leaned against her bedroom wall, blushing in her bed, trying to process what happened.

Reaching down for her clothes, she could feel

tightness growing in her muscles. Her lessons made their mark. She achingly slid into her shirt and pants, washed her face, and met Fleet outside her door.

"Mind explaining what that was all about?" she demanded.

"Ghaoithe asked me to come get ya," Fleet said. "Ya looked peaceful so I wanted to give ya a few more minutes."

"Thanks, but wait until I'm decent next time."

"Yer on a ship with seventy people. Yer ideas of decency are gonna change pretty quick."

Alex laughed. "I'll walk around naked when Ghaoithe does."

She meant it as a joke, more playful ribbing she'd come to expect with a man she saw as a mentor. His intrusion didn't bother her as much as surprised her. At the mention of the captain's insecurity, however, his face soured and he did not return the joke. Instead, he shook his head and bounded down the hallway. Alex quieted and chased after him.

Inside the captain's quarters, Ghaoithe paced around her desk, head down in thought. At the sound of the door, she shot the two a glance, then returned to her stride.

"Alex," she said after a minute, "what do you know about China?"

"About as much as I know about quantum physics," Alex replied.

Ghaoithe nodded. She paced for another moment, then turned to face them from behind her desk. "Good enough. We don't have anything else at this point."

Fleet glowered at her from beneath furrowed brows. "Lynn, ya best think this one through," he said.

The trainee looked at them both, caught by tension in the room. "Uh, someone mind filling me in here?"

Ghaoithe opened her mouth to speak, but Fleet interjected. "She wants to steal the vase back like a damn fool."

Alex blinked. "As in, break into one of their buildings and take it?"

"That would be the gist of it, yes," Ghaoithe said, clearing her throat.

"Despite the fact that they are heavily armed and rich and we have swords?"

"Close quarters won't be a problem, but, yes. I am taking that into consideration."

Another silence. "Ok. So why do I need to know about China?" asked Alex.

Ghaoithe shot her Quartermaster a victorious look, one that did not lift Fleet's mood. He huffed and sat down on a chair along the wall.

"This is a mistake, *Captain*," he muttered.

Ghaoithe ignored him. "Ethan and Deacon have been working as a team for years, making investments on your side of the fence to gain power. Their major company is located not far from Shanghai."

She reached down and unfurled a map of China. Alex recognized a few of the major cities, but most of the names and terrain were lost on her. The captain pointed to a spot near the eastern coastline filled with rugged mountains.

"That's all well and good, but I don't see where I come in on this. We don't even get decent egg rolls where I'm from," said Alex.

"Osiris is modernized," said Ghaoithe. "None of us are going to know our way around an office building. It's also secure. We can't really make our own entrance like we did at the hospital."

"You realize I'm a country girl who lived in a place where ten-story buildings were considered tall, right? It's not like I'm going to be able to hack into their security or anything."

"It's still more than we're used to. Even things you take for granted could make the difference here."

Alex looked to Fleet. He folded his arms and shook

his head, abstaining from the decision.

"Guess I better brush up on my Mandarin," Alex relented.

Shooting Fleet another victorious smirk, Ghaoithe rolled up the map. "Good to hear it. We'll be making a couple stops first, and then we'll take back what's ours."

Alex stood and left the room, confused and worried about Fleet. She heard him yell through the door after she closed it behind her.

"Yer out of yer goddamn mind, ya ginger, hot-headed..."

The outburst faded as she went down the stairs in haste. On one hand, Fleet had cause to be worried about Ghaoithe's plan. They still didn't know why exactly Pandora's Box was so important or what it contained. Yet, Alex didn't see breaking into an Osiris building as any more dangerous than a burning city or angry statues.

Ultimately, she felt like she was still living in a dream state. Walking back to her room, figuring out the tools she would need to invade an ultra-modern company... it sounded so outlandish as to be hilarious. She giggled to herself most of the walk, inviting strange looks from her companions.

In the evening, she stared at a blank page of parchment in a vain attempt to begin writing her story. The words failed to come, each new lede more ridiculous than the last. *Around the World with Sky Pirates* hardly made a case as a serious feature piece. So, she stared out her window, tingling with the possibilities of where their travels would lead next.

Her daydreams persisted well into their next port. In the week following Bimini, Alex got used to finding herself in strange lands, each day different than the last. Often, the ship only stopped for a few hours, a night at the most. Ghaoithe disappeared without a word before returning with a rush of orders. Alex practiced her fencing for a bit and the journey would begin again.

This time, the *Cloudkicker* came to rest above a village comprised of only a few solid structures. Every other building consisted of round tents made for a nomadic lifestyle. Yurts, Fleet called them as they spotted the tents from the bridge. Surrounding them were vast fields of grass opening up to boundless sky.

No lighthouse existed, so they relied on their rope ladder. The ship hovered only feet above the surface of the earth. Its crew stretched in the brisk sunlight, waiting for their equilibrium to adjust to standing still.

"We'll be here overnight, but don't overdo it. We need to head out first thing tomorrow," called Ghaoithe. Many of the crew were already well on their way to the ramshackle tavern, the largest of the permanent structures in the area.

Alex turned to ask a question, but Ghaoithe already walked several tents down from the ship, and Fleet was nowhere to be seen. She stood on her own among the crowd.

Deciding to explore the village, Alex turned down a path away from the tavern. Smoke rose from cooking fires, filling her with their pleasant smells and warmth. Noodle vendors called out as she passed, each with their own claim of colored broth. Men and women bowed to her in welcome, a rugged people with creased faces and cheerful, decorated robes.

After several minutes, Alex observed something unusual: few runes permeated the culture. Though a lantern shone through a doorway now and then, or the occasional cook's stove glistened with blue, most of the townsfolk bore the markings of traditional society. They were surviving, as they had for hundreds of years, off of the same basic principles as their forefathers.

One cook held out a steaming bowl of noodles for her as she walked by. She patted her pockets and shrugged, upset that she had not asked Ghaoithe for petty tradeables for the locals on arrival. The man smiled beneath a thick mustache and pushed the bowl towards her with a nod.

"Are you sure?" asked Alex. The man nodded again,

and she took the steaming bowl from him with a bow. She forgot her hunger, a theme more and more common on her journey and on her waistline.

She found a snug, dry section of ground to sit on. The noodles were thick, with a spicy brown sauce that made her insides glow. She decided she liked the village.

"Don't turn around and don't yell. We need to talk," said a voice behind her. Alex froze at its twang.

"Ethan?" she whispered. She stared into her bowl, daring not to look. She didn't need to see him to know the voice was his.

"I don't have much time. You're in danger, Alex. Osiris wants to help you if you're willing," he muttered.

"Help? Deacon seemed pretty bloodthirsty to me."

"Deacon is… eccentric, yes. He's just one person, and even his actions are for the greater good. You must believe me, Alex. Many of us do care about what happens."

"Why? You set fire to a city and threatened to shoot my friends. You're not making a very good case."

Ethan paused. After a moment, he said, "Ghaoithe knows more about the fires than she lets on. What she doesn't know is what she's dealing with when it comes to Pandora's Box. It's dangerous, Alex, and you could be caught in the middle of things she doesn't understand."

"What about Osiris, then? What are you planning?"

"To keep it safe. Look, I have to go. We'll see each other again." A hand reached out and squeezed Alex's shoulder then was gone.

Alex jumped up, letting her bowl fall to the ground, and searched the crowds for Ethan's lanky frame. However, only a few meandering locals roamed between the yurts.

By the time Alex entered the tavern, evening had set in. Rowdy cheers erupted through the sitting room. She welcomed the hearth, having been in progressively colder weather all day to clear her thoughts. After meeting Deacon firsthand, she acknowledged how dangerous Osiris could be. Yet, Ethan went through the trouble of warning her of danger. Did Osiris send him or was he acting on his own? Could he possibly still love her?

"Alex!" chimed a hardy voice. She turned to see Fleet and a few of the others at a nearby table. She stared, wide-eyed, expecting a reprimand about her meeting. Her mentor held up a hand of cards instead. "Come play a few rounds with us!"

Relieved, she took a seat. Shot glasses crowded the table, the players well past the point of caring about tidiness for their game.

"Where's Ghaoithe?" Alex asked upon noticing the

lack of her captain's presence.

"Ah, who cares? Probably off doin' somethin' foolhardy with that plan of hers," Fleet said, redfaced. He hollered for another round of drinks from the barkeep.

"You really don't like the idea, do you?"

A pitcher of ale arrived for the table. Fleet slammed his glass on the table, spraying foam.

"Course I don't," he shouted. "Damn fool is going to get us all killed at this rate. It's reckless!"

Trying to stay casual, Alex let a few cards go around before posing another question. "What do you think they'll do with the vase, anyway?"

"How should I know? Probably lock it up in a vault to be forgotten like all their other findings. Yer a right bugger tonight, aren't ya?"

She dropped the subject. Fleet avoided any talk about whatever their lead adventurer had up her blue sleeves. So, Alex continued for a few rounds, listening to the shanties sung through the hall with a half-hearted ear. When she left for her room, far earlier than the rest, restlessness set in.

She stared at the ceiling with doubt at the edges of her consciousness. Ethan's words were taken with a grain of salt, but they were enough of a seed to sprout questions.

What did he mean about Ghaoithe knowing about

the fires? Most of the crew were in the forest at the time. Ghaoithe's wrath during their escape had been palpable. It didn't make any sense.

Of course, the possibility remained that Alex listened to Ethan because she still felt attached to him. She wanted to believe he was still a great person. If he wanted to harm her, he could have done it by now with how easily he caught up to her. Did still loving him and hoping he loved her make her weak, a liability to the *Cloudkicker*?

She thought of one night in particular. Alex and Becky had a fight, the kind with no real cause that boils up anyway in a release of frustration and vindictive truths between two people tied to each other. Alex was supposed to go on a date with Jackson, barely making it to the restaurant on time.

When they met out on the sidewalk, he took only a couple seconds to ask if she wanted to go for a drive instead. With too much on her mind already, Alex absently answered yes. They took off, leaving their dinner reservations behind.

Only after some time and silence did Alex begin to worry. They drove for miles and were well into the dark country roads. The two had not been dating very long, a couple weeks or so at most, and worry fluttered within Alex's chest.

"Jackson, where are we going?" she asked.

"You'll see," he had said with a wink.

He raced on without saying anything. Out of her stupor, Alex's imagination went from Becky's demise to grim possibilities with a man she had only met a couple of times. What if he had been putting on a show for her, waiting to get her alone on some backwoods gravel drive?

"We should probably go back. It's getting late," she said as naturally as she could muster.

"You'll like this. I promise," he reiterated.

Just as Alex motioned to her phone, the two pulled down a familiar street. They passed a few small shops and homes before ending up in a large park. An old mill stood watch over a covered bridge, a small stream mixing with the sound of summer crickets.

"Bracket's Mill? Really?" Alex said. The landmark was filled with local history that served mainly to bore the minds of middle school children trapped on field trips.

Jackson smiled. "You mean an out-of-towner knows more about this place than you do?"

She rolled her eyes, but opened her door, happy to at least avoid being stabbed that night. They walked over to a wood fence guarding visitors from the stream. Humid Missouri summer wasted no time in clinging to their skin.

They stared out over the stream and into a wide field beyond, plains grass growing nearly as tall as Alex. It hardly met Alex's idea of romance until a flash caught her eye. Then another. And another. With the car's headlights turned off, thousands of blinking lights revealed themselves in the field. They swirled and bounced, a moving reflection of the stars above them.

"Oh wow. I haven't seen this many fireflies out in years," Alex whispered. She grabbed Jackson's arm and rested her head on his shoulder.

"Maybe you're just used to them. I'd never seen them before. They stand out pretty well," laughed Jackson. They stood at the mill, not saying anything for a few minutes as the world flickered before them.

"So, why did you bring me here?" Alex eventually asked.

"Only took one look to see you were having a bad day," he said with a shrug. "I figured being stuffed into a few walls wouldn't help much. Sometimes you just have to get out for a bit, you know?"

He struck a chord with those words. When so much of the world seemed against her that night, Alex denied the possibility that someone actually cared for her. She assumed the worst when Jackson meant for the best.

Dawn broke, lightening the sky after some time. The fields and fireflies faded away as Alex returned to her room in the tavern. Whether she had fallen asleep or daydreamed she couldn't tell; exhaustion wracked her body either way.

She splashed tepid water on her face and looked into the mirror. The bags under her eyes looked more akin to bruises. She tried to cover them with makeup borrowed from the dreadlocked Tory with moderate success. By the time she finished, she could hear Ghaoithe knocking on doors through the hall and met her there.

"Now you're looking like a sailor," said the captain as Alex stepped out of the room.

"Oh, just trying something different," yawned Alex.

"You didn't get a damn bit of sleep did you?" At Alex's silence, Ghaoithe continued, "You can catch up on the ship if you need. I won't call on you for a bit."

"Really, I wouldn't be able to rest if I tried."

"Suit yourself, but we'll take your lessons light today. Last I need is you passing out on the deck."

They filed through the tent village after breakfast. Alex wondered where Ethan fled to, if he crossed the open meadows in the thick of night. She hoped to spot him poking out from behind a warm kettle or rack of hides. Only the faces of the locals rising for the morning bid the crew farewell.

The *Cloudkicker* vaulted upwards. Alex made her way to the galley, ready to test her stomach with a cup of coffee. Her body craved the sleep that her mind would not give her, so she decided to treat the day just as she had treated countless nights during Final Exams. All-nighters were old news.

The galley was empty except for her. She normally relished the silence and thinking time, but it only compounded her issues as the caffeine settled in. She thought only of what secrets Ghaoithe hid within the ship that could be so damning.

It wasn't that Alex didn't believe Ghaoithe had a rough side. Watching the captain fight through Roanoke was proof that she could throw a few punches around. Yet she was never malicious or brutal. Nothing about her demeanor suggested anything but a mother protecting her litter. The Sky Thief did not seem the type to attack out of the joy of fighting.

Then again, they were flying towards an Osiris compound for no other solid purpose than vengeance. While Ghaoithe made every effort to be the honorable leader in their conflict with Osiris, she changed enough in her judgment to worry Fleet. Perhaps there was more to the captain than Alex had come to know in her brief time aboard the ship.

When Alex finally noticed the burly quartermaster staring at her from the doorway, her coffee was ice cold. She sputtered upon sipping it as he stepped inside for a seat.

"Ya look like crap," he said.

"Strange. Ghaoithe said I looked like one of the crew now," Alex replied.

"There's a difference?" Fleet's grin helped abate her sour spirits, if only slightly. "What's on yer mind, lass?"

She bit her lip, not sure if she should divulge her worries to him. Though Fleet and Ghaoithe disagreed about their current plan for China, Alex was certain that neither of them would take the news about meeting Ethan well.

"I'm just… thinking about something that happened in the fog in Bermuda," Alex said, carefully choosing her words.

"Now don't ya go putting any faith in those visions. The Triangle just wanted to claim another ship is all that was," Fleet said with a stern finger.

Alex shook her head. "No, I know. It shouldn't bother me but some of the things it said… Fleet, is Ghaoithe dangerous?"

His thick eyebrows furrowed at the question. Sighing,

he stood and poured a coffee of his own. "Guess yer trainin' can wait if yer in one of those moods," he said, taking a large swig from his mug.

Alex tempted a meager smile. "Sorry. I haven't mastered the pirate's stamina for partying yet."

Fleet's hands dwarfed the coffee as he sipped. "We've all done things we ain't proud of, and Lynn can say the same thing. But let's get one thing straight: nowadays she ain't much for fightin'. She's a goofy lug who wants to spend her time diggin'."

"I get that. What I mean is, do you think she's hiding something? Why's Pandora's Box so important to her?"

"Hmmm," Fleet stroked his tangled beard and looked up at the ceiling. "I can't tell ya. Truth is, I don't think this is about the jar anymore. She's trying to stand up fer everyone she loved in Roanoke. It's personal."

Alex shook her head. She placed her chin in her hands, letting blonde curls cascade through her vision without care. She could understand where Ghaoithe was coming from, but Fleet's words were not as reassuring as she hoped they would be. The ships till sailed on a suicide mission.

"Maybe it would be easier if we just let Osiris keep the damn thing," Alex said with a sigh.

"Well, ya know I don't like this plan either, but," Fleet said. He placed his elbows on the table and leaned in, "I will say this. I've known the captain fer a long time, and she is never wrong about things like this. It may be foolhardy to attack an Osiris buildin', but if she is convinced it's necessary, then she has a damned good reason to think so. We just gotta trust her."

They sat for a few moments, pondering the idea. Nagging at Alex's mind was the implications that Ghaoithe actually hid something in her pursuit of the artifact. She saw Ghaoithe's protective side, and it seemed implausible for the cautious leader to rush headfirst into an enemy building.

Clearing his throat, Fleet stood up. He said, "Why don't ya come with me, lass? I'll show ya somethin'."

He walked out of the galley door. Curiosity beckoned Alex to follow shortly behind.

They twisted through the *Cloudkicker*'s halls, eventually ending in the familiar archive room. Most of the shelves were empty, the artifacts having been cleared out in Roanoke or in one of their other desperate stops. Only the truly incredible pieces stayed behind for Ghaoithe's personal research.

When Fleet crossed to one of the shelves and picked up an object, Alex gasped. Though she entered the room several times to study the pieces, the book in her friend's hands went unnoticed. A layer of dust covered the binding, hiding it in plain sight.

Fleet opened the tome reverently. Upon seeing the contents, Alex burst out in giggles. "A photo album? Really?"

"Sure is! Some good times in here," he laughed. His eyes gleamed cheerfully as he peered at the book's contents. "Captain found a buncha old camera stuff and went nuts. Only time I've ever seen her excited over a piece of tech."

Many of the photos were group shots in different bars or uncovered ruins. Alex recognized her sword, freshly uncovered and surrounded by a small team. Roy's tavern was in another.

Though she had no idea what Fleet hoped to accomplish in showing her the book, Alex's interest held on to each page. The crew she knew looked fairly different in many of the pictures. They were younger, but also more vibrant. Even with Ghaoithe's normal energy, the woman Alex knew was downright gloomy compared to the radiant woman in the photographs. Ghaoithe's face was plastered with huge smiles at nearly every turn, her energy jumping through the pages.

"Wow! You were young once," Alex teased at a photo of Fleet from before the gray streaks invaded his beard.

Fleet tried to look stern, but his eyes lit with memories of the days held within the book's pages. "And I'll be damned if I grow older any time soon."

"How long have you been sailing with Ghaoithe anyway?" Alex asked as they flipped the page. A portrait of Ghaoithe, mid-bite into a breadroll, stared back at them without shame. She looked much the same, donning her blue armor and gold eyepatch, but her hair flowed down her back and the faint lines had not yet crept into her skin. She was gorgeous.

Fleet thought for a moment. "Hard to say. I guess about 17… 18 years?"

Alex's eyes widened in disbelief. "There's no way," she said. "How old are you guys, anyway?"

"Ya won't get anything about me, ya little snoop," he said with a grin. "As fer the captain, I don't know exactly. I don't think she even knows. She started sailin' young and already had a small group behind her when I met her. She was a bit younger than you are now, I wager."

Alex's mouth gaped open. Slowly, the truth in how deeply the crew's bonds were with each other came to light. She envied those connections. Becky flashed into her mind, and she felt her chest tighten ever-so-slightly.

Though she had been friends with Becky for as long

as she could remember, she had accepted, deep down, that school or careers would eventually drive them apart. They would remain friends, of course, but the fantasy of spending entire lives together never really took root. That such lifelong friendships were possible never crossed Alex's mind.

All of the camaraderie between Fleet and Ghaoithe painted a picture of life on the *Cloudkicker*. Several people told Alex of the captain's protectiveness over her crew, but it shined clear through the photographs in Fleet's hands. Alex felt foolish questioning the motives her guardians. She brought herself closer to the quartermaster and the book, interested at what other history it contained.

"Is there a reason for showing me all this? I don't mind skipping fencing practice, but y'all never seemed like the baby book type of crowd," she said.

Fleet flipped to another page. Alex's heart stopped, the air frozen in her chest. Standing in front of the *Cloudkicker* was a group of the crew's leadership. The photo lacked the aging of the rest. Fleet's salted beard grew in full force. Between him and Ghaoithe stood a young man with intense eyes. His nose was different, his hair a different hue, but the man in the photograph was unquestionably Ethan.

"That's why," Fleet said softly. "Ya ain't the only one invested in the boy."

"How long? Why?" Alex sputtered. Her mouth could not keep up with the questions running through her mind.

Fleet touched the photo, lost in memory for a moment. "He was with us a good while. Left to join Osiris a couple'a years ago, taking a lot of relics with him. It hit Lynn pretty hard. He was a good kid when we knew him."

Hands beginning to shake, Alex blinked away the tears forming at the corners of her vision. "And when were you planning on telling me this?"

Fleet stayed silent, leaving her to stare at the photograph. The longer Ethan's gaze reached out to her, the angrier she became. To make matters worse, she was not sure who to be angry at.

Staring at the photograph, Alex tried to feel shock at Ethan's image, but she could not bring herself to be mad at him. It was not that she necessarily forgave him for the past few weeks so much as she was no longer surprised at his secrets. Finding something hidden about his past started to feel like a daily occurrence.

However, she trusted Ghaoithe and the crew to be honest with her. She could not expect the captain to reveal everything, but Ethan's history on the ship was beyond her line of patience.

Alex did not register Fleet's calls to stop. She only

heard the sound of her boots hitting the floor in the same rhythmic pulse as the blood rushing through her head.

The slam of her chamber door startled Ghaoithe. Alex took it as a small victory, knowing she would not always be able to intimidate the seasoned adventurer.

"When were you going to tell me about Ethan?" Alex demanded.

Ghaoithe glared at Fleet, arriving with a huff at the door. He shot a pleading look at his friend but said nothing otherwise.

"I don't know what…" started the captain.

"Don't play that with me," said Alex. A flash of her mother's voice echoed in her head. She tried to push the memory out, afraid it would break her resolve.

Ghaoithe stood unmoving for a moment, her steeled eye not wavering from Alex's. The young woman matched it, unblinking. Finally, the captain grumbled and turned towards her table stocked with drinks. A glass of vodka in hand, Ghaoithe fell into her chair and took a swig.

"I'm guessing you looked at our photo album then?" she said.

"It was time she knew what this was all about," Fleet interjected. Alex felt her chest swell at having someone defend her.

"It's about getting back Pandora's Box," replied Ghaoithe. Her face began to blush, the only sign of nervousness Alex had ever seen from her leader.

Fleet folded his arms and glared at his friend. "Ya can keep sayin' that all ya want, but it ain't true and ya know it. If yer hellbent on sending us down this road, at least be honest with the girl."

With both Alex and Fleet staring her down, Ghaoithe relented. She downed her glass in one swig and slammed it onto the desk. She rubbed her eyebrows, stalling as best as she could.

"Fine, fine," she moaned. "Whatever."

Behind Alex, the quartermaster harrumphed in victory. The two sat down across from Ghaoithe. Alex's heart paced in anticipation of more answers. She took several deep breaths, hoping to calm herself down, but they helped little.

"You should have told me!" Alex blurted out, her anxiety boiling over.

"I couldn't risk you going off on a merry chase and pulling the same thing he did by joining Osiris," replied Ghaoithe. Her brows creased in the middle. Alex had never seen the captain so fidgety. Her tanned fingers were in constant motion playing with the globe at her desk.

Running her hand through her hair, Alex asked,

"Why would I join them? After what they did in Bimini? They burned that bridge."

The captain pursed her lips, causing the few age lines on her face to surface. She stopped spinning the globe and pulled open a drawer. After some shuffling, she placed several newspapers in front of the new recruit.

"The *Wall Street Journal*? You guys even know what that is?" Alex asked. She picked up one of the newspapers, its front page highlighted in several portions. Every page had similar markings as she flipped through.

Fleet pulled one of the papers across the desk. "We don't know much about yer modern businesses, but we do keep tabs on Osiris."

Alex continued flipping through the paper. One article mentioned a museum acquisition. Another wrote of a multi-billion dollar company buyout. Each article fed into a web of power and finance.

Whatever Alex had imagined Osiris to be was far off the mark. In her mind, it was just like any other big corporation with means and resources. However, the paper revealed it to be a massive undertaking of politicians, business leaders, and conglomerates around the world.

"Incredible. There's nothing that goes on without these guys being a part of it," she stated. "How do you know about all this? Surely someone else would have caught on."

"Not when they control what people see and hear. We know who they are because we aren't part of your world. They've struggled to find a foothold here because we don't follow any kind of system they can control openly," said Ghaoithe.

Thinking about it, Alex saw what Ghaoithe meant. In her short time in Lost Earth, Alex only learned a loose trading system that bordered on bartering. There were no newspapers or televisions to speak of, no standardized money system beyond precious metal coins of various origins.

Alex began to understand Ghaoithe's frustration over Ethan. The scrappy underdogs going against a massive empire had a turncoat. She didn't know how important her former lover was to the *Cloudkicker*, but he must have carried some weight if Ghaoithe avoided talking about him.

"Raiding one of their buildings is just your way to settle a vendetta, then," Alex accused. "You can't risk everyone here just to show Ethan what he missed out on."

"It's... not about that," Ghaoithe said. She stood up and began pacing across the room, her habit when in thought.

"Lynn..." warned Fleet.

"Ok, it's only partially about Ethan," Ghaoithe said. She ran her hands through her hair, fingers still in constant motion.

Alex's uncertainty got the best of her. "You two were never... you know, were you?"

For a moment, Ghaoithe stopped and looked at Alex, her eye clear with truth. She let out a soft laugh.

"Oh god no, dear," Ghaoithe said. The break passed and her eye lost its focus, returning to whatever hid in her mind.

"Something's been bothering me about Pandora's Box and why Osiris would go through desperate measures to stop us from getting it," she said.

"Did ya find somethin' then? You've been stopping at just about every lead since Bimini," Fleet asked.

"Nothing certain." Ghaoithe stopped pacing to stare at one of her numerous bookcases. Her hand brushed over the leather tomes idly. "I've heard some things suggesting that Pandora's Box might be more than just the vase we thought it was."

"Well, thanks for giving us the ominous warning there, Captain. It totally justifies attacking my ex-boyfriend that you knew for years without telling me," Alex sneered.

"No need to be sarcastic, lass," Fleet said. He placed a

firm hand on Alex's shoulder.

"Sorry, but it's a little difficult to see why you kept all this hidden from me. I am not Ethan, and knowing he was part of the crew here might have helped me work some things out."

"I'm sorry, Ms. Stirling," Ghaoithe said. "I know it must be hard for you, but I have my reasons for not telling you everything until I know what's going on myself."

Alex stewed in her seat, but the captain's tone did not invite a challenge.

The truth was, Alex was relieved to know Ghaoithe's disappearances at each stop on their journey towards Asia did have a purpose, that the captain wasn't just beating herself up over the loss of an artifact. If there was more to the vase than they thought, maybe it did warrant stealing back.

Ethan's words edged in ghostlike at the edge of her thoughts. He was right about Ghaoithe keeping secrets from her. She could only guess what else was going on behind the golden eyepatch. Despite all of the reassurances, the captain still did not trust her, which meant she couldn't fully trust the captain.

Not wanting to test the ire of Ghaoithe or risk being left out of the loop for good, Alex decided to play it safe.

"I get it," she said, crossing her arms, "but I can only

find out so much second-hand before my patience is gone. Do you want me to be a part of all this or not?"

"Yes," Ghaoithe replied, "I do. And I really am sorry. It's just... this situation is more complicated than we thought."

The two stared at each other for a few seconds, silently pleading each other to understand.

Finally, Alex nodded. "Ok. Then how long until we do this?"

"About three days. Since nothing has happened yet, I'm guessing Osiris is still figuring out what to do with the artifact, too," said Ghaoithe.

"Then what do we do for those three days?"

A mischievous smile crossed Ghaoithe's face. "I'll worry about the planning. You, however, declined my offer to take it easy today. Go get Excalibur and join Fleet on the deck."

Shouts clamored outside Alex's door. She stirred, lost in the world between dreams. The previous day's training session did not mix well with her fatigue, and her body lay stiff and sore in the morning light. She tried to roll over, covering her ears with a pillow, but one coherent word managed to pierce through her dazed state.

"Stowaway!"

Alex bolted out of bed and into her clothes. The commotion in the hallway had already moved towards the bridge when she opened her door. The crew's laughter echoed down the stairwell as she tried to catch up.

As she turned the corner to the bridge, she saw a crowd surrounding Ghaoithe on the balcony. She recognized Jonas, one of the men from the Bimini excursion, holding up a figure with little effort. Alex waded through the crowd until she neared the front of the uproar.

The man in Jonas' hands was tall and scrawny, with long strands of greasy black hair and a patchy beard that had not seen a blade in some time. He was young, no older than Alex, but dark circles under his eyes hinted at a hardened life.

He shifted as much as he could, but Jonas' grip on his collar held firm. His resistance stopped as Ghaoithe approached. She bent to greet him when a look of recognition crossed her face.

"Well, if it isn't Damian Locke," she said. She burst into laughter that bellowed throughout the room.

"Hello, Ghaoithe." Damian's voice was gravelly but gentle. He mustered up a weary smile.

"You've got some balls showing up here. Let him down, Jonas."

The sailor's grip eased, sending the stranger crumpling onto the ground. Damian made no quick attempt to rise.

"You know me," he grinned. "Nothing's worth doing

if it doesn't have some risk involved."

Alex looked on, confused. Their tone was friendly enough towards each other, but Ghaoithe's eye did not waver away from him for a moment. Her left hand stayed on the hilt of her rapier.

"Mind telling me how the hell you got onto my ship and what you're doing here?" Ghaoithe asked.

Damian sighed. He forced himself to stand, a task that took more effort than it needed. Alex wondered if he had been without food for some time.

"Got on when you stopped outside Ulaanbaatar a couple days back. I heard you don't turn down people who want to join your ship," he said.

Ghaoithe then had her turn to lift him. Tall as he was, his feet cleared the ground as the captain pulled him up to look at him directly.

"None of those people have a history of stealing from me," she growled. "Getting me once is impressive, but that doesn't mean I'll allow a second chance, Damian."

"Not even for a handsome face like this?" he said through his grin. His sickly frame had not inhibited a lack of fear towards the captain. Alex stifled a giggle at the man's daring.

"Sorry, but you're barking up the wrong tree,"

Ghaoithe responded coolly. A round of whistles and hoots sounded out from her onlookers.

Damian's face drooped. "So, that's it, then? I just walk the plank?"

"We don't have a plank. It's the brig until we figure out where to take care of you." Ghaoithe nodded at Jonas. They exchanged the man, who blew a kiss to the captain before disappearing behind the entry hallway. The crowd dispersed, leaving Alex and Ghaoithe alone on the balcony.

"You're totally going to let him stay," said Alex.

Ghaoithe shrugged with a smile. "Of course," she said. "I just need to let him sit for a little bit and get a couple meals in him first. See how he does and all that."

Alex's doubts over Ghaoithe's honesty were forgotten, at least momentarily. Whatever troubles truly went on in her captain's head, Alex remained surprised by how lackadaisy Ghaoithe could be at times.

The Sky Thief sat down in her chair, the morning light filtering through the bridge and igniting her hair. She was much more alive there than she had been since losing Pandora's Box.

"You're really something, you know," Alex said.

"Don't get sentimental on me," replied Ghaoithe. "I'm going to have you look after him for the first couple of hours. The real brig's one floor below you, far end."

Alex curtsied with a quick, "Yes, your majesty" before disappearing below deck.

The prospect of a new crewmate excited her, though she couldn't tell why. Even though she had been globetrotting ever since the hospital, she had become accustomed to life on the ship. Its faces were familiar now. Looking back, she never realized how monotonous arriving in new places each day could be.

I suppose if travel is your entire life, it's harder to surprise you, she thought to herself.

She ducked into the galley on her way downstairs, picking up a meager tray of breakfast and water for their new guest. She wanted to load the tray, but settled with a couple of bagels and some fruit lest anything more hurt his system. Witty as he was, there was no hiding the famine that wracked Damian's body.

When she finally arrived at his cell, Damian was sprawled comfortably on his bed, limbs enjoying a stretch away from whatever hiding spot he had been found in. The brig looked like any other jail cell, with thick bars instead of a closed door, but it was grimy and unused compared to the other rooms on the ship. Underneath Damian lay a bright pink comforter, hastily found once word spread out that the room would be needed. At the sound of Alex's footsteps, his head jerked up.

"Well if this isn't the nicest looking prison I've ever been in," he joked with a whistle.

Alex blushed and fumbled for a response. When nothing in her head worked, she settled with sliding the tray through an slit at the bottom of the bars.

"I, uh, brought you that," she said meekly. A stool waited beside the cell, no doubt placed for lonely guards like herself. Pulling it over, she sat down. "I guess I'm guarding you now."

Damian shot her a curious look and lifted the tray. "Thanks," he said before digging into one of the bagels. He started to shovel it into his mouth but thought better of it, pacing himself with each bite. "I'm Damian, by the way."

"I heard. I'm Alex."

He threw a grape into the air and ate it on its way down. "You're that new girl, aren't you? I heard Ghaoithe picked up another one of us."

"Wait, what? People have heard about that already?" Alex stammered. She couldn't recall meeting many people outside of the ship aside from the drunken night in Roanoke.

Damian nodded. "Sure. Word travels fast out here. Not too many people from the modern world know about

Lost Earth anymore. Plus, anything Ghaoithe does stirs up gossip."

Ghaoithe and Fleet had mentioned that switching sides rarely happened, but Alex never considered it a practice that made such larges waves. She began to wonder how many people like her existed in this realm of skyships and bawdy taverns.

"Well, that's me. 'Another one of us?' You're not from here either?" she asked.

"Nope. I'm from Los Angeles," said Damian. He finished his food and slid the tray back under the bars. "Thanks. Now, lovely to meet you as it is, I think I'm going to enjoy a solid roof over my head for a bit."

He stretched. Several pops clicked from his arms. He rolled onto the flat bed. Within seconds, snores rumbled from beneath the blanket. Alex sat with her mouth open, burning for more questions.

Alex nearly fell asleep herself by the time Sorin appeared. The sound of his footsteps nearby broke the quiet of the hallway, jerking her away from rest.

"You make a terrible guard," he said without humor.

"Hello to you, too, stranger. Where have you been lately?" Alex asked. Sorin spent most of his time either trapped on the bridge or disappearing with Ghaoithe on their land excursions, leaving Alex with little sight of him.

"We have been busy," was his only answer. He took her hand, helped her off the seat, then stood at attention in front of the cell door without paying its inhabitant any mind. "I am here to relieve you."

"Oh. I guess they want me on the deck for some training then?"

Sorin shook his head. "No. Go to the captain's quarters."

With one last cursory glance at Damian, still passed out in angles not meant for humans, she left Sorin to his guard post.

Ghaoithe's room was strewn about with papers and maps. The captain stood hunched over part of the pile on her desk when Alex stepped in. A couple maps of China were recognizable but little else. The captain's hair bristled in more ways than usual, as though she had not slept, but she kept nothing short of her full attention on her studies.

"Hey, Ghaoithe. Sorin sent me up here?" Alex said. She tried her best to step over the papers on the floor.

Ghaoithe's head shot up at the voice. She managed a weak smile. "Oh, yes, Alex. Don't worry about the floor."

Alex gave up on being sensitive to the mess and

stomped her way to her boss in a flurry of crinkled pages. "Fleet not here?"

"No. He's taking care of the bridge for a bit. I just needed to go over a few things with you."

Shaking off the last bits of paper under her boots, Alex looked at the figures Ghaoithe laid on the table. "I'm guessing these are the blueprints of the Osiris building?" she asked, unsurprised.

Its depiction was incredibly rough with only the basic information scrawled loosely in pencil. It hardly looked like an official blueprint used in so many heist films.

"What we know about it, yes," replied Ghaoithe. "Entrances, rough estimate of rooms and a general outline of a few floors. The rest is up to us."

The captain's words did not reassure Alex. A pit weighed in her stomach with the knowledge that they still had little to go on with only two days left.

"Well, we need to worry about getting in first, I guess," Alex said.

"I'm working on it."

"So you do have a plan?"

"Yes, but you're not going to like it."

Ghaoithe pointed towards the bottom of the structure. Alex stared for a moment, trying to figure out what

Ghaoithe was pointing when she saw the line, several stories above, marked 'Ground Level.'

"No. Just… no," Alex gagged. "I am not going in through a sewer."

"We don't have a choice. It was this or airdrop in."

Alex's imagination already kicked in, turning her skin pale. Ghaoithe was right; the sewer was a better alternative than falling through the sky but only marginally. How big did rodents get in other parts of the world?

You would have been through worse as a conflict reporter, she tried to remind herself. It stayed her initial disgust somewhat, but the dread lingered. She turned her thoughts to the task at hand, asking, "It doesn't seem very original. Surely they have it under surveillance or it's locked by runes or something."

Ghaoithe pulled another paper covered with the intricate symbols of Lost Earth onto the desk. She shook her head and pointed at it.

"This is the most they would have, and it's easy to break," said Ghaoithe. "Some of the upper floors might be powered by runic technology, but they're still a modern company. They have to keep up appearances. Osiris doesn't work by calling attention to themselves everywhere."

"So we just bust the seal and walk right in?"

Ghaoithe tapped her fingers on her desk. "Pretty

much. They probably already know we're coming anyway. Our main priority is to lose them once we get inside."

It sounded like a plan from a movie, which did not sit well with the less-than-clandestine recruit. A hundred problems popped into Alex's head. She bit her lip, trying to think of better ideas, but nothing surfaced. Instead, the map spread in front of her as an impenetrable fortress.

The crew would have to take the obvious route and hope for the best.

"So, say we do get in…" Alex started.

"We'll get in," interrupted Ghaoithe.

"Ok, *when* we get in, what then? Do we have any idea where to go to find this thing?"

"Do you still have your archives ring?" Ghaoithe asked.

For a moment, Alex had no idea what Ghaoithe was referring to. Then it dawned on her: the ring Sorin passed along to open the relic boxes when she first arrived. With most of the pieces unloaded from the ship, she forgot she had it.

Digging into her pockets, she pulled out the emerald ring and handed it to Ghaoithe. "What do you need that for?"

"I must have misplaced mine, and I don't have time

to dig through my room right now," she said, bitterness dripping in her voice. Losing things was an unfamiliar feeling for the relic hunter.

With Alex's ring, she crossed to a bookshelf in the back of her room. A small relic box waited among the collection. With a quick swipe, she unlocked it, palmed something in her hand, and returned to the desk.

"We'll need you to use this thing once we get in," said the captain. She tossed a tiny object at Alex. It was a plastic shell in black with a silver edge protruding from one end.

"A flash drive?" Alex's eyebrows scrunched as she looked at the miniature device. "Can't say I expected one of these to be on the ship."

"If that's what it's called, sure. Apparently we just activate that and it'll tell us where to go once we're inside the building."

"You have no idea how to use a thumb drive?"

At the captain's blank face, Alex burst into a fit of giggles. Ghaoithe's cheeks reddened. She tried to stammer out a feeble excuse about 'foreign technology,' but it did little to ease up the humiliation.

When Alex calmed down, she ran her palm over her eyes and placed the drive on the table. "How in the world have you managed to uncover so much without electronics?"

"I… we only needed building layouts. It's not like the Mayans or anyone used laptops when they hid these items," the captain said meekly.

Alex wanted to relish having something to hang over her leader, but her manners got the better of her. Grinning, she returned to the drive. "Do we need to open anything on this or use a specific computer or what?"

Ghaoithe shook her head. "I don't think so. The person who gave it to me said we just put it into any of the computers in their network and press the button on the drive."

Holding the drive up, Alex squinted at it as if trying to turn the black casing invisible. "Are you sure we can trust this thing?" she asked.

"Osiris isn't the only one with connections. I'm all out of favors now, but we can trust it," Ghaoithe replied. Whether the bravado in her voice was honest or simply a facade to convince herself was unclear.

Alex's stomach knotted with the knowledge that their plan would be carried out so soon. She had maintained a distant approach towards life on the ship, even through the fire and golem attacks. That changed somewhere along the road, and she could not say where. As they drifted closer to Ethan, her emotions grew increasingly more involved. The full weight of the stakes at hand were contained in the USB drive at her fingertips.

If their ideas didn't pan out, what would happen to them in that building? Deacon's merciless execution of one of his own soldiers flashed in Alex's head. Would they really do that to the *Cloudkicker* crew? Or would they be turned in to some secret society police, destined for torture for the sheer enjoyment of it?

Ghaoithe hunched over the maps, her eye unfocused and distant. Alex wondered if they were going over the same dreadful scenarios. Perhaps the captain was lost in justifying the impending operation. The Sky Thief's thoughts never manifested outside of her own head, and Alex gave up on trying to interpret them.

Whatever was going on in Ghaoithe's mind, she was not the same brash captain that created havoc in Roy's tavern their first night in Roanoke. Alex reached out to touch one of Ghaoithe's hands, warm and coarse without gloves.

"I know they upset you, and I can't pretend to know everything that happened between you guys, but it's not too late to call this off if you're not sure," Alex pleaded.

Ghaoithe squeezed Alex's hand before letting her fingers slip away. "Everyone's got their white whale," she said without looking up from the desk. "The question is whether you're willing to follow me to the depths of Hell? I won't force you."

"I ain't leaving. I'm in this, and I want to stay in this," Alex said, her voice level. "If I have to go out, at least it will have a more interesting story behind it than 'got old and went to sleep.'"

Standing up, the giantess' presence was alarmingly small for once. Still, she beamed at her young relic hunter with a weary eye. "I did well in keeping you on board," she smiled.

Alex laughed. "I'm a Missourian. We're stubborn."

"I've never spent much time there. Willing to tell me about it?" asked Ghaoithe.

Eager to spend more time with the captain, away from the realities of the future, Alex nodded. Ghaoithe strode to her liquor cabinet and poured two vodkas. With a clink, they toasted each other, enjoying the company as the ship bounced among the clouds.

"What do you want in life?"

Alex sat next to Jackson in the campus library, a mountain of books on their table. She leaned back and rubbed her eyes, the words in her notebook a blur in her vision.

Jackson looked up from his textbook. "Weird time to get existential, isn't it?"

"Maybe. I'm just tired," Alex said.

The library did little to help. They were the only ones among the shelves; the rest of the desks sat empty. Solitude became a way of life for Alex since the fire. With Jackson's arrival, the quiet became a prison more than the escape she once enjoyed, a box trapping her restless energy inside.

"That's mid-terms for you." Jackson said. He closed his book. Alex could feel her heart beginning to race as he stared at her, warm smile inviting her own. Whenever he looked at her with his sharp gray eyes, deep with concern, she lost control of her emotions.

It was a nice feeling, losing her grip, one she forgot existed. Each time, she wondered if she would ever even want it back, content to let others carry the load for eternity.

She stretched her arms over her head, her muscles relishing the slight movement. "That's the point, though. We're doing all this work and for what? To go join the rat race?"

Jackson reached and held her cheek for a moment before leaning in for a kiss. Alex closed her eyes, wishing for time to stop, but their lips parted just as her body began to sizzle with electricity.

"Something going wrong with your internship?" he asked. Alex had only been at the job for a couple of weeks, but she wasted no time in sharing her nitpicking with the boy who always offered an ear.

"It's not what I expected." Pressure squeezed her chest as she said the words aloud. "Maybe it's where we are or something. I don't know. I'm finally working in an environment where I thought I would be happy, but it doesn't seem like it will lead me anywhere like I was hoping."

"Well, we all have to pay our dues, I guess. Not many make it right out of the box," Jackson said. He scratched his chin as he spoke, choosing what to say carefully.

"No, I get that," Alex sighed and shook her head. "I just feel trapped here, like I'm working for nothing and that anything I do is just going into some empty void somewhere."

"Your work will pay off. You just have to keep at it. I'm sure somebody out there is watching."

"But how long do I wait? I can't keep doing this forever. I can't fight for years just to climb one more step of the ladder. I'm wasting away here, Jackson," Alex sniffed. Tears started filling her vision, a tide unleashed without warning. She rubbed her eyes with the palm of her hand. "I'm sorry. I don't know why I'm like this. Is something wrong with me?"

Jackson grabbed her hands, holding them tight. He locked his gaze with Alex's. "Don't give up, hon. You are great and smart and will do whatever you want to do in life. You have to kick ass with the jobs you're given and show them your real potential."

Alex blushed and looked at her feet. Her world felt so bright and awake after years of suffocation. When Jackson encouraged her, nothing else mattered. She was invincible.

Then he was gone. She looked up only to find Jackson's seat unoccupied. She sat next to a window, now pattering with rain. Nothing stirred but wind through the edges of the glass panes.

A presence tingled the hairs on the back of her neck. She stood and turned to see several men facing her. Each wore finely tailored suits and impenetrable sunglasses, despite the dim offering of the library's lights. Their faces were the same—chiseled, handsome, grim.

A scream caught in Alex's throat. She tried to back up, but tripped over her chair and had to catch herself on the table. The men did not move.

"We will find you, Alexandra Stirling."

The voices came from the direction of the men, though none of their lips moved. Alex panicked, searching the room for speakers or a sign of the strangers' master.

"Who are you? Why do you want me?" she called. Her voice fell flat in the dense air filling the library. She began to choke.

"It's no use, Ms. Stirling. You cannot escape us. We are everywhere."

The air thickened, causing Alex to cough as it stuck in her throat. "Please... don't hurt me. I don't know what you want!"

Light flickered behind the line of men as they watched Alex fall to the ground. They held their positions, unmoving, uncaring.

"We do not wish to hurt you, Ms. Stirling. You can stop all of this."

And then there was fire. Bookcases ignited. The air erupted with smoke. Alex could no longer see the men. She crawled, eyes stinging, towards the window. Cracks of splintering wood sounded behind her, growing louder and closer each moment. She clawed at the wall, desperate to pull herself up to the cool glass escape. Tears dripped down burning flesh as her vision went black. Hope was lost, powerless to stem the oncoming rush of flame.

A hand grasped hers, pulling upwards in her final moments of consciousness. Her eyelids flitted, seeking her rescuer, but darkness beckoned her with its cruel hand. With the last of her energy, she jumped towards the window and looked up.

The ceiling filled her vision. Her room swayed to the smooth glide of the *Cloudkicker*. The fire and strange men faded in her memory, but the echo of her fear prevented her from moving for some time.

After several minutes, her breathing slowed, returning her senses. Her covers were damp with sweat, and she pulled them off, nearly throwing them onto the floor with violent disgust.

Stumbling, Alex made her way towards the window panel. With a switch, she prepared herself for a rush of morning light only to see the sky outside nearly as dark as her room. Moonlight reflected off thick billows of fog. They were rolling slow over a mountainous terrain filled with pillars and masses dark with shadow.

Ghaoithe spoke about Mount Huangshan the previous night, filling the reporter's head with wild imagery. An ancient landmark, the mountain inspired countless pieces of Chinese artwork. Its mist-covered peaks reflected as much of the country's traditions as fireworks and martial arts films.

In the dead of night, however, their approach to the fabled area triggered anxiety within Alex. Whether it was the nightmares or reaching sight of the *Cloudkicker*'s goal that shook her limbs with electric force, she did not know.

So, she wandered the halls of the ship. Even without a direction in mind, she needed to move and breathe. Fleet's words about personal space came back to her memory. She wanted to be on solid ground again, outdoors and free, away from the enclosed walls of the ship.

"You're going to wear out your legs like that."

Alex jumped at the voice. She had been pacing beside the brig. Damian laid propped against the wall with his hands behind his head. His smirk suggested she had been pacing in front of him for some time.

She coughed, blushing with embarrassment. "Where's your guard?" she asked, trying to act nonchalant.

"Haven't had one in awhile," he said with a raised eyebrow. "We all know Ghaoithe's just keeping me in here for kicks. I guess she doesn't mind if I got out somehow."

"No, I guess not," Alex muttered. She stood for a few seconds, reaching for something to say, before resigning to sitting on the small chair beside the cell doors. "So why haven't you tried to escape?"

He shrugged. "Why would I? This is the first time in weeks I've had regular meals and a place to sleep."

Bags no longer swelled under his eyes, now awake

with life. The pallor had disappeared from his cheeks. He grinned from on top of the pink comforter, a healthy man once more.

Alex chuckled at the sight. "Maybe next she'll help you get some new clothes."

"Mud-stains are very much in fashion in Lost Earth."

Putting her chin in her palm, Alex puzzled over the man in the brig. Amid the solemn atmosphere of the Osiris chase, Damian's whimsy approached surreal.

When she didn't speak, Damian waved his hands in front of her. "Hello? Not a zoo here."

Alex shook her head to clear her thoughts. "Sorry," she said. "Got a lot going on."

The prisoner pulled himself upright. He stared at Alex through the bars of his cage. "I would guess so if you're up this time of night. Airsick?"

"No, not airsick. It's nothing," she laughed. She wanted to change the subject, to wipe away the remnants of her dreams. "So tell me, Damian, what did you do to the captain that landed you in here?"

"Oh god, I forgot you're a writer or some shit. You're going to interrogate me all night, aren't you?" Damian sneered. When Alex only replied with a smile, he sighed. "I managed to sneak off with one of her toys while they were unloading one day. She managed to snoop around and put me on her radar."

"That's impressive," Alex said, wide-eyed. She could only imagine the slight-of-hand required to make off with one of Ghaoithe's relics.

Damian stretched his fingers to drive home the point. "We all have our talents."

"Is that something you picked up in Los Angeles?"

"Yes. I learned it in the mean streets of Burbank," he replied. Alex could not read the deadpan expression until he beamed a goofy smile. "No, I did all right in LA. I used to do magic tricks for kids' parties. Was part of a club that had a castle and everything."

"That's cool," Alex said, though she did not understand anything about what he was talking about. Los Angeles to her was as foreign a place as the moon. "Do you miss it there?"

"Do you miss your home?"

Aside from a few moments wondering how Becky handled the explosive kidnapping, Alex gave Missouri little thought for most of her excursions. Having spent hours sharing stories with Ghaoithe, however, opened up a rush of memories. What would have been a resounding "no" a few days ago had become much more complicated.

"I don't really know," she finally decided. "I miss parts of it, I guess. Everything here is so new I haven't had time to think about my old life much."

Damian nodded in understanding. "I hear ya. Give it time, though. There's no going back once you get used to this place. It's total freedom. Like Alaska but with all the same sights and better weather."

"Maybe," Alex replied. She bit her lip. Her confidence wavered more than she wanted to admit. "How did you end up here, anyway?"

At the question, Damian's smirk faded. The energy exuding from his demeanor fell, and his eyes darted around as if searching for eavesdroppers. He shuffled towards the edge of the bed, leaning in closer to Alex.

"Hey, is it true you guys are going after Osiris?" he asked in a hushed voice.

Alex was taken aback by the change in his tone. Though she knew Ghaoithe was fine with Damian's presence aboard the airship, she didn't know how much information he should be privy to.

She decided to use caution. "I don't know what Ghaoithe is up to. Why? Where'd you hear that?"

Damian's eyes bore into her. An intensity rippled beneath the surface of his oily skin and casual personality.

She could feel him searching through her, reaching into cracks to find the truth. It caught her halfway between fear and awe.

Whatever he found in her, he leaned back, seemingly satisfied. His grin, however, did not return.

"Give 'em Hell, will ya?" he said.

"That seems to be the sentiment around here when it comes to Osiris," she replied. Her hands shook.

"You've never really noticed them have you? What they do to people?" He looked at her with something close to pity. "Well, I'm sure you noticed, but had no idea that anyone was really behind it all."

Alex took a deep breath to calm herself. She rubbed her hands through her hair, playing with her curls out of habit. "What do you mean? Not really much of an underground organized crime scene back in Missouri."

"That's the thing, though! They aren't even underground!" Damian stood and started to pace through his cell. Alex had been forgotten, lost to his ranting. "Osiris practically flaunts how powerful they are, that no one can stop them!"

"If they're so obvious, someone would notice."

"People notice, but there's nothing they can do. They can take small businesses and run them out of town, create as much spin as they want no matter how false their statements are. They create their own laws, exclude themselves from any serious repercussions when they screw up."

"You know this how?" After all of her interactions with the conglomerate, Alex dwelled on how such a coalition could come to be, but she wanted to remain skeptical, impartial. She believed in the power of the public. That that power was waning clashed with her upbringing, even if she admitted to its likelihood in the back of her mind.

Damian didn't acknowledge her, keeping his vision to the ground as he walked. His gestured at every word.

"I've been there. I've seen it happen," he said. "I was lost for a very long time, trying to prove that we were being deceived. Next thing I knew, I was stumbling through Lost Earth, picking coin bags from people for my meals."

Damian stopped pacing to stare at Alex, almost as if to test her reaction. She wondered if he was simply crazy, like a street preacher warning about the end-times.

"What do you want me to say?" she asked. "That I completely believe a strung-out homeless guy, no questions asked?"

"Hey, it's no crazier than jumping on an airship in the name of journalism," he replied. A wide, sinister grin spread across his face, like he was in on a joke only he understood.

"I'll have you know, I intend to write a fantastic story about all of this," Alex said.

"If that's what you keep telling yourself."

Damian strode back onto his bed and leaned against the wall. Between his vague undertones and sass, Alex could feel the heat forming in her cheeks. She stormed off with a frustrated grunt, feeling no better than when she arrived.

Damian called out behind her, "Hey, think you could bring me back a bagel?"

Biting wind forced Alex to pull her jacket tighter around her shoulders. Ghaoithe had found it for her, a leather affair with no lack of pockets in the lining, but little actual utility against the cold. Sorin and Fleet tried to look stoic, but Alex could see the mountain air sending shivers down their arms, too.

Excalibur straddled her back. Ghaoithe had hesitated on bringing it, fearful of tight crawlspaces or losing it to Osiris hands, but Alex insisted on bringing her steel companion. She refused to be dead weight.

They stood in front of a drainage pipe large enough to comfortably fit the party while they waited for Ghaoithe to return. The *Cloudkicker* already left for safer skies tucked in the protection of the mountain range. Beyond them, deep in a valley, the glass towers of the Osiris company gleamed as a bastion of the modern world among an ancient, wild land.

Alex wanted a rousing speech from the captain, words to keep her trudging on in the face of uncertainty. Instead, they walked with no words at all. They journeyed forward, listless against the rolling tides of war.

As the sun dipped below the horizon and Alex started to wonder if the air could get any colder, the Sky Thief emerged from the shadows of the pipe.

"It's clear for a ways in," she said. The three onlookers followed her into the tunnel, preferring the stale air over the wind.

The group trudged along in the darkness with Ghaoithe's armor as a guide. The air hung thick, choking Alex the farther they traveled from the entrance. She anticipated the sewers to smell worse than they did, but she still dared not to look at what splashed against her boots with each step.

A spot of light grew in the distance, eventually becoming a large channel lit with sickly green lights along the top. A murky sludge flowed through the center, lined with walkways on both sides. Ghaoithe motioned for the crew to halt.

Reaching into the folds of her sash, she pulled out three silver dogtags with a rune as the centerpiece. They each took one, placing the tags around their necks.

"These are one-off wards," Ghaoithe said. "If you get shot more than that, you're an embarrassment to my ship. They only help against projectiles, so don't start jumping into fires and all that just because you have them."

Fleet nodded, clearly impressed. "So this is what ya've been workin' on night and day."

Alex pursed her lips and said, "You couldn't hand these out before we started?"

"I hoped we wouldn't need them yet. Listen," commanded Ghaoithe.

In the quiet of the sewer, the only thing Alex could hear was the stream and buzzing from the florescent lights. She strained, unable to make out any noise at first. Then, far down the tunnel to their right, she could hear a faint hum. It droned on, blending in with the lights but deeper and pulsing. The hum lasted only a few seconds before fading away.

"What do you think it is?" asked Alex.

"This your realm, hon. I should be asking you,"

Ghaoithe said.

"I'm guessing it's not good, whatever it is."

They started their way down the walkway towards the noise. Alex held the middle, while Fleet and Sorin spoke in hushed rumbles in the rear.

The stench of the water became a reality. Alex forced herself to keep her eyes only on her next step, worried that the sight of the stream would empty what little she had in her stomach. Along the tunnel walls, ladders led up to the surface at random intervals, allowing Alex the distraction of imagining what lie at the top. A cyberpunk Osiris city? Chinese villages stopped in time?

Alex thought she had seen wonderful sights aboard the airship, but now she realized how much more remained out in the world. She did not want to miss any of it.

When the group reached an intersection branching to either side, they paused so Ghaoithe could listen for the noise. Whatever had created it had passed, though, leaving them alone in the tunnel.

"The walls must be echoing. No telling how far down that thing is," Ghaoithe observed, dissatisfied with losing the trail.

"Should we split up? Alex and I can take right," asked Sorin, folding his arms as he peered down the branching path.

"No," Ghaoithe responded sharply. "Not until we know what's down here with us and we find the complex."

Alex let out a breath of relief. Separating from the main group, even with a guardian like Sorin, terrified her. The last thing she wanted was to lose sight of the captain's armor.

Ghaoithe pushed down the left tunnel, oblivious to the murk she waded through to reach the next walkway. Sorin touched Alex's shoulder and indicated he would carry her if she wanted.

Grateful for the thought, Alex declined. She needed to press on for herself. The water was not deep, and she splashed swiftly across the channel. Fleet and Sorin trailed her by only a few steps.

The maps in Ghaoithe's quarters measured their path at a mile, but the labyrinth of the sewers made for slow going. Ghaoithe insisted on stopping at regular intervals on the route to listen for the distant hum. Several portions of the walkways were crumbling, forcing the party into the sludge. Alex stopped caring after their fifth foray in the channel.

Their journey shifted after an hour. Turning at one of the myriad crossroads, the architecture of the sewer system transformed from dilapidated to state-of-the-art. The water still churned with brown foam, but the walls were coated with fresh white paint. The green bulbs now shone bright white, illuminating every inch of the main passageway.

Ghaoithe stepped forward to begin scouting. Alex grabbed the captain's arm and pulled her into a alcove labeled for maintenance access. Alex raised a finger to her lips, and gave a slight nod towards their destination.

The tunnel led to a dead-end, the flow of water passing underneath the wall. A single ladder rose into the ceiling from the walkway. A few feet before it, embedded into an opening in the wall, a spherical machine hovered. The size of a basketball, a white bottom gave way to a reflective black shell, two poles jutting out from the sides of the seam. It made no sound as it bobbed in the air. The only sign of activity was a tiny red power light blinking under its dark glass top.

"What is it?" Ghaoithe hissed.

"A drone," Alex whispered back.

"A what?"

"Don't let it see us."

To Alex, drones contained nothing more than a few propellers and maybe a camera to be controlled by remote. She even had a friend or two that built them in their spare time for fun. Whatever Osiris had created outmatched those skeletal toys. She did not want to test whatever additions the organization fitted into their sleeker versions.

Ghaoithe eyed it, summing up the technology as best she could, when it emit a booming hum. The next thing Alex knew, she was under the water with the captain. The buzzing of five drones reverberated through the water as they passed overhead and into the tunnels.

Alex closed her eyes. Something soft and squishy brushed against her arm as it flowed past. Her stomach lurched as she held her breath with every ounce of will she could muster.

Once the drones disappeared into the tunnels, Ghaoithe released Alex. The young Stirling gasped for air and, no sooner could she see straight, proceeded to vomit onto the nearest walkway.

She finished, ready to yell at Ghaoithe, when one of the captain's hands covered her mouth. The Sky Thief nodded towards the end of the hall. A lone orb hovered in front of the ladder.

"What do we do with it?" Ghaoithe hissed.

Alex strained to look at the drone out of the corner of her vision. She sought anything familiar, clues to its inner workings that even a novice engineer could find.

The drone buzzed with its inner propulsion,

uninterested in the party. The twin prongs jutting from its side revealed no immediate purpose, the black visor too opaque to see inside. It almost resembled the security cameras dotting the ceilings of grocery stores...

"Motion," Alex muttered.

Ghaoithe's eyebrows crinkled. "What?"

"Motion," Alex repeated, her voice clear in the still air. "They use motion sensors."

"Are you sure?"

"I don't see any microphones on the outside. I'm pretty sure." Alex wanted to sound confident for Ghaoithe's sake, but the estimate was a shot in the dark. Flying orbs landed well outside her limited electronics expertise.

Ghaoithe leered at the drone, never taking it out of her sight. She bent down, cautious of going too quickly. The sewer water streamed two steps behind her. As though she were stuck in molasses, the captain edged backwards toward it, slipping in without the faintest ripple.

The machine continued to hover while the rest of the crew rooted in placed. Fleet looked wide-eyed at Alex, daring only point at the captain. Alex shook her head, as lost as he was about what Ghaoithe intended to do.

In the water, Ghaoithe crawled forward on her stomach, her head barely above the river's foam. Once positioned under the drone, she crouched and reached for her rapier. Steadying her breath, she struck.

The blade slid through the orb's shell with no resistance. Its humming vanished as Ghaoithe withdrew. It began to fall and, for good measure, Ghaoithe grabbed the ball, smashing it against the nearby wall, shattering it into several bits of metal and wire.

Standing triumphant over the metal husk, Ghaoithe slid her blade back into her sash. Fleet and Sorin let out relieved sighs as they rounded the corner. They pat Alex on the shoulder as they passed.

She wanted to join them, but her attention stayed on the husk of the drone. She forgot that she was holding her breath until she tried to speak.

"Uh, guys…" Alex said. The other three stopped chatting to look at her.

"What, Alex? Can this thing rebuild itself or something?" asked Ghaoithe, nudging a piece of scrap with her boot.

"Not quite, but you may want to get up that ladder."

Underneath the shattered black glass, the drone's motion sensor poked out. The red light on its side continued to blink, but with increasing intensity. It came to a stop, letting out a siren that reverberated through the tunnel walls, forcing the group to shield their ears.

Within seconds, the piercing screech ended, leaving only a ringing in the explorers' ears. They released their palms from their heads and looked at each other for an explanation.

Deep within the catacombs, the buzzing of the other drones sounded in response, rapidly rising in volume.

"Now would be a good time to start working on that ladder, Ghaoithe," Alex said, her voice shaking. Already starting, Ghaoithe's boots clanged against metal rails at the order.

Fleet and Sorin rushed by Alex to cover the corners of the intersection. They drew their blades, searching for the incoming wave of machines. The noise filled the tunnels, making it impossible to guess which direction the attack would come from.

Alex glanced at the two men, then back at the captain. Ghaoithe vanished into the access tunnel in the ceiling. Willing herself away, Alex reached for Excalibur and joined Sorin along the right wall.

"Do we stand still?" he asked.

"Yes," Alex replied. She had no idea if she was right and silently prayed that her friends could adapt if she wasn't.

The security drones entered from the left, creating ripples in the sewage beneath them. Alex counted seven as they made their way closer, more than she had anticipated. The three warriors held still, cautious to even breathe as they approached.

The first drone slowed to a cruise as it neared the intersection. It bobbed just inches from Alex's head, followed by the second drone, then the third, until they passed by and swarmed the ladder side of the tunnel.

Alex crept her head to the side, peeking through her curls as the drones ignored the group, hovering around the broken scrap on the ground.

Go away! Go back to your posts, she screamed in her head as though the sheer force of her will could be felt by the machines.

The drones turned from their fallen copy. They spread into a line at the far end of tunnel and turned towards the three crewmates. From the center drone, a thin red light pierced the air. It expanded, spreading from wall-to-wall in a narrow band, sweeping over the corridor.

When the red band reached the top of Fleet's head, the prongs of the drone sparked with an electric arc. The other machines followed suit.

The drones were almost on top of the crew by the time Alex let out an exasperated cry to run. She thrust Excalibur into the air in front of her, the force of splitting metal running up her arm. Another orb threatened to collide with her side, but Sorin's fist sent it crumbling into the wall. She gave him an expression of thanks before turning back towards the incoming attack.

On the other side of the channel, Fleet let out a sharp yell as one of the drones managed to graze his left arm with its taser. His hand dangled, useless, at his side. He whipped his free hand around, crushing it into the side of the drone with such force he staggered and fell into the water below. He sputtered, pulled his weight onto his good arm, and looked at Alex.

"Get to the captain! We'll take care of these buggers," he barked. When Alex did not move, he shouted, "I ain't askin'! Go!"

Alex tore herself away from the sight of her limping mentor. In front of the ladder, the remaining drones rocked forward, preparing another strike. Sorin lifted a hunk of scrap near his feet and tossed it at the cluster, sending them careening towards him.

Alex pumped her feet as hard as she could past the bots. Sorin's distraction worked; they paid little attention to the short blonde hugging the wall. She dashed towards the ladder, only stopping when her shoulder connected with the end of the tunnel.

Ghaoithe grasped the top rungs of the ladder. Their escape had been blocked, barricaded by a solid steel door speckled with runes. A piece of chalk in the captain's hand scribbled at a point on the door, pausing only for the rogue to curse before scrawling on another area when the lock did not break.

"What happened to this not being an issue?" Alex shouted.

"Now's not the time to be a smart-ass, Alex," Ghaoithe responded through grit teeth. Within a few hasty clicks of the chalk, the glow of the runes vanished. Ghaoithe shouted in victory and heaved the steel upwards, opening a passageway out.

At the first nudge of the door, the drones released another wail. A blistering shot struck the wall next to Alex, stinging her eyes with fine concrete ash.

One of the men shouted at her, but her focus narrowed on the three drones facing her, their taser prongs glowing with dangerous heat. More shots discharged with deadly precision and scorched blonde curls as Alex jerked away.

Behind the machines, Fleet and Sorin flailed in the stream, trying to reinvigorate life to their numb limbs, screaming at Alex to run. The drones ignored their distractions. Alex stood, fixated, as the drones charged for another round.

Ghaoithe sped down, hoisting Alex off her feet. Beams fired below them. As Alex lost sight of her two protectors beneath the edge of the access tunnel, she snapped out of her bewilderment, thrashing against the fist that held her. Ghaoithe's grip held firm, and the two ventured through the doorway above.

Once they were on the hard floor, Ghaoithe's grip eased, and Alex scrambled back to the doorway. She looked down only to see the drones flash into her narrow view. The captain shoved the girl aside, heaved the steel door shut, and cut off access to their companions.

It was Alex's turn to yell. She called after the two men, clawing at the door. Ghaoithe grabbed Alex's shoulders and faced her. Alex's eyes struggled to adjust to the dim chamber, only able to make out the faint glint of Ghaoithe's eye glaring into her.

"We have to go," said the rogue. Her voice projected calm, but her hands trembled.

"No. I'm not leaving them to die," Alex responded. She tried to shrug off Ghaoithe's hands but they held firm.

"They won't. The drones wanted whoever broke the seal. We have to go before whoever they signaled shows up."

Alex shrugged again with less conviction. Her sight of the men, limbs useless, conflicted with a vision of Osiris agents storming into the room. Neither option struck her as being better than the other.

"What if you're wrong?" she asked, checking her temper.

"I'm not."

After a moment, Alex nodded, mostly to herself. She knew Ghaoithe would never let her run back into the sewers, and they were as good as dead either way if Osiris reached them. She decided, as she had done so many times before, to place her trust in the captain and the abilities of the crew. Pandora's Box was the priority.

They were in a maintenance room, boxes and shelves piled high around them. Ghaoithe's armor spread its light over cleaning materials and tools. Their sight jarred Alex's senses after her time away from the modern world.

Ghaoithe stood, peering around the tight room. Lights from the outside outlined a doorway on the far end. She pressed her ear against it. Satisfied, she waved at Alex.

The door opened into a bright office hallway with a long mural of a dragon along one side. Bold red hanzi text offered encouragement to employees. Glass office doors spread along the other wall, most of them dark in the early hours.

Ghaoithe rushed to the first door to the left and tested the handle. It swung open without resisting, and the two women veered inside. Ghaoithe held a finger to her lips and pressed Alex beside the door, hidden from anyone looking in.

The two barely settled in position when footsteps pounded down the hallway towards their door. They ran past the office in militaristic unison, only stopping when reaching the storage room. Then, silence.

Alex leaned over Ghaoithe to glimpse at the action, but the captain nudged her back, resting a hand on the girl's shoulder. City lights poured into the office through a wall of windows, illuminating the captain's unflinching features with a phosphorous glow. Alex stared, breathless, registering only the warmth of the captain's presence beside her and the calloused hand on her shoulder.

When the boots failed to return, Ghaoithe eased up. She stretched her arms out and grinned at Alex.

"Guess those men are in for a merry chase," she said, placing her hands on her hips.

Alex could not help but smile, too, knowing that her friends were alive and causing Osiris trouble as they hobbled through the tunnels.

With their short break, the women stretched and relaxed. They smelled offensive, and Alex could only guess at what her thick hair looked like compared to Ghaoithe's matted, grimy crop. The blue armor shone as though it had not seen a drop of the murk in the sewer system.

Alex looked around the office, mesmerized by the twinkling of electric bulbs scattered through the city among the mountains. Though the furniture was sparse - only a desk, chair, a potted tree near the windows, and a few shelves with books - the modern room felt more unreal to her than much of her journey aboard the *Cloudkicker*.

"There's no computer," she said, startled once she noticed its absence.

"Are they usually that easy to find?" asked the captain.

Alex placed her palm on her forehead. "Yes, Ghaoithe. Computers are pretty much everywhere nowadays."

Unfazed, Ghaoithe continued, "Then, we find a room that has one."

She started to make her way back towards the door, twisting the handle when Alex called for her to wait. Ghaoithe looked back at the freshman sailor. Under the captain's gaze, Alex fidgeted with her fingers, looking everywhere but into the one emerald eye.

"You know I'm not going to leave you, right?" Alex muttered. The words took more strength than she had expected.

Ghaoithe eased off the door handle and tilted her head at her partner. "What do you mean?"

Alex let in a deep breath, heat rising into her cheeks. She said, "If we get separated, I know you would say I should go back to the ship, go back to Missouri, and live a normal life where Osiris would have no reason to bother me. And I am saying I won't do that. I won't leave you here if something happens."

Ghaoithe thought for a moment before flashing a smile at Alex. "Ok, Ms. Stirling. Guess we're stuck with each other then."

She motioned for Alex to follow and swung the door open. The acknowledgment swelled within Alex, lingering as they ran down the hallway. Many of the doors had been locked. The few that opened wide lacked computers as well.

As the final door of the hall yielded no results, Ghaoithe grumbled, "I thought you said these things were everywhere."

Alex rubbed her head. "They are. I guess they did know we were coming."

"Probably."

Another corridor, plain and uniform, branched off from the end of the hallway. Both Ghaoithe and Alex stared at the elevator doors at the other end, thinking the same thing: that if Osiris did move the computers, checking door after door would simply waste their time, that maybe Osiris had planned it this way from the beginning.

Ghaoithe started down the hall with a steady, slow stride, ignoring the doors around her. Alex kept the pace, racking her brain for ideas.

"Well, kid, this is your area of expertise, not mine," Ghaoithe said.

Alex pursed her lips. "If they know we're here, the only thing I can think of is to check floors randomly. Try to break any pattern they might expect."

Ghaoithe nodded, but her face remained flat. Uneasy anticipation crawled through Alex's skin. When they reached the end of the hallway, Ghaoithe stopped, reached into her sash, and held out the black USB drive to Alex.

"You need to take this now. Just in case," she said in a soft rasp. Her face had paled, and her shoulders drooped from when they had first entered the building.

Alex almost raised her voice to object but thought better of it at the sight of her tired captain. She took the drive from Ghaoithe and began to place it into her jacket pockets. With a second thought, she took it out and wrapped it snug into the folds her own blue sash, just like her companion.

Satisfied, Alex steadied herself and reached for the elevator button. Ghaoithe's hand clasped her arm, shaking Alex with surprise. When she looked up at her captain, Ghaoithe eased off the girl's arm.

"I… don't trust lifts where I can't see the pulley," she said. She blushed. "Can we take the stairs?"

Alex burst out in laughter. Ghaoithe shifted from foot to foot, stammering an excuse, but it only served to make Alex laugh harder. Ghaoithe soon joined in, starting with a snicker that swelled into a cackle of her own. Their voices echoed down the hallway, providing life to the sterile quarters.

When they calmed down, Alex hunched over to ease the pain in her stomach and wiped a hand over her eyes. She stared up at the captain, who stood tall again with her hands on her hips and color returned to her face.

"Yes, we can take the stairs," Alex said.

The stairwell entrance waited beside the elevator, familiar even with its red hanzi text. It spiraled up towards the heavens, beyond the reach of any reasonable person. The girls climbed with no aim or goal, no rush to meet their fate.

The clang of their boots against the stiff sheet metal provided the only soundtrack of their journey.

When they finally stopped at an arbitrary floor, just as Alex had suggested, they looked over the railing to see how far they had come. The floor had become no more than a pinpoint in the distance.

The door loomed before them, a sentinel to their success or failure. Alex expected the unease from the elevator to return, but, standing beside her captain, her heart beat steady and content.

Ghaoithe placed a hand on Alex's shoulder. "Thank you, Ms. Stirling," she said.

Alex returned a small nod, sweat-thick curls bouncing off her forehead. She reached for the handle and pressed it open.

On the other side, a mass of Osiris soldiers greeted them. Their guns aimed readily at Alex, daring Ghaoithe to make even the slightest twitch to protect her.

In front of the men, Fleet and Sorin rested on their knees, handcuffed and beaten.

XIV

The loss of freedom did not bother Alex so much as the casual efficiency in which she and her friends were held. Had she been placed in a dingy concrete bunker, her mind could have anticipated the horrors to come. However, their cell, bright with headache-inducing LEDs, had once been nothing more than a normal office space. Barred windows overlooked the lights of Huangshan's inhabited pockets. Temporary cots had been scattered over the paneled wood floors. Only a camera recessed into the corner above the door gave any indication they were imprisoned at all.

Osiris did not just imprison the crew; it mocked them, knowing full well the invasion only had one end by failing.

Alex paced through the cell, wringing her hands. Fleet looked up at her, squinting through a bruised and swollen left eye.

"Ya need to calm down, lass. Worryin' will just sap yer energy," he said, voice low and raspy.

Alex sighed and stood still in the center of the cell. She looked at Sorin, whose body collapsed onto one of the cots when they arrived and hadn't stirred since. Only the steady rise and fall of his chest gave an indication of life.

Osiris took Ghaoithe. They skipped the other three entirely, taking their weapons and tossing them into the cell without a second glance. Alex could see the shadows of armed guards moving through the frosted glass of their prison's door. She wanted nothing more than to charge through and find her captain, but the hours pressed on with vanishing hope.

"What if she doesn't come back?" Alex asked, returning to her pacing.

"She will," said Fleet. He leaned back against the wall to rub his leg. The guards had done a number on him, but the effects of the drones' shocks were at least wearing off.

"How do you know?"

"Because we're still here."

Alex grunted in response, on the edge of saying something snippy, but her energy failed. Fleet was right; if Osiris no longer needed Ghaoithe, the rest of them were expendable.

The lights of the valleys beyond the Osiris complex lured Alex into a trance as she leaned onto the window sill. They shone alone in a sea of black mountains, quiet and serene, a land of simpler lives than those in the corporation's complex. She imagined most of the people in the town rising early to go to work in nearby fields or the tourist attractions surrounding the landmark.

The lights reminded her of home. A pain shot through her chest and into her throat, a desperate panic to escape back to a life of homework and writing about building purchases. She could finally admit that her hometown frightened her less than her predicament with Osiris, and it made her sick, but not for her sake.

If she had not insisted on staying aboard the *Cloudkicker*, she never would have risked their lives by finding Bimini, never would have been a liability in Roanoke, never would have come to care about those she traveled with…

A click from the door sent Alex darting across the

room. The barrel of a gun poked through the opening, keeping her a safe distance away as the door opened. The guard, featureless in a black visor and gray fatigues, waited until the young girl stood an acceptable distance away before nodding off to another guard to the side of the cell entrance. They appeared with Ghaoithe, tossed her inside the cell, and wasted no time in locking the chamber behind her. Alex stepped towards her companion but stopped as nausea slammed her.

Ghaoithe lay crumpled on the floor, stripped of every piece of her clothing. Her skin, once hidden by her unmistakable armor, clung to her bones like ragged cloth, pale and worn beyond its intended use. Scars etched across her body like tattoos. Only a few of them flashed red with crimson; the rest acted as silent reminders of past mistakes.

Groaning, Ghaoithe pulled herself into a sitting position. Alex snapped out of her shock and joined Fleet in aiding their captain to one of the cots near a wall. Osiris had even deprived her of her eyepatch, revealing a mess of melted flesh that had once been her eyelid. Her good eye winced as they moved.

Once settled, Ghaoithe propped herself up against the wall behind her. She let out a dry cough and closed her eye until the pain subsided.

"What did they do to you?" Alex cried. Fleet rested a hand on her shaking arm.

Ghaoithe opened her eye and forced a weak smile at the two. "Don't worry, little Minnow. They found out the hard way they'll have to interrogate me from afar. They only managed a few bruises, and it cost 'em."

Her nonchalant attitude only forced the reality of their situation deeper into Alex. The young explorer tore away from Fleet and climbed into Ghaoithe's broad arms. Sobs heaved through Alex's body, but she no longer cared about keeping them contained. All of her fatigue and doubt flooded into her mind, breaking the dam that held them.

A hand stroked through her hair, weaving through the curls and tangles with matronly care. Through her cries, Alex became aware of a voice in the distance, low and enchanting. It grew louder, a flowing song easing her frustration. The voice quieted her weeping until she stopped completely to listen.

Alex rested against Ghaoithe's chest, feeling the captain's breath with each lyric, letting it reverberate through her. She couldn't understand the Gaelic words, but they were nonetheless beautiful with their calm, flowing rhythm. They slipped into Alex's mind, erasing her surroundings and melting away the uncertainty they faced.

When the song finished, Alex held her eyes closed, not wishing to move from her comfortable spot away from reality.

"What's it mean?" she whispered to Ghaoithe.

"It's a lullaby I used to hear back home," replied Ghaoithe, still combing through Alex's hair. "It's a song to make the birds sleep."

"What was your home like?" Alex opened her eyes and peered up at Ghaoithe's battered face. Even without her eyepatch, the captain maintained a regal glow.

Another click from the cell door shot through the silence. A guard stepped through and pointed at the two.

"The blonde! Now!" he barked.

Alex's grip on Ghaoithe tightened. The captain lifted the girl's chin with a reassuring palm.

"Go. Do what they ask. Don't do anything stupid," said Ghaoithe.

Alex hugged her leader and made her way to the guard at the door. He shoved her into the hall and slammed the cell behind her. With his rifle pointed squarely at her back, they marched down the white corridor and into an elevator at the end.

As the lift maneuvered its way up the tower, Alex steeled herself against the possibilities that awaited her. She ignored the guard, staring only at her reflection in the elevator's door. Her hair had grown even more wild, her skin darker. The stocky nature of her build had trimmed, toned in her arms and lost completely in the unnecessary areas around her waist.

The elevator shuddered as it stopped. Alex straightened up, focused on whatever waited beyond the doors as they slid aside.

"Alex! Are you ok?"

Ethan, sleek in a pale blue button-down and dress pants, rushed forward to greet her as she stepped out of the elevator. His hug left her paralyzed, uncertain that he really existed. Tugging her hand, he nodded for the guard to leave and led Alex out of the elevator.

They stood in an ultra-modern suite near the top of the tower with glass walls overlooking the complex. White carpet met with black furniture surrounding a clear conference table. In the center of the table, a small fire greeted them. A plate of fruit had been laid out beside it.

Ethan eased her into a seat before sitting down next to her, leaning his chin onto clenched fists. Conflicting emotions fought for Alex's will. Ghaoithe's torn body remained fresh in her head. Yet, Ethan, with his familiar tussle of hair and penetrating eyes, called for Alex to talk. She wanted to scream and cry and yell all at once.

"Who are you?" she asked, careful to keep a deadpan voice.

"Cutting right to the chase," Ethan said. He rubbed his eyes and leaned back in his chair. "At least have something to eat. You look like you're starving."

Ethan reached over to the fruit tray, picked up an apple, and offered it to her. Alex did not flinch, only grasping the fruit when he placed it in her hand. It stayed there.

"You lied to me. I deserve an answer," Alex said.

"Yes, I suppose you do," he replied. The drawl she had loved so much had disappeared. "My name isn't Jackson. It's Ethan Holt. I work with Osiris."

"Why couldn't you have told me?"

Ethan shifted in his seat. "It's complicated. Osiris is a complex organization. Telling you would have made you a liability. They don't like loose ends. And, honestly, would you have believed it anyway?"

"I might have!" Alex yelled. Her fingernails dug into the skin of the apple. She fought for control, inhaling deep before adding, "I trusted you. You could have just told me. I would have gone with you."

"It was risky, Alex. It was best for you not to know. You would have moved on and lived a quiet life. I didn't expect Ghaoithe to be so close on our heels," he said.

At the mention of her captain, Alex slapped Ethan square on the jaw. It stung her palm, and she relished the feeling.

"Did you love me?" she asked, eyes dark with fire. Ethan rubbed his jaw and turned back to her.

"Yes," he said, "I did. I still do. That's why you're still alive. Deacon wanted to dispose of your crew."

"If you're willing to leave Ghaoithe for his kind, that tells me plenty," Alex said.

Ethan reached over to her and grasped her hands. Her instincts told her to pull away, but Ethan locked his eyes onto hers, pulling her into his world.

"Alex, I'm being honest," he said. "When I said I would protect you, I meant it. Osiris has its hotheads, yes, but they are doing very important work for humanity. They will listen to me when it comes time to keep you from harm."

Alex's head spun, boiling for a reason to fight Ethan. She knew he had betrayed her, but he was sincere in the moment. His hands held the same gentleness she remembered. She desired nothing more than to lean over and cry into his shoulder, knowing everything would work out in the end. She looked into his eyes, searching for an excuse to relent and found none.

Doubt lingered too strong to sway her, pecked at her conscience with an irritable buzz. She straightened herself and let her hands slip away from his.

"I can't trust you or Osiris," Alex said.

Ethan thought for a moment, then let loose the charming smile that enraptured Alex from the start, melting her resolve. "Then, let me show you. Tomorrow. Will you give me that?"

"Will you call off Ghaoithe's interrogations?"

"Already done once I heard what was going on."

"And what about the *Cloudkicker*?"

"They've been boarded and the ship confiscated, but the crew is unharmed."

Alex considered for a moment, searching for a drawback. When she could not think of none, as if she even had a choice, she gave a short nod. She moved to stand when Ethan coughed her to attention.

"There is one small thing, though," he said. "I need that flash drive you're carrying."

"I don't know what you're talking about," Alex stammered.

"You and I both know I can't let you leave with it. Please, Alex. You can't use it now, anyway."

Shaking with failure, Alex fumbled at her sash and

pulled out the black drive. She had barely handed it out to Ethan when it disappeared into one of his pockets.

"Thank you for not making this harder, Alex," Ethan said.

They strode back to the elevator and waited as Ethan called for the lift. When it arrived, Alex stepped in with the guard and turned to face her former boyfriend.

"See you tomorrow," Ethan said and the doors closed.

Alex heard the guard's steps well before he unlocked the cell door. Sleep had eluded her throughout the night. She stared out the barred windows, watching as the sun rose through the valley. Her companions slept, the only sound in the building.

Before leaving, she gave one look at her companions, still passed out. Ghaoithe had been given spare clothes, barely long enough to reach her joints. At least she looked decent again.

Alex followed the guard back into the elevator. Their trip lasted only a few seconds. They exited on a different floor than the suite. Despite her hate for Osiris, Alex gasped.

Along the right wall, a wall-wide hologram looped with images of smiling businessmen and slogans in languages from around the world. Between the commercials, a large O with a green branch growing into the center splashed across a white background.

"Building tomorrow from yesterday," a cheerful female voice cooed through the speakers.

People buzzed behind glass walls on the other side of the hall in their designer suits and cutting heels. Many worked with paper-thin panels at their desks or video chat with associates on screens projected directly into their walls. Several of the drones from the sewer sputtered about, retrofit not with tasers but with mechanical hands and trays to carry goods about the halls. No one stopped to glance at Alex as she was shuffled down the hall. No one stopped for anything in those offices.

They reached an office midway down the hall. Ethan, feet on his desk and attention on his phone, waved at her through the clear wall. The guard abandoned her side, and she was left as the only person standing still on the floor as Ethan finished his conversation.

"Glad you could make it!" Ethan said, pulling the doors to his office open wide. "Welcome to Osiris!"

"What did you want to show me?" Alex snipped. She was far too tired to condone his chipper attitude.

His attitude did not falter. "I wanted to show you

what we do here. Help you understand. This way."

The two walked towards the end of the hall and back into the elevator. Once inside, Ethan pressed a button, eyes flickering to a security camera in the corner, and the elevator took off.

"What do you know about us?" asked Ethan as they rose.

"That you burned a city and tortured my friend," Alex said.

"Alex..." Ethan sighed. "If we're going to do this, you need to hear me out and not jump to conclusions based on assumptions."

"Fine," she grunted. "I know you are a multi-national organization that controls most of the wealth in the modern world and that you compete with the *Cloudkicker* for lost relics."

"And Ghaoithe never told you what we do with that money or those relics?"

"No," Alex replied. She was loathe to admit that Ghaoithe had been vague about Osiris's operations.

The elevator lurched to a stop and opened its doors. They entered another glass hallway, but it was darker, lit with blue phosphorous light. Workers in white lab coats filled each room, hunching over long tables and tech equipment.

Monitors oversaw all of their work with charts, graphs, and images in constant motion.

"Welcome to Floor 52: Relic R&D," Ethan said, spreading his arms in welcome. "This is where we work to better humanity."

In the first room they passed, two men holding tablets scribbled notes over a stone plate etched with markings. The monitor above them cycled through letters next to a picture of one of the markings. In another room, a massive scimitar blazed with fire.

"You actually use artifacts here?" Alex asked. Aside from Excalibur, she had never actually used any of the relics kept in the *Cloudkicker*'s hold.

"Reverse engineer, actually," Ethan replied. He made no effort to hide the pride in the statement. "Here. This room."

They stepped into a room filled with more of the thin monitors, each on different news channels around the globe. Some flashed with stock reports while others featured downtrodden societies meeting with aide workers.

"This is our media room. It's where we get to see the fruits of our labor," Ethan explained. The table beside them did not feature any ancient find but instead an array of remote controls. He picked one up and began flipping through channels.

Alex began to catch on. "So, you find out how these items work and then create new technology for the modern world."

"Exactly!" Ethan pointed at her. Enthusiasm built in his words. "We use these to create new jobs, help people. The work we do here changes lives, Alex! We've engineered plants for drought-ridden countries, new sources of energy... and there's still so much we don't know!"

"For a price, I assume."

"Well, of course this isn't cheap." Ethan straightened the collar of his suit. "Which is why we've had so much trouble with Lost Earth. They reject our help. They say we're robbing them of their opportunities when we're the only ones with the resources to give them those chances."

"They have the sigils."

"Yes, but those only go so far. We don't know much about how the runes work, but we know they are very limited in scope. Yet, the people of Lost Earth refuse to see that, staying content with all the troubles a lack of modern technology brings."

"So you burn their cities, knowing they can't fight back."

Ethan lowered himself into a chair beside the

remotes. With a press of a button, the multitude of screens went mute.

"Look, you need to understand that we're a collective, not one single company," Ethan said. "What happened in Roanoke was the work of a few extremists I was there to stop, and I was too late. They've been dealt with. We do our best to keep things civil, but we do have some that would rather use brute force for their objectives. That was extreme, even for them, and not something we could ever apologize enough for."

Alex's temper flared. "You expect me to be ok with that? Just a quick 'I'm sorry,' and everything's fine again? You've either got balls of steel or shit for brains if you expect me to just accept that."

"I don't expect you to accept it right away. All I can say is that what happened was extreme even for our bullish types. We want to help people, not scare them. Something got out of hand. Tensions have been high lately between us all."

The landscape of the two worlds, old and modern, began to fall into place for Alex. That Osiris held a monopoly on technology, its creation, and how it was thrust into the world would certainly clash with Lost Earth ideals of communal sharing and simple, if wild, living.

Hearing about the workings of Osiris from Ethan did little to ease the frustration in Alex. If anything, it complicated matters, giving neither side a clear victory over the other. She enjoyed living among Lost Earth and Ghaoithe's crew, but she could not deny the benefits projected onto the screens in the office.

Roanoke's end could not be forgiven so easily, but Alex knew she had few details on the workings of either side of the conflict. All she could say for sure was that she trusted Ghaoithe, and that Osiris had a long way to go to be redeemed.

"Why are you telling me all this now? What's changed from when you ran away?" Alex asked. She appreciated Ethan's openness, but Osiris hardly seemed the kind of people to be candid about their operations.

Ethan's hands clasped onto hers. "Because I can protect you now. You have options here. You can stop running."

"Options? What are you talking about?"

Ethan released her hands and stood. "Come back with me to the suite. We can talk business there."

She followed him out into the hall, not taking her eyes off of him, trying to read his game. She felt uneasy in the pit of her stomach, like something had been lurking in the corners of her vision, waiting to rip at her if she let her guard down for even a second.

Ethan's eyes flickered towards the end of the hall, a subconscious reaction out of habit. Alex let him lead the way past her, then glanced at what caught his eye. A room, blackened with cloth along all sides, created a pit of darkness among the neon glow of the neighboring research facilities.

"That's Pandora's Box, isn't it?" she asked, her curiosity bubbling over.

"What, that? Oh, no. Getting maintenance done for a new piece we just found in Greenland. The object we found in Bimini turned out not to be the urn at all," Ethan replied with only a quick look back. He walked down the hall towards the elevator. Alex lingered on the room then turned to join him.

In the suite, the fire in the table burned low and the fruit tray had been replaced by elegant trays of cream, coffee, pastries, and juices. The daylight coming through the windows bounced off the carpet with blinding intensity, making the room appear to glow with heavenly light. A screen lowered from the ceiling and displayed morning news from across the Osiris empire.

"Hey, did you want to see your big moment?" Ethan asked as they crossed the room. Without waiting for an answer, he picked up a remote from the table and flipped the channel on the screen.

A camera with a major news logo in the corner captured a familiar hospital building with the *Cloudkicker* positioned outside. From the ground, the airship dwarfed everything around it, and Alex fully realized how much of a miracle it took for Ghaoithe to avoid toppling anything in the area. The camera zoomed in to the hole blasted in the side of the building just in time to showcase Fleet hauling Alex onto his shoulder and crossing out of sight.

The screen went blank, leaving Alex longing for another few seconds to view her hometown. Ethan placed the remote on the table, sat town, and began chewing on one of the sugary pastries on the tray.

"You know, that was a pain to clean up," he said between bites. "The big news networks were easy, but your little paper was another story. We never bothered with small-town press, but it may have to go in the pipeline after that incident."

Alex decided she did not like the suite. She became angry every time she entered it.

"What's your point?" she asked, closing in on Ethan. "What are you trying to prove here?"

"Alex, calm down."

"No. Whatever you're doing to intimidate me… I've had enough."

Ethan finished the last bite, wiping his hands on the sides of his suit. "Do you know why we are called 'Osiris?'" he said. "Osiris was the God of Death, but he also represented life and rebirth. He was the manifestation of the cycle of all things. That is what we do: we aide that cycle, take the negative, the discarded, and turn it into something positive for humanity's benefit.

"I want you to join us in that cycle, Alex. This is your chance to start fresh. I can offer that to you here. You can do some good work."

"You called me up here to give me a job offer? After all that you've done?" Alex's temper flared. She couldn't stop herself from yelling, from shouting out at the world holding her captive as though she were nothing more than a chess piece.

"Think about it, Alex," Ethan replied. He remained composed. "Think of what you can do, what you've always wanted to do. New York? Chicago? Any of the major international networks? We can set you up wherever you want to go. You can tell the stories you want, carte blanche. I just have to give the word. It will keep you safe."

Alex could not decide whether to feel insulted or

thankful. She knew the offer was real. The rational side of her mind reeled with the possibilities she could make use of. But Ghaoithe and the *Cloudkicker* forced their way back into her head. She would not make the same mistake Ethan did.

"I don't know what you're trying to do," Alex said. She leaned over and placed her hands on the armrests of Ethan's chair, trapping him. "Maybe Osiris does have some great, moral plan to help people, but you are an idiot if you think I will just abandon my friends for a job I didn't earn. I'm not you."

Ethan's mouth flickered with a frown, his veneer of concern broken ever-so-slightly. He pulled his chair away from her grasp and stood.

"Are you sure you won't even consider it?"

"Positive."

Sighing, Ethan rubbed his forehead. Then, in his perfect Southern drawl, he called out, "Hey, hon! I got a surprise for you!"

From behind Alex came a high-pitched squeal. "No way!"

Another room branched off from the side of the suite. In the doorway, wearing a shining purple dress under perfectly-styled bangs, stood Becky. She ran for Alex, embracing her in a choking hug.

"Oh my god! Jackson said you got called away on assignment, and then I didn't hear from you. I was so worried!" Becky said with a trembling voice. "What in the world happened? You look like you've been through Hell."

Alex leered at Ethan, all of the love she had for him draining from her heart. "Sorry," she said, "things got a little crazy for a while. I'm fine."

"I'm so glad you're safe. I expect a full rundown later." Becky let go of her friend and smiled wide. "Why didn't you tell me Jackson's family was so well-connected? He called me up the moment I got to Chicago and got me a huge internship! They flew me out here for work and everything!"

"Funny. He didn't talk about his family much," Alex hissed. She hoped the malice in her voice would hint to Becky of her dire situation.

Ethan stepped up to them, his posture returned to the meek student they had come to know from home. Even in his fine attire, no one would have guessed he headed a branch of a massive hidden conglomerate.

"I thought I'd surprise you by flyin' Alex here out for your first big show," he said as he placed his arms around the two girls. "I know you're busy Becky, but we should all get together for dinner while you're here."

"That sounds great!" Becky cheered. She clasped Alex in another hug. "I can't wait to hear all about your trip."

"Wouldn't miss it," Alex said. Patting on her shoulder, Ethan led Alex back to the elevator, Becky waving innocently behind them.

By the time Alex returned to the cell, her three companions were awake and digging into plastic bowls of oatmeal. Sorin nodded to her as he lifted his spoon with a sore arm, hand shaking with the effort. She placed a ginger hand on his shoulder before picking up her own bowl left out on her cot.

"How did it go?" asked Ghaoithe.

"Not good. They have Becky," Alex replied. She swallowed her breakfast without tasting it.

Fleet threw his bowl onto the ground, leaving a spray

of water on the floor.

"Figures," he growled. "Bunch'a thugs. All of 'em.'"

"What do they want with your roommate?" Ghaoithe asked. She sat cross-legged on the floor, rubbing her chin.

Alex recounted the meetings with Ethan, the relic rooms, and the appearance of Becky. The other three listened patiently, hanging on to every detail she could remember. Occasionally, one would ask her to clarify something with painstaking detail.

When she finished, they sat quiet, listening to the chirp of birds from outside the window. Eventually, Ghaoithe let out a groan of exasperation.

"I don't get it," she said. "What's his game? He knows you're too smart to accept an offer like that."

"I don't know," Alex said. "It was all really strange. Like he was purposely trying to upset me."

"Do you think he was lying about that room in the labs?"

"I thought so at first, but would they really keep it somewhere so open if they knew we were after it?"

"No," Sorin spoke. He sounded as if he had swallowed thumbtacks. "They would keep it locked. Only Ethan and Deacon allowed."

"Not much we can do about it right now, either way,"

Fleet said. He stood and stretched life back into his limbs. His bruises had already started to heal, turning his face and arms into a pallid yellow.

"Fleet's right," Ghaoithe said. "Just humor Ethan. You have to be our spotter. We'll be fine in here for now."

Alex hated waiting. With Becky involved, she doubted that Osiris would keep the *Cloudkicker*'s crew as leverage for long. Worse, they were no closer to finding out about Pandora's Box. Such an artifact would not stay in one place for long.

In the midst of figuring out their strategy, two guards entered the cell. One stood watch over the doorway while the other addressed the group.

"Women with me. Men with him," he shouted.

Ghaoithe shook her head, as taken aback as the rest of them. The crew quietly obeyed, grouping around their assigned guard. The two ladies followed their escort out of the cell and into a winding path of hallways in the complex. They arrived at an empty doorframe with a skirted stick-figure plaque next to it.

"Facilities. You have 45 minutes. I will be watching from here," said the guard.

Alex stepped in behind Ghaoithe, nervous about their guard peeping in. She exhaled when the restroom revealed private stalls, a countertop island, and, best of all, individual showers with curtains.

Just think of it like the campgrounds you visited when you were young, she told herself. *In fact, this is probably cleaner than the ones in the Ozarks.*

After using the washroom, Alex sneaked into one of the showers, conscious even in her clothing. A small caddy for her clothes rested on a shelf. Miniature bottles of soap, shampoo, and even plastic sandals waited inside. Ghaoithe entered the stall next to hers. Alex laughed; the adventurer's frame cleared the showerhead by several inches.

Alex moved to unbutton her jacket when she grasped a piece of metal at her chest. The bullet-warding dogtags, ignored by the Osiris guards in their haste to haul Ghaoithe to her interrogation. She held her hand over it, eyeing the guard and then her captain.

Ghaoithe noticed Alex's taught expression and frowned. She motioned with her eyes towards the back of the restroom. There, smaller than the others in the building, a black orb spied down on them. Alex stopped moving, afraid that she had given away the crew's ace-in-the-hole.

"Just assume they can see and hear us everywhere. You can't be shy in prison, Ms. Stirling," Ghaoithe said, taking off her own ragged shirt.

Nerves took hold of Alex knowing Osiris watched from afar, but she knew she had to take advantage of Ghaoithe's lead. She took off her top, careful to slide the necklace off with it so that it was bundled among the folds, unseen by the security camera. With one last look at the black orb, she placed the rest of her clothes in the caddy, slipped on the plastic sandals, and turned the shower handle.

Uncomfortable as she felt, Alex admitted to herself that she needed the relaxing steam. It burned her raw. The scalding spray washed away her insecurities and the terror of the past two days. With a cleansing, she felt powerful.

Alex turned to Ghaoithe, who crouched low in order to rinse her hair. With her evening planned by Ethan, she knew that they would not have many more chances to talk before their situation could change for the worse.

"Think the Great Wall is that far from here?" asked Alex as she lathered shampoo into her curls. She projected all of her will into hoping Ghaoithe would catch on.

"Shouldn't be hard to find if it's so great," Ghaoithe joked.

A moment. "I wonder why they built such a large wall. You can protect yourself with smaller things just fine," Alex hinted.

Ghaoithe's eye flickered at the pile of Alex's clothes

and smiled. She bent down again, humming a tune that bounced over the steaming hiss of the pipes. Alex closed her eyes, letting the shampoo wash out of her hair and run down her back, every drop a worry gone.

It was up to Alex. She had the only eyes outside their cell, but with the crew awake and healing, the makings of a plan had been seeded. When the time came, they would risk freedom.

She just had to find Pandora's Box first.

Alex slept through the afternoon, her energy expended in a sleepless night and the giddy excitement that an escape plan could still come together. She still feared the dinner with Ethan, unsure of what other cards he had yet to play, but she at least approached it with focus. No longer would she allow her frustrations to cloud her observations.

As Alex came to, she noticed her three crewmates busying themselves around the cell. Ghaoithe had cleared out a corner where she could do push-ups with clockwork timing. Fleet and Sorin worked together for their exercises, making sure the other did not overwork still-sore limbs. The rugged Transylvanian only finished a few mild sit-ups before taxing himself.

Seeing the others bide their time, Alex realized she

had not spent much time with them since their imprisonment. Whatever their thoughts on her constant escorts to Ethan, they kept them private.

"Are you guys ok down here?" Alex asked, suddenly feeling very left out of their company.

"This is nothing," said Sorin as he eased himself back down onto his cot. "We have been trapped worse places."

"Like that time in Turkey," Fleet said as he stretched an arm behind his back. The reminder of lost adventures made even the dour Sorin smile.

"You had honey in your beard for weeks," he said.

"And it was damn good for my complexion," Fleet replied. At Ghaoithe's guffaw, Fleet pointed at her. "It was your idea to go after that hive in the first place!"

"Bees are nature's miracle bugs," the captain called from across the room. She lifted herself into a handstand, balancing against the wall, feet nearly touching the ceiling.

The group bickered for a while more. Alex smiled and listened to the friendly rhetoric, enjoying the presence of the boisterous crew she had come to know. With nothing else to lose, the tense attitude among the shipmates could be briefly set aside. Their exchanges reminded Alex of long nights with her clique, before her parents had left her, when hours would be spent on gossip, boys, and trashy romantic comedies.

Osiris may have been able to lock the group's bodies away, but spirits didn't break as easily.

Alex almost forgot they were imprisoned when the turn of a bolt signaled her back to the present. She maintained her composure as the group settled down to watch her leave; Osiris no longer scared her. She wanted to learn what secrets they held, to shove Ethan's attempts to manipulate her right back in his face.

Running a hand through her now-dry curls in an effort to look presentable, she stood proud and followed the guard into the hall. As he closed the door, she caught sight of Ghaoithe. The brigand's eye lit with a cunning understanding of Alex's determination. She nodded before disappearing behind the locked door.

Alex's heart pounded in the elevator with excitement. She fidgeted with her sash and smoothed over the folds in her shirt several times. Somehow, she knew Ethan had set up their shower break and silently begrudged him a thanks for the rejuvenation, even if it was just for his own selfish reasons.

As the elevator stopped with a ding, the aroma of sweet meat filled the air. Alex's stomach rumbled. She thought of the meager oatmeal for breakfast, the only semblance of food she could remember having in some time. She began to debate the merits of refusing Ethan out of spite or taking advantage of the opportunity to recharge in preparation for the next step in the escape plan.

Caterers bustled throughout the suite, a steady stream from a hallway to the right of the elevator. In front of their hideaway, a bar had been fully stocked, a gentleman awaiting their orders with it. Through the observation windows, sunset cast deep shadows over Osiris territory, giving the diner's view a painter's quality.

Ethan, dressed casually in dark jeans and thin button-down, sat engaged in conversation with Alex's roommate. Becky sparkled in a rose dress that could only have matched the model figure inside. She looked natural in the lavish environment, as if the old Becky had simply been a cocoon for the butterfly inside now released.

At seeing her friend arrive, Becky jumped out of her seat to give Alex a hug. When she pulled away, she smiled at Alex with lips to match her dress.

"I'm so glad you're here! And you even cleaned up! This really is a special occasion," Becky teased. Alex returned the hug and sat with a plastered smile aimed at Ethan.

"I told you I wouldn't miss it," she said with as much insincerity she was willing to risk.

Ethan ignored her tone. "Just wait until the cooks finish, hon. You'll be glad you stopped by."

"Jackson says we're getting duck. Actual peking duck! Can you believe it?" Becky asked with clear excitement. The only fancy dinners she had experienced in rural life were at the local Red Lobster for prom.

They sat, Alex stuck next to Ethan on her right. Their table had been set with fine plates stenciled with vines around the edges. Silver bowls of sauces, breads, and rice covered most of the area around the lit firepit in the center. Ethan reached over to one of the plates of appetizers and picked up a gelatinous wedge tinted black and green.

"Try this with some ginger on top. It's a century egg," he said, offering it to Alex. The smell of ammonia struck her nostrils, and she recoiled from the slice.

"Don't be mean," Becky reprimanded. She turned to Alex. "It tastes like cats."

Laughing, Ethan shrugged, sliced a dab of ginger from a nearby tray, and downed the wedge in one bite. "Fine with me. If you don't want to enjoy local culture, that's your problem."

As they bickered back and forth, Alex took in how smoothly Ethan transitioned into his old self. Becky only met him a handful of times and would never be able to guess anything was off about him as they sat at the table. If Alex had never boarded the *Cloudkicker*, she doubted she would even notice. His performance could have fooled anyone.

She thought of all the times he lied to her, hid right in front of her. Thoughts of meeting him in quiet hallways after class, his hands never releasing hers. Echoes of phone calls late at night, calling for her name.

"Alex."

She drifted back to the table in Huangshan, unaware of how much time had passed. In front of Alex, the duck had been served, steaming with dark glaze and crepes. Whatever fortitude she built in denying Ethan any satisfaction disappeared. She gladly lifted a knife and began cutting at her plate.

"Slow down there, Chief," Becky said. She stared at Alex, wide-eyed, with a glass of red wine in her hand.

Alex slowed down, biting down with a satisfying crunch. "Sorry. There wasn't much to eat... on assignment."

"Oh, I was so worried about you! I got home and Ethan said you were assigned to some kind of ship for work? It's been weeks!" Becky picked up her own utensils, cutting into the meal delicately, as if she had rehearsed how to eat at a formal event. "I got your letters, though. Ethan made sure to pass them along."

"Something like that. I, uh, went up the river for a bit," said Alex.

Nausea overtook Alex from the intake of food as the night wore on. She slowed herself, resigning to munching on a small, sugary roll filled with red bean paste. The sweet pastry tasted unreal, a gift after the Hell in the sewers. Becky and Ethan chat on, letting Alex relax without the pressure of conversation while her stomach eased.

"How's the show coming along?" Ethan asked between mouthfuls of rice.

"Wonderful! You guys have every kind of fabric a designer could want. I may have to steal some samples away before I leave," Becky replied with a chuckle. She turned to Alex. "You won't believe the people my bosses are working with. This show is going to be amazing."

"Wait until you see next year's line. We're working on it on the 52nd floor. Right near the front so employees can view our handiwork," Ethan said. He turned to Alex. A smile crossed his lips, staring at her with an intensity that lacked humor. She stared back, trying to read his expression. She expected malice, but instead found something she could not quite place.

"Will you show me? I'd love to see it!" Becky remained oblivious to Ethan's glances at Alex.

"Maybe. I'll need to clear it with Deacon first. He can be a bit of a pain," Ethan laughed. Then, that look again, stripping Alex of her shield to reveal the frightened girl out of her element. Hearing Deacon's name only added to her discomfort.

Sickness continued to slam into Alex's stomach. Her head spun, and she was sure that it was more than just eating too much. Her hand clutched a napkin. She could sense her throat tightening as her insides swirled when Ethan's hands met her own.

"Hon, you alright?" he asked with false concern.

Alex focused on him. He still aimed the peculiar expression her way. She struggled to make sense of it when she felt her hands moving underneath his. Gently and with as little movement as possible, he gripped her hand into a ball. All except for her index finger.

Following the direction he had her pointing, Alex tilted her eyes up to see a camera mounted on the far end of the ceiling behind Ethan. The truth dawned on Alex with brilliant clarity. The strange openness about the company, the ruse about a job offer, the odd expressions he gave her.

Ethan never left the *Cloudkicker*. He was Ghaoithe's contact in Osiris.

Alex bent over, torn between her wrenching stomach

and the new revelation presented to her. She knew her sudden pain was no coincidence, but what did Ethan hope to accomplish by making her sick? She wished they had a way to communicate beyond coded phrases. How much had she missed in his words due to ignorance?

"You don't look so hot. Everything ok?" Becky asked. She rubbed Alex's back with a worried hand.

"Ate too much. Bathroom?" Alex choked out.

"Through the bedroom. On the left," Ethan said.

His words still peppered the air as she ran from the table and into the bedroom. The entire room had been decorated in monochrome, making the porcelain of the restroom all the harder to find. Once she reached it, she lifted the lid of the toilet and emptied her stomach.

When Alex finished, her stomach no longer turned, almost as if she had not been sick at all. Her legs still shook, and she wobbled to the nearby sink to wash her face, noting with bitter acceptance that another camera bore down on her in the mirror's reflection.

Whatever Ethan had placed in her food did a number on Alex. In the short time since leaving the elevator, her skin had taken on a dingy hue, and her eyes sunk into dark circles. Her stomach settled, but a nagging instinct told her she needed to continue acting for the cameras.

Alex stumbled back into the bedroom. Its glass walls hid the setting sun through an electronic tint. She imagined Ethan, laying among billowing white sheets, coming to terms with being trapped within Osiris of his own volition. How hard he must have had it, cutting off contact with Ghaoithe and the *Cloudkicker* for an unknown end.

Back in the main room, Becky and Ethan argued in raised voices. Alex's roommate apparently worried that their food had been contaminated, while Ethan struggled to reassure her they were both fine. At Alex's entrance, they hushed and turned to her.

"I'm fine. Really. I just had too much," Alex croaked.

Becky rushed over, placing her hands on Alex's cheeks. "Oh, hon, you look awful."

"I'll have her taken down to the medical office," Ethan said with concern.

"I'll go with her," Becky said.

"You need to worry about your show. It's ok. I'll have a guard take her down."

Alex could sense the tension rising between the two. Ethan obviously did not want anyone following her downstairs, which could only mean he had set something in motion. Alex needed to diffuse Becky's worry and fast.

"It's fine," Alex said, stepping back to hold Becky's

hands. "You need to work. I probably just need to sleep it off."

Becky bit her lip. "If you're sure."

"I'm sure." Alex squeezed her friend's hands and nodded to Ethan.

They walked to the elevator, each step raising the dread within Alex. She felt as if she were marching to war, making her task of appearing ill all the easier. By the time the lift's doors slid open, she wanted to throw up again of her own volition.

Becky threw one last hug around Alex. "I hope you feel better."

"I will. I'm sure I'll see you again soon. Sorry for ending our dinner early," replied Alex with a weak smile. She stepped into the elevator and waved as the doors closed. The guard pressed for the prison cell's block and stepped behind Alex as the elevator plummeted down the building.

An arm grappled Alex, pinning her against the guard's body as a sharp prick stabbed her neck. For a moment, her vision spun as she tried to make sense of the sudden attack. She began to thrash, kicking at the walls and jabbing her elbow into the guard's stomach with no luck.

An empty syringe rolled between her feet. Whatever the guard injected her with had no effect, and she knew then that her sickness had been Ethan's countermeasure. She let herself ease up, slowly going limp in the guard's arm.

He loosened up as she began to sink to the ground. The break in his grip allowed her to spin around, putting everything she had into kneeing the soldier in the groin. He doubled over in a combination of pain and surprise.

Alex reared back to punch him again when the deafening bang of his assault rifle rang out. She shut her eyes as her ears burst with pain, leading to a steady ringing. When she opened her eyes, the guard lay in a bloody pool on the floor, a hole ripped through his helmet. Beside him, the snapped chain of Alex's sigil necklace lay depleted.

Alex's throat tightened. She wanted to gag, but glancing at the camera in the corner reminded her she was out of time. She reached down and rummaged through the soldier's pockets until she found the keys to the cell door. She lifted the gun. It straddled uneasily across her back as the doors dinged open.

Alex ran, scrambling to find which door led to their cell, wishing she had paid more attention the previous days. When she found it, she steadied her shaking hands. Fumbling, she fit the key in the lock. Ghaoithe, Sorin, and Fleet stared with wide eyes as her short frame entered the doorway, assault rifle on her back.

Alex unstrapped the gun and threw it to Ghaoithe. "Remember what we talked about in the shower?"

"Yes?" Ghaoithe said, fiddling with the gun in her hands. It looked like a plaything in her care.

"It's happening."

Ghaoithe ran down the hall first, rifle ready to blast any Osiris soldiers coming to intercept them. Alex figured they only had a couple of minutes before the hall would be swarming with them.

"Now will you consider getting guns for the ship?" Alex asked Ghaoithe in short breaths as they neared the elevator.

The captain punched the elevator button. "I'm taking it under advisement. This lift fast?"

Alex nodded. "Yes. You gonna be ok?"

"I'll get over it."

The doors opened, and they piled into the elevator as best they could. Ghaoithe had to duck inside. For once, Alex thanked her stature as she slipped next to the two stocky men.

Ghaoithe stared at the button panel in confusion. "What floor?" she asked. Alex pressed the button for the 52nd floor, and they rode up in silence, lost in creating an exit strategy on the fly.

The doors opened into the artifact laboratory. The researchers from her last trip had disappeared, either called away or off the clock. Alex stepped out, having anticipated the haunting blue glow of the floor, while the rest stood back to let their eyes adjust. She scoured the front of the room, certain that Ethan's mention of clothing on the floor had been important.

To their right, hidden in the far corner of one of the glass rooms, Ghaoithe's armor glowed from beneath a tarp. Excalibur rested alongside it. Alex let out a victorious cry and ran in to lift her sword.

Ghaoithe and Sorin followed behind while Fleet stood watch over the door. Ghaoithe tossed the assault rifle onto a nearby table and began stripping off the rags she had been given by their captors. Sliding her runed leggings on, she gawked at Alex.

"How did you figure all this out?" she asked with a grin.

"I figured out Ethan was still on our team. He's been hinting at us this whole time. Why didn't you tell me?" Alex replied.

"Osiris has eyes everywhere. It was too much of a risk for anyone other than me to know," Ghaoithe said, tightening the red sash at her waist. She slid the chestpiece over her head, the golden sigils drowning out the oppressing blue haze around them. Sifting through the tarp, she found her eyepatch. The relic hunter Alex had come to admire looked complete and stronger than ever.

A piercing click sounded from behind Alex. She felt the barrel of a gun nudge the back of her head. She stood still as Ghaoithe stared at Sorin.

"We've gone far enough," Sorin said. He shifted his hands, the weight of the gun unfamiliar to the brawler.

"So you're the one. I was hoping I was wrong," Ghaoithe said simply. She wanted to be angry, but her face sagged with disappointment. Near the doorway, Fleet readied to charge, but Sorin jammed barrel of the gun harder against Alex's head.

"Don't bother. Her necklace is gone," Sorin said.

"What's going on?" Alex's voice trembled as she tried to make sense of the trouble at hand. Part of her understood what was happening, but the other half refused to believe that the man she helped save in Roanoke now aimed a gun at her.

"When did they get you?" growled Ghaoithe. Her fist clenched the hilt of her rapier, waiting for Sorin to make the slightest hesitation.

"Not too long. In Roanoke," Sorin said with his deep timbre. "The fire was my first job."

"What's that got to do with the girl? Leave her be," Fleet roared from the doorway. His face fumed with crimson.

Sorin shook his head. "Sorry, Minnow. Your necklace is gone. You were the only choice."

"Glad to be of service." Alex aimed for sarcasm, but the bite had left her words, replaced with an overwhelming sadness at the loss of a friendship. "Why, Sorin?"

"My family cannot live on grain and lamb forever," he said.

"Well, what now? You kill Alex, and then you have us to deal with," Ghaoithe threatened.

"She is the one they want," Sorin replied.

Silence took over the room as they reached a stalemate. Neither side budged, with Sorin and Ghaoithe staring each other down to no end.

Their stand-off ended only when the elevator doors slid open and a stream of Osiris guards flooded into the lab. Each aimed into the glass room, ready to fire at the slightest movement.

"Don't move!" shouted their leader. "We're taking the girl!"

Fleet straightened, daring the guns to test his necklace, counting in his head how many guards he could take down before the protection wore off. Deep inside, he knew it would not be enough. Alex shut her eyes, hopeless in the face of an upcoming onslaught.

A ringing in her ears forced Alex's eyes open. At first, she thought it was an echo of the gunshot that killed her escort. Then, everyone else on the floor began to look around in search of the noise's source, as well. The sound bent, taking shape, streaming into several pitches that harmonized and glowed.

It wasn't music, not in the traditional sense, but it was more than white noise, filling Alex with warmth and bright enthusiasm. She felt like she was floating, like the gun no longer existed, like the room had melted to reveal sunlight streaming in from boundless sky.

The music reached a pinnacle. Shattered glass chimed

from the far end of the lab. Alex turned her head to the commotion, her mind hazy as though she watched from beneath a crystal-clear lake. Each room exploded in a hail of shards, blasting one-by-one towards the stand-off with each blow. None of the people around her motioned to run, trapped in awe by the vibration in the air.

When their room dissolved, the blast rocked the guards. Most toppled over into a pile of gray camo, but others flew off their feet, slamming into the walls. A deep, primal portion of Alex's brain screamed to brace herself. Instead, she grinned. She may have even laughed, completely absorbed within the music.

Then, like the crack of a whip, the lab quieted. Alex regained control over her mind, groggy and confused. Fleet and Ghaoithe stumbled around her.

"You heard it too?" Ghaoithe asked. She rubbed her ears.

Alex nodded. Against the wall, Sorin sat slumped over the assault rifle. His chest rose and fell, deep in unconscious slumber.

Grabbing Excalibur, Alex made her way to the other end of the lab, following the trail of destruction. Glass crunched beneath her heels. Nothing stirred beyond the three escapees and the hum of the electronics around them.

They reached the curtained room. No longer constrained by solid walls, sheets of black cloth fluttered underneath air vents. Through the edges, light pierced the glow of the lab.

A large hand patted Alex's shoulder. Ghaoithe stood beside her, staring at the veiled room before them.

"You did good, kid," said the captain.

Ghaoithe pulled back the cloth, and the three stepped into the room. White, antiseptic light bathed them. Mobile trays lined the walls, piled with syringes of various colored fluids, some of which had broken in the shockwave. Curved, sterile tools reflected the crew in chrome. In the center, a mass of wires and monitors surrounded a long table.

Resting on top, a young girl rubbed sleep from her eyes.

Alex gasped. Ghaoithe and Fleet shot looks to each other, just as stunned as Alex. The girl sat up, arms pulling several monitor wires with them, and squinted groggily at the newcomers.

"You aren't the clock makers," the girl said. She tilted her head and let out a gaping yawn.

Fleet snapped out of his daze. Rushing to the girl's side, he began pulling the needles from her skin. She watched without a hint of pain through curious blue eyes. Her straight, silver hair fell in translucent strands over his arms as he worked.

"No, hon. We didn't find no clock," Fleet said, smiling at her with rose cheeks. "We'll help keep ya safe, though."

"What are you doing, Fleet? You saw what happened to the guards," Ghaoithe said. Her fingers drummed the hilt of her sword. She made no attempt to get closer to the captive child.

"I ain't leavin' her here. If we was supposed to get hurt with the rest, we would have," Fleet replied. Pulling the last cord from the girl, he lifted her up, a bundle of white gown in his tanned arms.

The girl giggled and tugged at the sailor's beard. "Itchy!" she squealed.

Ghaoithe rubbed her forehead as she lost her words. Whatever she expected from Pandora's Box, a child had not been part of the equation. Living relics were not her forte.

She threw her hands up in the air in surrender and turned to Alex. "All right. You're the one with the clues. Where to next?"

Ethan had only clued Alex in on the location of Pandora's Box. The crew would need to improvise an escape plan from there. Alex's thoughts turned to the only other place she knew within the building.

"The suite on the top floor. We have to get Ethan and Becky out of here," Alex said.

"We'll be trapped if we go that high," Ghaoithe argued.

Alex planted herself stubbornly in front of the captain. "I lost Ethan and Becky once. I'm not leaving without them."

Ghaoithe's eye twitched as she considered her options. Alex, unflinching in her stare, made no effort to back down in her resolve.

"You know," Ghaoithe relented, "you can be a pain in the ass." She stepped out of the room and made her way to the elevator. Alex and Fleet followed, the pale child cheering for a ride in Fleet's arms.

"Where'd ya come from, missy?" Fleet asked her as they waited for the lift's doors to open.

"From the temple," the girl said as if the answer should have been obvious.

"Do ya have a name?"

The girl peered up to the ceiling, humming in thought. "Ellie," she said.

"Nice to meet ya, Ellie. I'm Fleet." He bundled Ellie in one arm and extended the other hand to her. She shook it in feigned formality before erupting in more giggles.

"I like you. You're fun," Ellie said.

"How old are you, Ellie?" Alex asked with a smile.

"Seven." Ellie paused. "Hundred. Thousand." She burst into mischievous laughter again, leaving the crew to shrug at each other. The elevator opened, and with one final look at the unconscious Sorin, they piled in.

Anticipation swelled within Alex. Images of reuniting with Ethan, the Ethan that had always been on her side, swirled in her head. In a few minutes, she knew she would be safe and sound, outside of the Osiris building and with her lover by her side.

Ghaoithe felt differently. Crammed inside the lift, she breathed rapidly, no longer certain of any outcome. A small hand reached out to hold her arm.

"Don't worry. It's almost over," Ellie said sweetly. The captain looked at the girl, noticing far more knowledge than any seven-year-old should have locked within her oceanic eyes. Ghaoithe placed a hand over Ellie's, but the words failed to soothe her nerves.

The elevator stopped. Alex's muscles tensed, ready to run into the suite as the doors opened. She found herself yelling instead as the crew exited to see Deacon standing with a pistol aimed at a kneeling Ethan. A fresh gash across

Ethan's forehead stained the pristine white carpet beneath him.

At the arrival of the relic hunter, Deacon rolled his eyes. "About time. We have been waiting ever so patiently for your arrival," he said. "Though I am surprised to see a lack of bullets about your bodies."

"Go back down! Run!" Ethan yelled. Deacon swiftly planted a cream-suited leg into the captive's side. Ethan fell over, gasping for air.

Alex's hand shot towards the hilt of Excalibur on her back, but Ghaoithe stopped her from going any farther.

"What's going on here, Deacon? Burning a city wasn't enough so you moved to torturing kids?" Ghaoithe yelled.

Deacon smirked and straightened his round glasses. "Torturing? Oh dear, no. This is the first time I've seen her awake! I'm afraid have no more inclination to her origin than you do."

"That's no excuse!" Alex bellowed. Her knuckles turned white from gripping her sword, but she paid no attention.

Deacon raised an eyebrow at her, turning as though he only just saw her appear from thin air.

"Ah, you! After our last encounter, I had a feeling of deja vu towards us," he said. "Then I remembered! You're the little girl with the poster that started all of this. I must apologize for your family. Had we known you moved the directions to Bimini to a new home, we could have spared your parents. A costly error on our part."

Alex's lungs purged themselves of air. Besides her, Ghaoithe screamed obscenities at Deacon, but they may as well have been miles away to Alex's ears.

"Oh, you didn't tell her? Well, well, Ms. Loinsigh, that's your misstep. The girl should have been told long ago. How disrespectful of you!"

Memories of the fire tore through Alex. She could feel the smoke, suffocating and toxic, filling her being. Then, a hand, calloused and firm, pulling her out of Hell and into dark sleep. She turned towards Ghaoithe, who fumed with seething hatred at the man on the other side of the room.

"He's not lying, is he?" Alex choked, her tongue numb in her mouth. "You knew Osiris caused the fire."

"We'll talk about it when we're out of here," Ghaoithe spoke softly. Her tone only confirmed Deacon's words. The punch of betrayal, of more hidden secrets, sapped the fight out of Alex. She lowered her sword, wishing she would wake up, back in her cell or at the end of a cul-de-sac in Missouri.

"That's enough, ya snake. Let the man go. We still

outnumber ya!" Fleet growled.

"About that," Deacon said. Gun still pointing with one hand, he lifted his cane in the other, planting the butt of it firmly on Ethan's temple.

"Ethan here has officially caused us more trouble than he's worth," Deacon continued. "We were content to let him play his little secret agent game with the young woman and your crew, but with the captain and the child now at risk, we must part ways with him at this juncture."

Deacon pressed on the trigger, sending a crack throughout the suite. Fleet covered Ellie's eyes, but not before she let out a terrified scream. Alex watched with blurred vision, transfixed as Ethan's body went limp on the ground.

Alex remembered screaming, the leather hilt of Excalibur rubbing her hands raw, and Deacon aiming the pistol at her as she tore across the room. As he started to pull the trigger, she became vaguely aware that her life would be over, and that she had to make one final push to take down Deacon's smug expression with her.

Alex jabbed the sword forward, closing her eyes, waiting for the shot to ring out, to release her from the desperate agony whirling inside her chest. The gun exploded next to her ear. The pain and ringing from the sound squashed her hope, signs that she still lived. Deacon gasped beside her as windows shattered around the room.

Opening her eyes, Alex squinted at the bright runes of the *Cloudkicker* parked next to the suite.

A voice boomed from the ship. "Hey, Ghaoithe! Sorry, but I kind of picked your key ring the other day."

Ghaoithe beamed. "I think you just earned your freedom, Damian," she yelled back.

The distraction provided just enough of a window for Deacon to move. Alex, turning to face him again, keeled over with a blow to the stomach. Deacon leaned in close as she gasped for breath.

"I will find you," he whispered. Satisfied, he darted to the left edge of the room, vanishing into the servant's hallway behind the bar.

Ghaoithe made a step to follow him, but stopped with a curse. She turned to Alex and ran over to place a hand on the injured girl's back. Alex shrugged off the captain's concern.

"Don't touch me," Alex hissed. She needed time to breathe, not because of Deacon's sucker punch but from the crashing of her world around her. From the corner of Alex's vision, a hand lay inert on the floor in a pool of red. She refused to look, to acknowledge that Ethan existed once. She knew her companions stood, waiting for her to break down so they could swoop in and make things right.

"We need to bury him," Alex said, listless. She started towards the ship hovering in the night, where she could be alone and away from Ghaoithe's suffocating presence.

As Alex walked up the gangplank, Fleet trotted to the captain. Ghaoithe's shoulders slumped and her eye took a red tinge, but she stayed the tears. She lingered on her retreating student and the body no longer recognizable on the ground.

The quartermaster reached up and gave a quick scratch to the back of Ghaoithe's cropped hair. He strode towards the ship, burying Ellie's head in his shoulder and whispering to her not to look as they passed Ethan.

Shortly after, Ghaoithe followed. She squatted over the corpse on the ground and closed her eyes in a silent prayer. With the care and patience of ages, she lifted Ethan over her shoulder and carried him aboard the ship.

Alex watched the funeral from inside the bridge, placing the deck's windows firmly between her and the life she thought she wanted. She sat rigid in Ghaoithe's chair as the rest of the crew gathered among the clouds outside.

Ethan's body had been wrapped in cream linen and placed on the gangplank. The captain stood at the front, her hands gesturing as she spoke to the crowd before her. Several times in her speech, she stopped, hanging her head as the words failed to come. When she finished, those gathered on the deck hung their heads in silence.

Fleet stepped forward, sprinkling a fine powder over Ethan's wrappings. The linen began to sizzle, then burst into full flames. The gangplank retracted, sending Ethan's body overboard, dissolving into ashes in the sky.

As Ethan careened into nothingness, Alex wished to be able to cry out her frustrations. However, nothing came. Stone-faced, she sat until the crew members moved back inside the ship. Alex made her way out of the bridge to avoid her peers. The quiet moment aboard the ship gave Alex an opportunity to eat. Her stomach rumbled, empty since her meeting with Ethan and Becky the day before.

Becky. She had not escaped with Alex. Likely, she had no idea anything out of the ordinary had happened, only that Alex and Ethan were whisked away again. She probably sat in some workroom in the complex, assisting a famous designer, unaware she had become a pawn in a much more elaborate game. Alex could only remain optimistic that her roommate was either innocent enough or held enough value as collateral to remain unharmed.

In the galley, Alex paused as she entered to see Ellie munching on a bowl of cereal. The girl paid Alex no mind, happy to dig spoonful after spoonful. Even fully awake and no longer hooked up to machines, Ellie's skin lacked any semblance of color. Alex worried she was cold, but the girl continued to eat without any complaints.

"I didn't know we had cereal," Alex finally said, taking a seat across the table.

"Fleet found some for me. It has frosting on it," Ellie replied through a full mouth.

Alex leaned into her hand on the table. Her curiosity with the girl melted away her thoughts of Ethan and Ghaoithe. Aside from her strange looks, Ellie seemed no different than any other child. Why had she been in Bimini?

Alex sat up and smiled. "Can I have some?"

Ellie nodded enthusiastically and held up her spoon for Alex, oblivious to the milk she splattered on the table. Alex bit down, letting the sweet crunch take her back to her own childhood. She couldn't remember the last time she ate Frosted Flakes.

Ellie tilted her head, judging Alex. "You don't have to be so sad," she said.

"What do you mean?" Heat rose into Alex's cheeks, as though she had been caught stealing.

"You just seem sad. You don't have to be. Your friends here like it when you smile."

When Ellie spoke, she teemed with sincerity. The world bent to the simple truth that she spoke. For some reason, it embarrassed Alex, like she had been stupid not to realize her friends cared for her.

Alex flashed with images of Ethan's slain body. She wanted to be mad, to let her hate remain in her mind, but she only ended up conflicted between her desires and the pensive effect of Ellie's attention. Both options lured her away from reason. Somewhere, the sight of Ghaoithe before Bimini, her head glowing with fire in the Caribbean sun, flashed into her thoughts.

"What are you?" Alex asked with a frustrated sigh.

"A girrrl," Ellie replied with a devilish grin, the kind reserved solely for children who have outsmarted their superiors.

Trying to get any more out of the girl would be useless, Alex decided. She watched Ellie eat, imagining the possibilities of the girl's origin, when someone knocked on the galley entrance. Ghaoithe entered, but waited just inside the frame, eye pointed at her feet.

Alex pursed her lips. "What do you want?"

Shuffling from foot to foot, Ghaoithe ran a hand through her hair. "We should talk," Ghaoithe said without looking up.

Alex's first reaction was to scoff and yell out a no, but Ellie's words left her biting her tongue. She did not want to disappoint the child, at least while they were all in the same room.

"Ellie, can you go play for a bit?" Alex asked sweetly.

Ellie nodded with a bright smile and picked up her bowl. Leaving it on the return counter, she disappeared into the hallways of the ship, leaving Ghaoithe and Alex to themselves.

"What do you think she is?" Ghaoithe asked, head following Ellie out the door.

"If you're going to dodge serious conversation, why did you bother to come down here?" Alex snapped.

"I'd say she is serious conversation," Ghaoithe replied sharply. She flashed her usual, powerful self before catching her words and blushing. She hung her head and sat across from Alex. "You're right, though. I'm sorry."

Alex let out a huff, but did not object to Ghaoithe taking a seat. The two let the silence grow between them, each forming their arguments for the debate at hand.

"Your parents... what were they like?" Ghaoithe spoke into the table, her words barely audible.

Alex seethed at the mention of her family. "Don't even..."

She wanted to reach out and strike at the captain. The question stung her, calling pent up anger and tears to form. However, she also knew that the question didn't make her mad because Ghaoithe kept the fire a secret from her, but because she didn't know how to answer. She had lived for so long simply accepting her lot in life, letting herself waste from the inside out, that she no longer believed herself to be a real person.

The *Cloudkicker* changed that, gave her purpose and acceptance. Alex allowed herself to believe that her old life had actually been the dream and that her true calling had always been to fly among the clouds. Finding out that those two lives were not just the same but directly connected washed away the thin fabric that veiled her shaken well-being.

In truth, Alex spent many of the years since her parents' deaths holding back memories of them, as though forgetting them would make it heal. Now, faced with the reality of their demise, she needed those moments more than ever, yet they wouldn't come. Alex's self-reliance had been built so much on their deaths that she had now forgot much of their life together.

Even though she had her fists ready to swing, to punish Ghaoithe for intruding into her life yet again, Alex could only slump and weep.

"I don't remember," she sobbed. "I can remember their faces. That's it."

Ghaoithe motioned to hold Alex's hand, hesitated,

and pulled it back to fidget with the corner of the table. "I'm sorry I've put you through all of this, Alexandra. I never wanted anyone to get involved, let alone hurt."

"What happened? Why me?" Alex dried her eyes with a palm.

Ghaoithe looked at her for the first time since entering the galley. Her eye sat deep in her skull, ringed with weariness.

"Like Deacon said, it was their mistake," Ghaoithe began. "We were both tracking the poster. You live in a small town that Osiris didn't bother with much. I guess they didn't know you had moved houses. They set fire to the place since the poster would have been protected by runes.

"By the time anyone in Osiris realized their mistake, they would have drawn too much attention to themselves going right back after you. So, they sent in Ethan. I'd hoped he would just get the letters, bring them to me, and that would be it. But, we heard Osiris was planning something big with Pandora's Box, and things got more complicated. So we needed to get the lead to Bimini ourselves. I wish you would have let me take you somewhere safe after you gave us the coordinates."

"Then why'd you let me stay? Don't tell me you felt guilty," Alex said with a bitter tongue. She hoped the truth would help her move on, but it only saddled her with frustration.

"I do feel guilty," Ghaoithe said. "If I had been a few moments sooner, maybe none of this would have happened. But, I wasn't. As for why you're on the ship, I don't know. I guess it's my way of trying to fix what happened."

"Oh, thanks. I really appreciate it." Alex's sarcasm cut through the air. At seeing Ghaoithe's face fall, she regret her harsh treatment of the captain.

Ghaoithe allowed Alex to vent, the words carrying their weight into silence. When the air cleared, she hunched over the table.

"You have every right to hate me for not letting you know earlier, but please tell me, would that have changed your decision to stay?" Ghaoithe asked.

Whatever her thoughts towards Ghaoithe's secrets, Alex could not say that knowing them would have changed her answer. She squirmed in her seat, trying to find a way to argue, but each avenue turned up the same answer.

Whether she wanted to acknowledge it or not, by owning the directions to Bimini Road, she had become a part of Ghaoithe's world. Maybe Osiris would have stolen it away in the night. If Ghaoithe had beaten Osiris to the poster's whereabouts, maybe Alex's parents would have lived. Maybe they wouldn't have or maybe Alex would have perished instead.

Joining the *Cloudkicker* changed her life for the better. Debating what-ifs wasted energy and drove a gap between Alex and Ghaoithe for the worse. It distracted them from the man they now knew to be the real enemy.

"No, it wouldn't have changed anything," Alex sniffed. She wiped her wet cheeks with a sleeve.

"That's good. Having you here has been... it's been nice," Ghaoithe said. For once, it was her turn to blush at an open revelation.

Alex tempted a soft chuckle. "You still should have told me, though."

"I should have, yes. I promise I don't have any other secrets to hold. At least not about you," Ghaoithe said with a weak smile.

A wave of relief washed over Alex, happy that her past now remained the past. She knew she still had a lot to discuss with Ghaoithe, but Alex was willing to leave the bridge alone for the time being. She reached out a hand and grasped Ghaoithe's calloused fingers.

"So, what do we do now?" Alex asked.

Ghaoithe's hand closed over Alex's. "Well, we get you cleaned up, have a few drinks, and keep flying. Not necessarily in the order."

"Drinks sound nice."

Overhead, the endless blue expanse filled the windows of the *Cloudkicker*'s bridge. Below, a stretch of sand and dunes, the rumbled folds of a soft blanket covering the Earth.

They fled China with all the haste the ship could muster. By the time they slowed down to assess their needs, the great Saharan Desert became their hideaway, free from the cities and technologies Osiris could use to find the ship.

Alex and Fleet sat on their perch playing a round of poker. Ghaoithe had locked herself away within the holds of the ship, searching for clues about their newfound child passenger. Though they had reconciled, Alex had not interacted much with the captain for the past three days, though not for lack of trying. With Mt. Huangshan behind her, the Sky Thief became obsessed with solving the mystery of Ellie.

"Don't give her too much mind," Fleet drawled over their card game after Alex lost herself in worry. "She's just persistent about these things. Probably the happiest she's been in a while."

Alex nodded and revealed her hand. Though Fleet

certainly helped hide the situation with her past, Alex found herself unable to hate the gentle, bearded warrior. She had confided in him about her chat with Ghaoithe, and he never failed to ease her doubts. Alex admired his ability to speak his mind with some measure of objective truth.

When Ghaoithe did arrive to her seat, her brows furrowed in thought, she threw a paper down onto the card table. In the corner of the front page, an article regarding an arson near the Thames had been circled in red ink.

"I found out about the clocksmith Ellie mentioned when we woke her. Poor fellow named Hubert Thomas," Ghaoithe stated. "Guess Osiris would have beat us to the punch anyway. Whatever code was on that clock hid access to Ellie's hiding place in the temple."

Fleet passed over the article. "Well, we got her now. That's all that matters."

Taking the paper from Fleet, Alex asked, "Yeah, but what do we do with her?"

Ghaoithe sat in her chair, face lighting up with a wicked grin. Noticing her look, a groan bellowed from Fleet in objection.

"You have got to be kidding me," Fleet said.

"Why? What's going on?" Alex asked, glancing back-and-forth between the two.

"We're going to Dilmun," Ghaoithe cackled. "If anyone knows what Ellie is, they'll be there."

"Dilmun? Doesn't our book say that was originally thought to be the Garden of Eden before we found Bimini?" The excitement in Alex started to spew forth with the promise of a new destination. "That sounds fun!"

"It ain't," Fleet said as he crossed his arms. "It's lures people in with its looks and then strangles 'em."

"Oh, it's not that bad," Ghaoithe waved off Fleet's concern. "Big man like you will scare off most of the troublemakers."

"Den of thieves is what it is!"

Ignoring the argument with a grin, Alex imagined what the ancient city looked like. She had read it to be a paradise among the desert, an ancient trade post where members of every civilization gathered to shuffle their wares. It sounded like a well-deserved vacation after fighting through the Osiris complex.

Footsteps echoed down the entry hall leading into the bridge. From around the corner below the captain's deck, Damian entered, all too pleased with himself to no longer be contained in a cell.

"Kid's tucked in. Had to tell her a story a few times in a row, but she's out like a light," he said. "She's a handful, for sure."

"I don't trust her," Ghaoithe said. The rest of the group turned to stare at the captain.

"What, ya want I should lock her up like Osiris did?" Fleet laughed. "I'm sure that'd go over well."

Ghaoithe pursed her lips. She said, "No, I just... she's obviously connected to Pandora's Box somehow, and after what she did to Osiris' goons, we'll have to handle her with gloves on."

"She's a kid," Damian said. "You feed her, you let her sleep, you give her some toys. It ain't rocket science. I don't know what happened in that tower, but if she were dangerous to you, I don't think she would have helped you escape."

The group looked to Ghaoithe for a response. Her cheeks blushed as she looked to the ground and murmured, "I still don't trust her."

The bearded quartermaster threw an arm around Ghaoithe's shoulder and walked her to the captain's chair. "Then let us worry about takin' care of the kid, and ya worry about keepin' us out of Deacon's eye."

"You're right. We need to get to Dilmun," nodded Ghaoithe. She straightened up and shouted "Set course!"

As the *Cloudkicker* drifted forward to the forgotten

city, Alex turned to stare out the bridge windows. For as far as she could see in any direction, the carpet of sand welcomed them, almost daring them to cross its expanse.

She couldn't wait to see what future awaited her beyond those dunes.

ACKNOWLEDGMENTS

After nearly three years of work, it's nice to finally be able to write a thank-you section for the first of what I hope to be a few smattering of words on paper. Though the life of a writer usually sounds solitary and lonesome as we sit hunched before our computers, it turns out that publishing a book is quite a bit of work!

Every author needs support, and my parents have shown nothing but in my time writing, querying, and dealing with paying Los Angeles rent all the while. They have always been my biggest fans, and I can finally say that after a lifetime of giving them Hell. I could never have powered through without their support.

To my Beta readers who provided such great feedback to make sure this all came together. Adam Davis and Kit Peterson for telling me it didn't suck. Adam Dotson for being willing to put that Masters towards improving my words. Edlin Lopez and Karina Alos for making sure my women stayed women. I hope I did a good job.

To Brad Holten, for over 20 years of friendship, fights, video games, and long nights.

ABOUT THE AUTHOR

After taking his turn in traditional journalism with stories and photos seen on CNN.com, the L.A. Times blogroll, and the LACC Collegian, Wes Smith has taken the leap into fiction writing with *The Sky Thief*. When not writing fiction, Wes is the founder and Editor-in-Chief of geek news site ActaDinerda.com. He currently lives in Los Angeles with his computer and far too many issues of *National Geographic*.

For upcoming news on Wes's novels, check out:
Thecloudkickertrilogy.wordpress.com
Twitter: @Weszor

www.ingramcontent.com/pod-product-compliance
Lightning Source LLC
Chambersburg PA
CBHW050507110726
47899CB00005B/1362